ALSO BY SUSAN GABRIEL

FICTION

The Wildflower Trilogy:

The Secret Sense of Wildflower

(a Best Book of 2012 – Kirkus Reviews)

Lily's Song

Daisy's Fortune

Trueluck Summer

Temple Secrets Series:

Temple Secrets

Gullah Secrets

Grace, Grits and Ghosts: Southern Short Stories

Seeking Sara Summers

Circle of the Ancestors

Quentin & the Cave Boy

NONFICTION

Fearless Writing for Women:

Extreme Encouragement & Writing Inspiration

Available at all booksellers

in print, ebook and audio formats.

DAISY'S FORTUNE

SUSAN GABRIEL

WILD LILY ARTS

This is a work of fiction. Names, characters, places, and incidents either are the product of the author's imagination or are used fictitiously, and any resemblance to actual persons, living or dead, business establishments, events, or locales is entirely coincidental.

ISBN: 978-0-9981050-2-4

Cover design by Lizzie Gardiner, lizziegardiner.co.uk

Wild Lily Arts

Printed in the United States of America

For seven generations

CHAPTER ONE

Wildflower

The smell of honeysuckle fills the mountain path. I am a girl again in Katy's Ridge. Thirteen. A time when everything changed. The sun has fallen below the mountain, and shadows creep along the forest floor. Three crows sit atop the gate at the back of the cemetery. We exchange looks. One of the crows points her beak toward the ground, drawing my attention to something shiny on the path. It is the gold medallion I used to wear for protection, covered in Johnny Monroe's blood. Yet in the dream, it now belongs to Daisy.

The telephone rings. I gasp awake. For weeks now, I have been dreaming of Katy's Ridge.

"Wildflower?"

Is Aunt Sadie part of the dream?

No, I decide. Does this have something to do with the nudges I've been getting from my secret sense? Nudges I keep ignoring? Nudges that tell me I need to go back to Katy's Ridge?

"It's your mama," Aunt Sadie says.

A beat of silence follows. Then another. Unspoken words communicate a lifetime of history between us.

"I'll be there by lunchtime," I tell her.

We end our call.

In the early-morning light, I put on the coffee and stand at the kitchen window overlooking a small courtyard behind my apartment building. A lonely red maple stands in the center surrounded by boxwoods, a feeble attempt by the management to add a hint of nature amid all the brick and concrete.

The small wooden cat Daniel carved for my thirteenth birthday sits on the windowsill. After Daddy died, Daniel—my sister Jo's husband—was like a father to me. A wave of homesickness catches me by surprise. It is 1982, twenty-five years since I left Katy's Ridge, and even now the thought of it causes a physical ache deep inside me. A lingering longing. Longing that nudges me in the middle of the night when I can't sleep and sends messages in my dreams. The landscape is what I miss the most. The hills and valleys of my childhood. Mountain streams so sparkling clear they reflect a person's soul. My soul.

After pouring my first cup of coffee, I telephone Bee, who is in Baltimore for a teacher's convention. Her big presentation is today. The one about at-risk children in Appalachia. The one she worked on for almost a year and practiced in front of me a dozen times while trying not to look at her notecards. The operator at the Holiday Inn stifles a yawn before connecting me to Bee's room.

"What's wrong, Lou?" she says before I have time to identify myself.

"It's Mama. I have to go to Katy's Ridge."

Silence. She knows what this means. We were friends for years before we became more, and she knows how difficult my relationship with Mama has been at times.

"You okay?" she asks. Just hearing her voice soothes me.

"Not really." Anchoring the portable phone between my shoulder and ear, I pour the rest of the hot coffee into my work thermos, though I won't be working today. It is a telephone that Lily bought and had installed. Not only for our weekly telephone calls, but for her long calls with Daisy whenever Lily travels.

"I wish I could go with you," Bee says, and I wonder if this is true.

"I'll call you tonight and let you know how Mama is," I say.

I imagine Bee in bed, her book and reading glasses a placeholder for where I used to be. On the bedside table, her pink windup travel alarm is probably set to go off soon.

"Good luck with your speech," I tell her.

She thanks me, confessing how nervous she is. At this moment, it feels like we are still together.

After we left Katy's Ridge, a hairline of distance opened between us. A tiny fissure that grew over the years until it felt like a chasm. A chasm that neither of us quite knew how to cross. A memory comes of Daniel and Nathan, my brothers-in-law, rebuilding the footbridge on the way to the cemetery. The same path as in my dream. Bee and I needed to build a bridge between us, too. For a while, that bridge was my daughter, Lily, but after Lily left home, there wasn't much to hold us together as a couple. For years I wondered what happened to us, tracing back every thread of disagreement to find where the weave loosened. Unfortunately, endings don't always make sense.

In the stack of mail on the table by the front door, I find the itinerary Lily gave me before she left on her latest singing tour. She is in Scotland for the next two days. When I can't reach her business manager, I call Jerry, her ex-husband, who is also her record producer, and leave a message on his answering machine:

Hi, Jerry. This is Wildflower McAllister. Could you please give Lily the message that Aunt Sadie called, and I have to go to Katy's Ridge today? We were supposed to talk on the phone later, and I want her to know why I won't be here.

I thank him, though I have never liked Jerry. Something about him has never sat right with me.

Daisy, my only grandchild, turned thirteen yesterday. We went out to dinner at a local restaurant, where I discovered that trying to get Daisy to talk is like lowering a heavy bucket into a deep well and not knowing if you will come up with anything after all the effort.

While Lily is on tour this summer, Daisy asked to stay with me instead of her father—a change that surprised everyone concerned, including me. Touring is a big part of Lily's singing career. She performed in small venues for fifteen years before her fourth album became a gold record and her music found a wider audience.

Lily admits her success is a blessing on the best days and a curse on the worst. She has told me how much she misses Daisy when she is away. She telephones whenever she can and sends concert T-shirts and coffee mugs with *Lily McAllister* on them. Yesterday a box arrived for Daisy's birthday containing a leather-bound diary and a fountain pen, and they talked on the telephone for over an hour. I tried not to worry about how much the long-distance charges would cost Lily. Evidently, she can afford it.

After getting dressed, I gather a few clothes in a suitcase, thinking of Mama. Aunt Sadie wouldn't call unless things were bad. I walk into the small second bedroom full of houseplants where I set up a twin bed for Daisy to sleep. A sheet covers her head, her hair a mess of blond curls. When calling her name doesn't work, I give her shoulder a gentle shake. She sits straight up, as though breaking through the water's surface after a deep dive.

Daisy's wide eyes blink at me, their blue-green color reminding me of Sutter's Lake in Katy's Ridge on a cloudless day. She looks around the room as if to determine where she is.

"What is it?" she asks, vigilant.

Except for the curls, Daisy looks like Lily at that age, but their temperaments are oceans apart. While Lily was inquisitive and outgoing at thirteen, Daisy is quiet. Too quiet, in my view. Even as a young child, she was challenging to get to know, her play more solitary than communal. If we played hide-and-seek, she preferred to stay hidden.

"I have to go to Katy's Ridge," I say.

Daisy falls back onto the bed and covers her head with the sheet.

"You have to come with me."

Daisy sits up again, her wide eyes narrowing. "Why?"

"Your great-grandmother isn't well," I say, probably an understatement given Aunt Sadie's call.

Daisy looks at me as though the name has no meaning to her.

"Your great-grandmother," I repeat. "Granny McAllister."

I remind her that she has an extended family, even if she rarely sees them.

While Lily was also an only child, she had plenty of cousins to keep her company. I doubt Daisy could even name all her cousins. Not to mention the aunts and uncles that are practically strangers to her.

"I hate it there," Daisy says, her sullenness waking up for the day.

It occurs to me that Mama's prolonged grief after Daddy died may have skipped two generations and has now taken up residence in my granddaughter. But Daisy's pain seems a different animal. I remember the dream, the blood-covered gold medallion that had somehow become Daisy's. A slow shiver walks up my spine.

The truth is, neither of us knows the other that well. Age doesn't help. While I cling to the outer edges of middle age, Daisy is making her slow, painful-to-those-around-her journey through early adolescence.

"It doesn't matter whether you love it or hate it," I say to her. "We're going." My voice leaves no options.

Daisy huffs and tosses off the covers, mumbling something about unfairness. At the same time, she seems relieved to have someone else in charge.

In the kitchen, I call the plant nursery where I work and tell them I have a family emergency. I have enough sick and vacation days saved up to leave for a good six months. It never occurs to me to go on a vacation. Mama and Daddy never took a vacation in their lives. Nor has Aunt Sadie, my role model for all life's essential things. Not that going home to be with Mama is a vacation.

Since a hungry teenager might worsen matters, I scramble Daisy two eggs and make toast. I am not the greatest of cooks, but eggs and toast I can manage. Lily is the cook in the family. She learned from Mama. After we moved to Nashville, it was Lily who cooked most of our meals, with an ease I always envied.

Moments later, my granddaughter slumps onto a kitchen chair as I place her food and a glass of orange juice in front of her. She eats without commentary. My thoughts travel again to Mama. Every morning of my childhood, I woke to the comforting sounds and smells of Mama cooking breakfast. A pot of coffee was always on the stove and biscuits in the oven. Eggs gathered from her chickens were scrambled or fried, depending on Mama's mood, and served in a bowl on the kitchen table, covered with a plate to keep in the heat. The memory makes my mouth water as I take a bite of bland toast.

After Daisy finishes breakfast, she washes her plate, silverware, and juice glass in the sink and puts them in the drainer. I credit Lily for teaching her this thoughtfulness. At my request, she gathers a few clothes to take with her, along with the diary and pen Lily sent her for her birthday.

Minutes later, we get into my small pickup and head to Interstate 40, which will take us east toward Knoxville. My thoughts merge with different trips I've made from Nashville to Katy's Ridge over the last twenty-five years. Most of my visits home these days have been quick visits on Thanksgiving and Christmas. Trips where the family gathers and time is spent catching up, without in-depth conversation. Trips that feel like crumbs when what I need to satiate my hunger is an entire loaf of Mama's homemade bread.

Staying connected to the family from a hundred miles away isn't easy, and in truth, I have made little effort except for occasionally answering Mama's letters. I think I blame

Katy's Ridge for my exile, something I wouldn't have done if people had treated me better. Perhaps that is something that can begin to heal while I am home this time. Forgiveness is needed. Forgiveness of place and people.

An 18-wheeler passes in the left lane of the interstate, and the entire pickup shudders in its wake. The thought of Mama not doing well shakes the ground underneath me. Ground that usually feels solid. Daisy looks over at me as though aware of my unsettledness. With one hand, she holds her shoulder-length hair to keep it from flying in the wind from the open window. The distance between us feels like miles instead of inches. She reminds me of an abandoned barn I saw out in the country once, totally overtaken with wisteria vines and aflame with purple blooms. Beautiful, solitary, and somehow secretive.

Another truck passes, this one carrying new cars strategically balanced. Even while in a rush, I am slower than most. A result, perhaps, of growing up in Katy's Ridge. In those days, time passed at an inchworm's pace. I became an expert at moseying, a southern art form I would like to become good at again. After moving to Nashville, time raced by like those calendars in old black-and-white movies. Months flying by, ripped off by an urgent wind. Lately, I've begun to long for a simpler time.

"Why are we going here again?" Daisy asks, not looking at me.

"My mama is sick," I say. "Your great-grandmother."

Could Daisy fill out even a short limb on her family tree?

"Mama has always been a strong woman, so it's hard to think about her being sick and weak." *Maybe even dying,* I want to say. But I am not about to try to explain my complicated relationship with Mama to a teenager, and a new teen at that.

Daisy's disinterest peaks with a sigh.

On the ancestral airwaves, I send Mama a message to not go dying on me before I can get there.

In my imagination, I hear her say back to me: *That is just like you, Louisa May. Only thinking of yourself and wanting me to hold off on resting in peace so that it will be more convenient for you.*

My relationship with Mama is not something I get homesick for. We are too different to appreciate each other. Although the older I get, the more I wonder if we may be more alike than I realize. I can be stubborn like Mama. A dog with a bone. A trait that can be helpful at times when things need to get done, and not the least bit helpful when letting go is required.

To go from Nashville to Katy's Ridge—doorstep to doorstep—takes two hours. My pickup rattles its need for a tune-up. If Daniel's son Danny is available, I'll have him look at it while I'm home. He owns a gas station in Rocky Bluff.

The warm June wind rushes through the windows of the pickup. I have never owned a car with an air conditioner, and on days like this, I wish I did. The radio is on a Nashville country station when one of Lily's songs comes on. I turn it up.

"Turn that off!" Daisy says, coming to life.

When I protest, the look she gives stops me midsentence. I turn off the radio.

"Does it make you miss your mama?" I ask.

Without answering, Daisy pulls her diary from her backpack and opens it. A furious flurry of sentences follows. The fountain pen scratches the page like a flock of angry chickens pecking the ground. In ten minutes of writing, she expresses more words than I've heard her say in her lifetime. I smile, imagining all those pent-up sentences finally free from Daisy's mind.

"Do you like the diary?" I ask, looking over at her, determined to make conversation with my only grandchild.

Daisy offers only a quick shrug, not looking up. Her writing slows and then pauses. She flips to the front and rereads the inscription Lily wrote in the book, wishing her a happy birthday and telling her how much she loves her. Then Daisy closes her diary and pulls a paperback novel out of her backpack. It is the same book she was reading yesterday. Dog-eared, with loose pages. A girl on the cover holds a spear and stands on a cliff at the edge of the sea. Blue dolphins jump out of the water below her.

"Did I ever tell you about the first time I heard one of your mama's songs on the radio?" I ask.

Daisy turns her head away to look out the window, her curls parting from the wind like the Red Sea.

"I pulled over on the side of the highway to listen to her," I continue, not one to be deterred. "An old farmer and his wife thought I had car trouble and stopped to see if I needed any help. I told them that my daughter was singing on the radio. I can still remember how excited they were."

Daisy turns toward me. "You sound so country."

"Is that a bad thing?" I ask.

She rolls her eyes. I used to be fluent in eye rolls myself back when I was Daisy's age.

"They were coming from church," I begin again, refusing to let go of that bone. "They wrote Lily's name in the back of their Bible with a yellow Putt-Putt golf course pencil so they could remember her name and get one of her records."

Daisy stares out the side window, as though considering jumping from a moving vehicle. When I was Daisy's age, Daddy had been dead for almost a year, and Johnny Monroe was standing at that crossroads, ready to pounce.

"Why are you so unhappy these days?" I ask her. Directness is not a trait practiced south of the Mason-Dixon line, but at this rate, I'll be dead and buried before Daisy gets around to telling me anything.

She doesn't answer.

"Is it Lily being on tour? Or did something happen at school?"

She twists a curl.

Unlike Daisy, Lily talked practically nonstop and asked endless questions. I was the one keeping secrets. It took months of Lily asking who her father was before she finally found out. She still wouldn't know if she hadn't persisted.

Daisy's parents split up before she was old enough to remember them together. She has always had two bedrooms, one at each parent's house. Always been one of the few children in school whose parents were divorced. Despite this, she is well-adjusted. Yet something has ahold of her right now. Something that feels deeper, dark, and somehow familiar.

I lean over and touch her leg.

She jumps as though I've slapped my open palm across her face.

"Sweetheart, what's going on?" I ask.

Lips stern, she returns to her book, as if the act of opening the pages will close the issue. Gripping the wheel tighter, I steer clear of the hopelessness I feel. At this rate, this is going to be a long summer. Even though Daisy stares at her book for the next several miles, no pages turn to advance the story.

I think of Mama again, hoping Aunt Sadie told her I am on my way. We were like mixing vinegar and soda, Mama used to say, and we are running out of time to understand each other. When Sadie called, I was so focused on the dream that I didn't think to ask more questions. The truth is, it may be time to say goodbye to the woman who carried me into this world. A woman who could be difficult even on her better days. A woman who was not only my biggest challenge but my greatest champion.

CHAPTER TWO

Daisy

My book is my protective shield, cover for whenever I don't want to talk, which is often. I have already read *Island of the Blue Dolphins* six times. I have the pages practically memorized. I want to be like Karana, the main character. I want to need nobody and live on a deserted island.

Sometimes I hear voices in my head. They don't talk to me; I just listen to them, like a television playing in the next room with the volume turned up. I only hear the voices at certain times. Sometimes I wish they would leave me alone.

I am also good at overhearing actual conversations. It is unreal what grown-ups say when they think a kid is reading and not listening. Last weekend I heard my father tell my second stepmother that my mom should be paying him child support instead of the other way around and that he should take her back to court now that she has made it big.

It is hard to imagine my parents married, much less

happy together. My father likes to push people around, and sometimes my mom lets him do that. He doesn't have talent like she has. Not many people do. Any skill I have is hidden. Unless hearing voices counts.

As far as grandmothers go, my mom's mom—Gran—is okay. People call her Wildflower, which I think is weird. The McAllister side of my family is funny about names. Gran's nickname is Wildflower. My mom's name is Lily, and mine is Daisy. What's with all these flower names? I guess I'm lucky I wasn't called Tulip or Daffodil. But Daisy is easily the most boring name on the planet.

Thankfully, Gran doesn't require a lot from me when I stay with her. We usually keep to ourselves. But not today. Today we are driving out to the *sticks* to see my great-grandmother. My mom hates going back to the place she grew up. As a result, I have only visited a couple of times, and I was not the least bit impressed.

"You sure you don't want to talk?" Gran asks me.

I press my lips tighter, not willing to give her what she wants.

The first time I heard my mom singing on the radio, it was no big deal. By the time I was five years old, I had listened to all of my mom's songs a million times. When I was a little girl, she took me to her concerts. As the family story goes, after she left my father, I slept backstage in car seats and strollers. To this day, I can sleep just about anywhere, even with loud music playing.

Even though my mom was up for a Grammy last year, I don't tell people that I am Lily McAllister's daughter. As far as I can tell, the best way to get by in life is to not draw attention to myself, especially when I am staying with my father. Thankfully, I don't stay with him that often unless

Mom is touring. She used to travel only in this country, but now she tours in Europe, too. This summer I asked to stay with Gran.

"Here's the exit." Gran puts on the turn signal of the old truck she drives. Grandmothers aren't supposed to drive old pickups that have dents and chipping paint. They are supposed to drive shiny Buicks or Chryslers or something respectable. My father drives a Mercedes because he wants people to think he's hot shit. Evidently, Gran doesn't care what people think.

When we reach the interstate exit for Rocky Bluff, the sign looks like someone has used the *O* in *Rocky* for target practice. A spattering of holes bleeds rust. Whoever did this was a good shot.

"Rocky Bluff is practically New York City compared to how it was when I was a girl," Gran says.

You've got to be kidding, I think.

Gran pulls her silver pocket watch from her jeans and checks the time. It makes a soft click when it closes. Grandmothers are not supposed to carry men's pocket watches, either, or wear faded blue jeans for that matter. But Gran isn't like most grandmothers. I still haven't decided if this is a good thing.

Fast-food joints litter the main road, alongside gas stations servicing travelers coming off the interstate. A huge billboard, next to the sign for the city limits, announces that the Rocky Bluff High School Bobcats were the 1979 State Football Champions—three years ago. A circle of stadium lights towers over the ball field and the blue-and-gold bleachers. Looming behind it is a metal water tank that could use a coat of white paint.

"I attended a lot of football games there," Gran says. "Your mama had a big crush on one of the players on the team. His name was Crow Sector."

Crow? What is it with these country people and names? Can't they call people Jill or Jack or something?

Gran taps the steering wheel of the old truck.

"What was he like?" I ask, knowing this is what Gran wants. She wants me to talk to her. Show an interest. Not hide. However, hiding is what I do best. If gifted superpowers, I would choose invisibility every time.

"Crow was charming," she begins. "His hair was jet black. Still is, I imagine. That's why his nickname is Crow." She pauses. "Come to think of it, I don't know his real name." She smiles. "His mother, June, is a good friend of mine. She helped me through a really rough period in my life, and she was the only friend who knew about Bee."

Gran's smile fades. I wonder if she misses Bee as much as I do. When I was younger, I was closer to Bee. Bee taught school and was off every summer and took me to museums and art galleries. If we walked in a park, she taught me about photosynthesis and the water cycle. Bee was cool that way and didn't mind if I was quiet. She told me I was always wearing my thinking cap. Once we spent an entire afternoon making thinking caps with construction paper and magic markers. Mine still sits on the desk in my bedroom at Mom's house. I miss my bedroom when Mom's away. I have a bedroom at my father's house, too, but it's all frilly and pink from my first stepmother decorating it. I hate that room. It's like being trapped inside a cotton candy machine.

Bedrooms aside, Gran is different from Bee. If Bee is like an open door, Gran is a closed one. Gran has secrets. Secrets that nobody, including a granddaughter, is allowed to know. I have secrets, too.

"It's ugly here," I say, matter-of-fact.

She smiles. "It was the center of the universe when I was a kid."

We drive past empty buildings, signs of a small town worn out.

"Rocky Bluff is experiencing a slow demise," Gran says.

"It doesn't seem that slow to me," I say.

She smiles again.

The two times I came to Katy's Ridge, I didn't even notice this town. It seems sad in a way, and lonely.

Gran slows down and points. "One of my sisters has a seamstress shop on that corner, next to that run-down Revco."

She never talks about her sisters, and I wonder if they are close. I would give anything to have a sister. Or a little brother like Karana has on the island at first. Being an only child isn't horrible, but it's intense to only be around grown-ups all the time. It's like you forget you're a kid, and your parents do, too.

Gran drives through the small town at a turtle's pace. Even though no one is behind us, I pretend to jam my sneaker on the gas and get us out of here. I remind myself that in only three years, I will have my driver's license. This fantasy rescues me with growing frequency.

Gran stops at a long red light, and when it turns green she presses down the clutch and coaxes the pickup into first gear. I study the moves. Could I drive a stick shift if I had to? First gear looks like the gearshift is standing at attention. With second gear, you press in the clutch and pull the stick straight down. Third gear goes up and to the right to find the sweet spot, which evidently isn't always easy to find in Gran's truck. Sometimes it takes her two tries. With fourth gear, you move the stick straight down again. My father's Mercedes is automatic, which seems dull in comparison.

Looking into the side mirror, I catch myself frowning. Stepmother number one always told me that I was unattractive when I frowned. She also said that I should start saving money for a boob job.

Meanwhile, Gran is my tour guide for the most dilapidated main street I've ever seen.

"That furniture store over there used to belong to my Aunt Chloe and my Uncle John," Gran says. "They both died in the early seventies."

A yellowed SALE sign stretches across the big front window. In some ways, it feels like I am in the middle of a ghost town, held captive by a nostalgic grandmother. I imagine there are worse things. And as long as she keeps talking, I don't have to.

"That old theater closed several years ago," Gran says. "I saw *The King and I* there with my sisters and Bee." She takes a long, slow look, craning her neck as we pass. The sign out front announces the Masons' Christmas party in 1967.

I wonder what kids my age do for fun in this town—not that I see anyone my age.

Gran looks at her watch again. "Why am I wasting time?"

Sometimes Gran says her thoughts aloud, not requiring an answer. She speeds up, but not by much.

"Tell me something you dread." She looks over to me.

Gran is always asking dorky questions that are not even questions.

Sheer boredom pushes me to respond.

"For starters, I dread going to the boonies to see a bunch of people I don't even know."

She laughs a short laugh. "Fair enough."

To my surprise, I say more. I tell Gran about how I dread going back to school in September, and how I dread tests, and Monday mornings, and seeing Mom pack before a trip, and spending the night at my father's house. I stop. I didn't plan to say that last one.

"That's a lot of dread," she says, tapping the steering wheel again.

My awkward smile leads to my ugly frown, and I wonder if she thinks I need a boob job. But why would I need a "job" for something that barely exists?

"What do you dread?" I ask her.

"Death." She grins, as though she's caught herself saying something she didn't intend to, either.

For a few seconds, the heaviness in my chest lightens. At least Gran is trying to get to know me. Most people don't even try.

We leave downtown and turn onto a county road. Potholes provide an immediate obstacle course, and the truck squeaks with every bump. Gran talks about bucking broncos and how the road needs taming. She swerves to miss a pothole and cusses. "Shit" is her favorite cuss word. Grandmothers aren't supposed to cuss, either.

"This morning, when the phone rang, I was dreaming that I was walking an old trail in Katy's Ridge that I used to walk when I was a girl. And now here we are," Gran says.

I don't tell her that I was dreaming about being stalked by killer sharks when she woke me up. It might spark another conversation.

"Did you like growing up here?" I ask. The question sounds lame. But I'm grateful Gran has agreed to let me stay with her this summer.

She pauses before answering. "It was my home, you

know. I didn't think anything of it. But looking back on it now, I feel like I grew up in the arms of mountains."

I imagine Karana held in the arms of her island.

"Why did you leave?" I ask, surprised by my interest.

She shifts into a lower gear to get up the hill we're climbing. "Well, I thought I'd be living in Katy's Ridge my entire life. But then, people found out about your Grandmother Bee and me."

Growing up around Gran and Bee meant I never gave their relationship a thought. I didn't realize it was different until I went places with them and saw the disapproving looks they got sometimes. It made me angry. A line in one of the songs Mom wrote says that finding love is a miracle and that you can't make love wrong. I always wondered if she wrote that song for Gran and Bee.

"I can't imagine how my sisters are taking Mama going downhill," Gran says, more to herself than to me.

I begin to wonder what *downhill* looks like, and if this is something I want to watch. The only thing I remember about my great-grandmother is that we had a staring contest, and I lost. She kind of scared me. I was around seven at the time. That was the last time I was here, and I suddenly wonder why, if Katy's Ridge is only two hours away. The only reason I remember that particular trip is because Mom took pictures that are in the photo album in the den.

"My family and I haven't been that close since I moved to Nashville," Gran says.

I nod, watching the scenery out the window.

For the next few minutes, Gran is silent. We go deeper and deeper into the country. Traveling the mountain roads feels like being rocked as a baby, and I try to imagine being held by these mountains like Gran was.

Every now and again, I glimpse the river below. Sunlight sparkles off the water's surface. We drive through pockets of shade that cool the car in an instant before the warm sun returns. It is an ordinary day, yet it somehow also feels extraordinary. When I look over, Gran wipes away a tear. I hear her unspoken words: *I'm home.*

CHAPTER THREE

Wildflower

Memories rush to greet me at the faded welcome sign to Katy's Ridge: Daddy teaching me to read long before I went to elementary school. Mama combing my tangles with a less-than-gentle touch. My sister Jo coming to look for me at the cemetery after Daddy died. Then my mouth waters with the memory of Mama's chicken and dumplings the first time Jo brought Daniel, her future husband, to the house. When the memories darken, I think of Daniel carrying me home in his arms after Johnny Monroe attacked me. A time that feels like a thousand years ago, and also only yesterday.

Sunlight winks through the trees, reminding me of the gold Mary—the angel that appeared to me as a girl, bright as the noonday sun. It has been years since I thought of her. Years since I realized how much I missed her. More than I've even missed Mama.

Mama never believed in ghosts or visions. Spirits went

against her practical nature. They were nonsense that got in the way of the hard work of life. If asked, I imagine she might say that seeing spirits was pure laziness, just like anything else that caused a person to ponder life.

Meanwhile, driving into Katy's Ridge is like going back in time fifty years. People aren't the only ones to mosey. Progress does, too. Especially here. Living in a city is different from living in the country. They are complex in different ways. Instead of high-rises worshipping commerce, the forest adores the mountains. Instead of avenues criss-crossing, running in straight lines, a river meanders south as it has for millions of years. Mountain streams swell with rain and push their way to the sea as they have for centuries.

Daisy stares out the window, her book now in her backpack. It is cooler here. Thick trees are in competition as they reach for the sun. Day after day, I rode the school bus to and from the high school in Rocky Bluff, watching the familiar scenery pass by. The same scenery that Daisy appears to be taking in for the first time.

After I moved away, nostalgia accompanied me everywhere I went for months, if not years. Perhaps that's because Bee and I had no choice about leaving. Not when our livelihoods ended. A mob with pitchforks chased us out of town. Imaginary pitchforks, but ones dipped in the poison of judgment and fear.

A new stretch of road stops my reminiscing. It bypasses the high bluff and travels alongside the river, elevated just enough to avoid flooding. Remnants of the harrowing old road along the cliff appear periodically. A reminder of the old way of entering and leaving Katy's Ridge.

To my surprise, I miss the thrill of driving the narrow and dangerous old road. Undivided attention was required to avoid a fatal swerve off the cliff into the rocky riverbed below. I still miss my first pickup, which I learned how to drive on these curves. A vehicle I drove until the engine fell out one day while I was waiting at a red light on Church Street in Nashville.

The road tames, and we enter the valley where little has changed.

"Down that dirt road is the sawmill that I used to run."

Daisy glances. Weeds have grown up and hidden the sign.

"You ran a sawmill?" she asks.

"Me and your Great-Uncle Daniel," I say.

Katy's Ridge is like a tea bag steeped in history. My history. By a miracle of grace, the tea has not turned bitter.

Daisy observes, her eyes wide as if swallowing Katy's Ridge whole.

We pass the dirt road that goes to the Sectors. Though the house isn't in view, I beep my horn in greeting. I will visit with June when I can. I imagine she knows what is going on with Mama. All of Katy's Ridge probably knows. The grapevine has never been more vibrant, according to Mama's letters.

Moments later, I pull over and leave the truck idling.

"This is where Bee used to live," I tell Daisy.

At the end of a short gravel road sits a small house that Bee still owns and rents out to a young family from Chattanooga.

A colorful mess of big-wheeled trikes covers the yard. A clothesline stretches from a maple tree to the front porch, the line full of clean clothes blowing in the mountain breeze.

"Bee used to sit under that maple and read in the summer," I say.

I look at Daisy, and she nods as though imagining it. She is a deep thinker like me.

I pull out my watch again. In an hour, Bee will give her speech in front of several hundred teachers at a conference in Boston. I imagine her nervousness is kicking in about now. She has never spoken in front of that many people. But she couldn't pass up the opportunity to bring attention to the small schools here in the mountains. Schools with outdated textbooks and no community resources for the most impoverished children.

"I miss Bee," Daisy says.

"I do, too," I say, more wistfully than I intend.

Sometimes I forget how close Daisy and Bee are. Bee has always treated Daisy like a favored grandchild. Bee and Lily are close, too, and sometimes I think Lily was more devastated than I was when Bee and I parted.

At the main crossroads, street signs now give the names of the roads. When I was growing up, they were unmarked. Everyone knew the names already. I brake at a shiny new stop sign at the intersection where Johnny used to throw rocks from one side of the road to the other while spitting tobacco juice into a peach can. I wonder how many days Johnny stood at this crossroads waiting for his life to change, and how many times I have wished I never walked by that day. Probably more than I can count.

All of a sudden, I turn, taking the road to the right, away from Mama's house. I can't bear the thought of seeing her lying in bed, possibly saying goodbye to this life. I want to run like I did the day Daddy died. I want to run to the river and pretend that endings don't exist.

New gravel covers the road leading to the elementary school where I spent eight years of my life. It is summer vacation, and two men clear brush from around the playground. Why is it that the places we grew up always seem smaller than we remember them?

"The school has two buildings now, but it used to have only one," I say to Daisy.

She narrows her eyes, as though trying to imagine it. "Mom went here?"

"She was top of her class," I say.

"I wish I had inherited her intelligence."

"You're plenty smart," I say. "You just haven't found your passion yet."

A wry smile crosses her face, as though she has spotted my affinity for self-help books.

"Lily's passion was to get out of Katy's Ridge and travel the world."

"Well, she got her wish. She's never home." Daisy's moodiness returns for an encore.

"Singing is her job, honey. You know she loves you more than anything."

Daisy crosses her arms as if a drawbridge has suddenly closed. I question again if she is somehow in trouble. Trouble that she refuses to discuss. At least for now. She will be staying with me for the rest of the summer. A summer that feels suddenly momentous.

"Bee was just out of teachers college when she taught me in that one little building," I begin again, sticking to more comfortable subjects. "There were twelve of us, ranging in ages from first to eighth grade. My best friend, Mary Jane, and I were the only two students in our grade. Everybody else was either younger or older. Years later, she taught Lily, too."

"What happened to your best friend?" she asks.

"I have no idea," I say. "Last I heard, Mary Jane had moved to downtown Little Rock."

My pickup idles, and I suggest we go. Mary Jane is a part of the past. A past that I don't care to remember.

As I drive toward Mama's house, the smell of honeysuckle and wild roses fills the car—the aroma of summertime in the mountains. I come to the three mailboxes next to the big boulder at the bottom of the driveway. Mama's is in the center. Jo and Daniel live across the street, and theirs is to the right. Amy's mailbox is on the left. After her husband, Nathan, died, my sister moved to a small house next door to Jo and Daniel. Meg lives farther down the road past the church.

I pull up Mama's gravel driveway, which now extends halfway up the hill and ends at a clearing just below the four redbud trees that Daddy called the Redbud Sisters. Daddy could be silly about naming things, but as girls, my sisters and I loved it. While working at the nursery, I continued his tradition, although mine is a secret naming.

The engine off, I take a deep breath. My childhood home sits atop the rise, barely visible behind the trees. A couple of years ago, Lily had Mama's house renovated with money she made from her gold record. Around the same time, she offered to build me a new home in Nashville. My refusal created a sore spot between us that hasn't quite healed. The truth is, if given a choice, I wouldn't want to stay in Nashville forever, though I'm not sure where I belong anymore.

Our old house is now a much grander version of its original self. The front porch, no longer rickety, stretches around the house. A small barn is in the side yard, next to a new chicken coop. New windows and doors smile into the forest. The best in indoor plumbing replaced aging pipes throughout, along with new kitchen appliances, and a room built onto the back of the house for the new washer and dryer. In the old days, the washer and dryer lived on the back porch.

For months, Mama's letters were full of the news about all the changes, as well as her complaints of workers underfoot. I wish Daddy could see the transformation of the old place. But maybe he has.

"Why are we just sitting here?" Daisy asks.

With all the memories rushing toward me, I forgot she was even there.

"It's always strange to come home again," I say.

She sighs.

The thought crosses my mind again that this could be a long summer.

"It's going to be a long summer for me, too," she says.

My eyes widen as I turn to look at her. How does she know what I just thought?

However, there is no time to solve this current mystery. Mama is waiting. After getting out of the pickup, I toss my keys onto the front seat, something I would never do outside my apartment in Nashville. Here in the country, I have no worries about anything getting stolen. Not that my pickup is anything of great value.

The sun directly overhead, Daisy and I begin our trek up the hill. In the distance, Aunt Sadie stands on the porch. With the simple sight of her, tears spring to my eyes.

Years ago, after Lily and Bee and I moved away from Katy's Ridge, it was Aunt Sadie I missed the most, along with Daniel. Not Mama, or my sisters. A fact that surprised me at the time. I brush away tears and return a quick wave. Meanwhile, Daisy drags herself up the hill as though sentenced to an unfair prison sentence nowhere near completion.

"Give these mountains a chance," I say to her.

She doesn't question what I mean, her quota of words possibly fulfilled for the day.

Meanwhile, I wonder what I will find at the top of the hill. It seems I have been approaching this moment my entire life. A moment where I must give Mama a final goodbye, just like I did with Daddy forty years ago.

In my memory, I hear the stretcher dragging as Simon Hatcher's mule pulls Daddy up the hill after his sawmill accident, the life pouring out of him. Death makes everybody useless. Useless as the day we were born. The only thing those left behind can do is to witness it.

After Daddy died, I ran like a wild animal down the river road to forget seeing him take his last breath. In some ways, it feels like I am still running. And now, here I come again, donning my running shoes for Mama.

Daddy's memory kisses me in the same place he always kissed me, my forehead a monument to his love. My scalp tingles. I never feel alone here in the mountains as I do in Nashville. The spirits of the dead are everywhere, like the negatives of old photographs. Imprinted forever on my mind. Ready to be restored to full color with a sound, a smell, the sight of home.

I think of the last words Daddy said to me on his deathbed: *Take care of your mama. Promise me.*

At that moment, I would have promised him anything. But did I keep my promise? Mama has always been prickly and not the easiest to take care of without getting pricked.

Sorry, Daddy, I think. *I wish I'd done better.*

Whistling travels on a summer breeze, a faraway memory. Daddy always whistled when he walked this path, and I suddenly wonder if he has come to greet me. Seconds later, I smell the aftershave he used to wear to church. My sisters and I saved our pennies and nickels for an entire year to get him a bottle one Christmas, and he wore it in abundance as if to show his love for us.

"Daddy?" I stop on the trail and look around.

Daisy turns to me, a question in her eyes.

I tell her it is nothing and wonder if it is.

The first time Daddy appeared to me in spirit form was when he came to get me that day that Johnny hurt me. It seemed crazy then, and it feels crazy now. But he felt as real as anything those many years ago, just like he feels as real as anything today.

In the distance, Aunt Sadie holds up a hand to shade her eyes from the sun. She smiles. Not everyone coming up this hill is welcome. I think of Johnny's sister, Melody Monroe, staggering up this same hill to find Lily, her brother's child. I've thought before about how life can turn on a dime. If Melody hadn't traveled to Katy's Ridge that day, I might still be living here, and Bee and I might even be together, though living a secret life. The older I get, the more I realize how one incident can alter a life forever. A road you thought you would travel forever becomes the road left behind.

Daddy's aftershave fades, and the smell of lavender take its place. He planted lavender to keep the deer away from Mama's flowers. Daisy lingers in the yard while I approach Aunt Sadie, whose hair has been solid white for as long as I have known her. Her eyes crease into little branches like one of the ancient oaks behind the house. Sadie is Daddy's sister and was my age when he died. She is ninety-six years old now, but when I step into her arms, her embrace is strong. After Daddy died, I relied on Aunt Sadie to love me no matter what, because Mama was no longer available.

Our embrace ends, and I miss her closeness instantly. I ask her about Mama.

"I'm glad you're here," she says.

Sadie looks behind me and smiles at Daisy, who hasn't come within hugging distance. Instead she stares at the laces of her tennis shoes.

"Let her be," Aunt Sadie says, her words soft. "She can stay out here while you say your hellos."

And goodbyes, I can almost hear her say. She takes my hand and squeezes courage into my palm as we cross the threshold into the house. A threshold that leads to a lifetime of memories.

CHAPTER FOUR

Daisy

An old woman stands on the porch waiting for us, easily the oldest woman I have ever seen. I may have met her before, but it has been six years since my mom brought me here. When the old lady looks at me, I turn away. It feels as though she can see right through me to every thought and feeling I have ever had.

Moments ago, when Gran called out for her father, a chill rushed up my spine, and all sorts of conversations from the past rushed at me. This place is alive with stories. Voices I don't recognize and can't put faces to except for Gran, who sounds young but still like herself.

An old black dog sits at the old woman's feet. His muzzle is gray, and he makes no effort to bark when we approach. A dollop of drool drips from his mouth onto the porch as he pants and smiles. The old woman gives Gran a big hug, and I hear Gran sigh. I usually complain about Gran's hugs and try to duck away. But in truth, I don't mind them.

When the old lady greets me, my face flushes hot, and I lower my eyes.

"I'm Sadie," she says. "You don't have to do anything here that you don't want to do. Is that clear?"

When I look into her eyes, I find softness there. My shoulders relax, a wild thing suddenly tamed.

"Why don't you wait out here on the front porch while Wildflower visits with her mama," she says. "Or you're welcome to come inside, too. You get to decide."

I look at Gran, who has her hand on the door.

"I'll stay out here," I say.

"Don't you want some iced tea or a bathroom?" Grans asks.

I tell her I don't.

After Gran and the old woman go into the house, I sit on the white porch swing and push off with my legs. The swing squeaks to life. It is old but newly painted, just like the house. What a strange place this is. I don't think I've ever seen so many trees. Surrounded by forest, I breathe deeper. A moment's peace leads to something unsettled. Whenever Gran asks me what's wrong, I tell her I'm fine. The truth is, nothing is okay. Nothing at school. Nothing at home. Nothing.

I twist a strand of hair and put it into my mouth, tasting a bitter remnant of my apricot shampoo. My mother grew up here, and she never talks about this place. When I try to imagine her as a girl playing on this porch or out in the yard, I can't. All the photographs of her start when she was my age and lived in Nashville with Gran and Bee, not here.

Alone on the porch, I continue to play with my hair. If Mom were here, she would ask me to stop, but playing with my curls gives me something to do while I think about the mess my life is in.

The house smells old and new at the same time. The outside is painted white. No designer colors like stepmom number two insists on in their big home in Nashville. This house is much simpler. The old black dog smiles at me. I pat my leg to call him over. With great effort, he pulls himself to standing and comes. Fur flies as I pet him. I am usually scared of dogs, but not this one.

A voice startles me. When I look up, a girl about my age stands at the bottom of the porch steps looking up at me.

"Where did you come from?" I ask.

"I was out back gathering eggs," she says. "I'm Nellie."

I look at her blankly.

"My mom is Jo," she says. "Wildflower's older sister."

I translate Wildflower to be Gran.

"I live across the street. My daddy is Daniel. I'm a change-of-life baby," she continues. "Mama and Daddy call me their 'sweet little surprise.'" Nellie laughs. "Isn't that tacky?"

I agree that it is tacky.

She waits for me to say more, and maybe give the conversation a spark. But I have never been good at sparking talks.

"You're Lily's girl, right?"

I imagine this is something she already knows, but I play along and answer in the affirmative. She cocks her head as though I may require studying.

"It won't be long now," Nellie says, her curiosity turning serious.

My confusion is genuine.

"You know." She motions her head toward the door. "It's almost Granny McAllister's time," she whispers.

"You mean, Gran's mother is going to die?" I say, forgetting to whisper.

Nellie puts a finger over her lips to shush me.

"Does she not know she's dying?" I whisper back.

Nellie comes up on the porch and plops herself into the rocking chair next to the swing where I sit. She wears cutoff overalls and sneakers without socks. She has an abundance of freckles, and her legs are tan even though it is only June.

"Do you sing like your mama?" Nellie's hair is longer and much straighter than mine and is pulled back into a red hair ribbon, though her shirt is pink.

"No, I don't sing," I say. It has never occurred to me to call my mother Mama instead of Mom.

"What's it like to live in Nashville?" she asks, her southern accent turned up on high. Kids at my school would make fun of Nellie if given a chance.

"Busy," I say. "And loud." I take note of how quiet the mountains are at this moment. No car noises. No machines running. Only birds giving a chirp every now and again and the sound of clucking chickens in the backyard.

"Can you tell me what that sweet smell is coming from the woods?" I ask her.

She sniffs and smiles, not hiding her surprise. "It's honeysuckle, silly," she says. "Don't they have honeysuckle in Nashville?"

My face momentarily warms, but to Nellie's credit, I don't feel judged. Her look is of a botanist with a new specimen.

"I've always wanted to go to Opryland." Her expression lightens.

"It's nice," I say, not mentioning that I have been to Opryland so many times I could puke. "What's she sick with?" I motion toward the house as Nellie did.

"Old age."

"Old age?"

"It's her time. That's all." Nellie sounds like the old lady with the old dog. "It's almost Rufus's time, too." Nellie pets the dog who has left my side to be closer to her.

"His name is Rufus?" I ask.

She nods. "Rufus is over a hundred years old in dog years. He's been with Aunt Sadie forever."

In the distance, a man comes into view, ambling up the hill with a cane. He waves a greeting when he sees us. A short, high salute.

"That's my daddy," Nellie says. "He's coming to see Wildflower and check in on Granny."

I wonder if I will get used to Gran being called Wildflower.

When Nellie's father stands on the porch, he towers over me, but not in a threatening way.

"We've met before, but you were tiny," he says, extending his hand. "I'm Daniel. Jo's husband. How's your mama doing?"

"She's fine," I say, though I have no idea how she is. I got a phone call on the morning of my birthday, and she was getting ready for a performance and couldn't talk for long. She sounded tired. But these days she always seems tired.

"Isn't she over in Europe right now?" His face is wrinkled by the sun, though he looks younger up close than he did walking up the hill. I wonder what happened to his leg.

I tell him that yes, my mother is in Europe, but I'm not sure where. I leave out how tired she is.

When he kisses Nellie on the forehead, she smiles up at

him—a daughter's love unhindered. It would never occur to me to smile at my father that way.

"Is Wildflower inside?" Daniel asks.

I nod.

He leans down to kiss my forehead, too, but I lean away. His thoughtful look hints at bewilderment. He bows his apology, his eyes closing as he bows. He reminds me of a prince in a storybook. A weathered prince, perhaps, but one who has fought many battles and grown in wisdom. I wish now I hadn't ducked.

In the meantime, Nellie looks at me as though I am a thousand-piece puzzle that may take more time than she realized to figure out. I can't say that I have come anywhere near to solving it myself. But being here feels important, as if the mountains are somehow magical and a lifetime of mysteries might be resolved in a single afternoon. In agreement, Rufus looks at me and wags his tail.

CHAPTER FIVE

Wildflower

A quilt with hummingbirds graces the top of Mama's bed. A quilt that Mama and Aunt Sadie made together in the evenings when I was growing up. It is a replica of another quilt that was in the family for ages, one that my Grandma McAllister brought over from the old country. The first hummingbird quilt was wrapped around Daddy and went with him to his grave. The McAllister family doesn't have family heirlooms. No gold jewelry or silver or china plates. But according to Sadie, this hummingbird quilt will pass to me someday, and then to Lily, and then to Daisy. I'm not sure how she and Mama decided this, given I have three sisters, but I am grateful that it will.

Mama looks small, lying on the bed. Why is it that people who are dying always look smaller than when they were alive and well? A formidable woman, Mama could evoke fear in me with a single look. A look that could convey her instant disappointment in me, and her secret wish that I was different. Quieter. More controlled. Less emotional.

As I approach, I remember Daddy lying on this same bed when he left this world for the next one. A leave-taking that at the tender age of twelve woke me up to the randomness of life and death. It didn't matter if you were kind or how much you were needed, you could still be taken away in an instant, never to be seen again. Carried away by a God who supposedly kept good people for himself. This consolation never made sense. The world needs all the good people here, not in heaven.

When I look down at Mama in her bed, I realize how strange it is to see her without her apron. As long as I have known her, she took turns wearing three aprons that lived on wooden pegs on the back of the kitchen door. All were too faded and nondescript to be such a critical uniform in her life. Mama seems somehow naked with only a nightgown showing beneath the quilt, her pale chest covered in wrinkled age spots. Her hair is now white with streaks of gray running through it, and it still reaches to her waist. It is down instead of up in her usual bun. This, too, adds to the strangeness.

Aunt Sadie looks over at me as if to give me strength. After Daddy died, she stepped in to help fill the space her brother left behind. She showed up on anniversaries, birthdays, and holidays and insisted we take her homemade tonics to avoid colds every winter. Sadie was loyal to all of us, not just Mama. Mama and Sadie have lived together these last few years. More like sisters than in-laws sharing meals and companionship. Playing cards, working on quilts, and watching a television show or two.

For the longest time, we stand at her bedside and watch

Mama sleep. For years I tried to get her to go to a regular doctor and have tests run so we could get some formal kind of diagnosis and know what we're dealing with, but she refused. If Aunt Sadie couldn't fix it with her herbal remedies, Mama didn't want it fixed. Perhaps there is wisdom in this choice. Maybe not. Mama can be more stubborn than the most stubborn mule. At the same time, Aunt Sadie, at ninety-six years of age, has been an expert in mountain plant cures for over half a century.

"Will you be okay staying here if I go and get lunch started?" Aunt Sadie asks, her voice just above a whisper.

"Of course," I whisper back. When I hold Mama's hand, I notice that she has clear nail polish on her fingers. I imagine Meg painted them, since she won't even walk to the mailbox without a fresh coat of polish, and I anticipate seeing my sisters later for lunch.

"Our job is just to try to make her transition as smooth as possible," Sadie says, patting my shoulder.

"Smooth as possible," I repeat, not having a clue what that means.

The room smells of Aunt Sadie's blackberry spirits, mixed in with other elixirs in nature's medicine cabinet. Remedies used to make Mama more comfortable in this grandest of transitions.

"I'll check on Daisy on my way to the kitchen," Aunt Sadie says.

I thank her as she leaves the room, quietly latching the door behind her. I feel suddenly claustrophobic in the closed room and take a couple of deep breaths, willing myself to stay calm and be here for Mama.

Then I think of Daddy and how I could feel him on the path up to the house. Being back in Katy's Ridge is like having a family reunion with those who have gone on before, and those who are going soon.

Mama stirs. She lets out a soft moan before opening her eyes. She appears to focus, and then she smiles her delight at seeing me. I have experienced her irritation many times, but I can't say I have ever experienced her joy. My heart opens to the miracle of finally being seen by the woman who gave birth to me. A girlish giggle escapes my lips. Mama's eyes fill with tears before she sweeps them away. The McAllisters have never liked to be seen crying.

She takes my hand.

"I didn't think I'd ever see you again."

"I got here as fast as I could," I say. I move closer, squeezing Mama's veined hand, her skin tinted gray rather than flesh tone. Her hands are callused as someone who has worked hard her entire life. They are cool to the touch, almost cold.

Most importantly, her smile, through tears, hasn't waned. I soak in the sunshine of her approval. A gift I have waited my entire life to receive. I have always thought that I was too much for Mama to handle. Too talkative. Too imaginative. Too *everything*. However, at this moment, I feel I am exactly who she needs.

Mama looks at me, gathering her strength to speak. "I've missed you so much, Joseph,"

A slight gasp escapes my lips, as Mama's approval feels suddenly snatched away. She always said that I looked just like Daddy, that we were two peas in a pod.

Mama's cheeks blush a dull pink like a young woman awaiting her beau. Her smile makes her look decades younger. It seems that Mama—like Aunt Sadie—has been old forever, but when I left Katy's Ridge with Bee and Lily, Mama was younger than I am now.

"I knew you'd come," she says, her gaze unwavering.

A shiver tickles my spine as I remember the smell of aftershave on the trail and the whistling I heard on the wind.

"Come closer." Mama takes my hands, squeezing them weakly to test their realness. I am the ghost of my father. This belief animates her.

"It's not like me to take to my bed," she says to her long-dead husband. "I only did this on the days our babies were coming. Remember?"

I nod and smile, an unwitting stand-in for my father.

"All our girls came quickly once the pains started," she begins again. "Even Jo was shorter than the usual first labor. Then eighteen months later, Meg came. Then Amy. Then—"

Mama's voice grows softer. "A month doesn't pass that I don't think of our baby Beth." Her eyes glisten with new tears.

I squeeze her hand again, wishing I knew what to say. Beth was the baby whose tiny grave is right next to Daddy's in the cemetery.

"I remember," I say, wanting to give her something—anything—to comfort her.

Her voice changes again, from soft to stern.

"A year later, Louisa May came. She whooshed out of me like she was late for supper. A meal that child has never been late for a day in her life, I might add."

The last girl, I was to be named Louisa May because all the character names in *Little Women* were taken. But instead of being honored to be named after the author, Louisa May Alcott, I felt like I had missed out on being one of the sisters. Years later, it was Daddy who nicknamed me Wildflower for my wildness and supposed beauty. Daddy was the one who always saw me as I was.

"The hardest part to having Louisa May came later," Mama continues, "whenever I tried to keep that strong will of hers in check." She looks as though she's tasted something bitter. "You were the one who always knew how to handle her. How dare you leave me just when I needed you the most." She shoots a scolding look in my direction.

"I'm sorry, Nell," I say, pretending to be my father. "It wasn't my choice to leave. And you did the best you could."

Mama's fury softens into a faint smile. "I did do my best, Joseph." She closes her eyes again, as though exhausted by the memories, and begins a light snore.

A knock on the door pulls my attention away from Mama. Daniel steps inside, and we embrace. I will never forget the night he rescued me in the woods and carried me home. I crawled inside his smell that night. A scent that reminded me of Daddy. A mixture of sweat and sawdust, river and earth. Years later, Daniel would work with me at the sawmill and help me keep the business going. Until people found out about Bee and me.

"I'm glad you're here, Wildflower." His low voice resonates through me, soothing everything that ails.

"She doesn't recognize me, Daniel. She thinks I'm Daddy."

He looks at Mama sleeping. "She comes and goes right now. It's just the way these things are." Aunt Sadie said something similar, and I realize that they have been dealing with this a lot longer than I have.

Mama fidgets, restless. Life and death play tug-of-war. She opens her eyes again. Daniel steps forward.

"You need anything, Nell?" he asks.

She narrows her eyes as though trying to decipher who he is. Memory wins. "I'm fine, Daniel."

"Spoken like a true southern woman," he says. "Everything's fine, even on her deathbed."

A slight smile crosses her lips. She has always said that she can trust Daniel to tell her the truth. Mama knows it's her time.

"Joseph was here, Daniel. We had a nice chat."

Daniel and I exchange a quick look.

"Wildflower is here, too, Nell." Daniel steps aside to reveal me standing near the end of her bed.

A flash of irritation crosses Mama's face. "It's about time."

I was always the one to catch Mama's wrath. A fact that is hard not to take personally, especially now. She looks at me only briefly before returning to Daniel.

"I wouldn't let Sadie call her until the last minute," Mama says to Daniel. "Louisa May moped around here for a solid year after Joseph died, reminding us all how life had dealt her the worst of blows. But life had dealt the same blow to me," she continues. "Of course, it never dawned on her what Joseph's death was like for me. Or how hard I worked to keep from collapsing in a heap on the floor and never getting up again."

Her bitterness surprises me.

"I was twelve, Mama," I say. "It wasn't my job to understand. I couldn't have if I'd tried. I was a child."

She doesn't appear to hear.

One minute Mama sounds lucid and in the present day, and the next minute it is 1941, and she is grieving her newly dead husband.

"Wildflower came as soon as she heard," Daniel says in my defense.

"Louisa May always wore that big heart of hers on her sleeve," Mama says, as if this is the worst of sins.

Daniel starts to correct her, but even weakened, Mama will have none of it. His look tells me that she isn't herself, she doesn't know what she's saying.

Now that I am Louisa May and not Daddy, Mama hasn't looked at me once. I can't tell if she knows I am in the room or not. I hang on to the thin rope of knowledge that she loves me and would move mountains for me if she could. Yet her words tell me a different story. A story of grievances held on to for years.

But then Mama's words soften again. "Truth be told, I let her down, Daniel. I need to apologize for that before I go. That's why I need to wait until she gets here."

"Wildflower is here, Nell." Daniel motions for me to join him at the bed, and Mama appears to see me for the first time.

"Is Lily here, too?"

"She's on tour, Mama. But Daisy is here."

"Daisy?"

"Lily's daughter," I say. "Your great-granddaughter."

Mama nods. "Next time I see Joseph, I want to tell him about Lily being famous."

"Were you dreaming earlier?" I ask. "You looked so happy."

"Joseph came to me," she says. "He says I get to go with him soon." Mama closes her eyes as if practicing her leave-taking. I wonder if she has fallen asleep again, but then she mumbles something about having things she needs to tell Wildflower.

Daniel and I exchange another look. Mama's confusion fades in and out like an old-timey radio station.

"Mama, I'm here," I say, holding her hand.

"I'm glad she's on her way," Mama says, not opening her eyes. "I need to tell Joseph that Lily is famous," she repeats.

Mama has been one of the most dependable people to ever walk this earth, and for her to be this confused is hard to witness.

"Would you like me to bring you some of Aunt Sadie's special tea?" Daniel says to Mama.

"I hate that 'special tea.'" Mama spits out the words as though spitting out the tea. "But it does make my memories come alive."

Daniel leaves to get Sadie, and Mama appears to be sleeping again. I suddenly realize how tired I am. It has already been a long day, and it's barely lunchtime. It is Sadie who returns, not Daniel, carrying a cup and saucer.

"What do you put in that special tea of yours?" I ask Aunt Sadie.

"Just things to help her rest," she says.

The smell of blackberry spirits fills the room again, and Mama opens her eyes.

Sadie places the cup to Mama's lips, and Mama takes small sips in what I can only guess is a rare act of obedience.

"I don't know what I'd do without you," Mama says to Sadie.

"I don't know what I'd do without you, either." Aunt Sadie caresses Mama's hair like a mother touching the head of a sick child.

For the longest time, the three of us listen to the clock on the nightstand click the moments of Mama's life away.

Then Mama tells Sadie about seeing Joseph. I sometimes forget that Daddy was Sadie's younger brother. She asks how he looked.

Mama pauses, as though picturing him. "He looked the same as the day he left and never came back."

Sadie looks out the window as though remembering that day, too. "When he first told me about you, he couldn't stop smiling," Sadie says. "He was so smitten."

"I was smitten, too," Mama says. "I can't believe I was ever that young and that in love."

"That young woman is still in there somewhere," Sadie says to Mama, and then looks over at me and winks.

"I doubt it." Mama offers a gruff chuckle.

Growing up, whenever Daddy made Mama laugh—that was the only time I saw the young part of her. Now she looks tired. Worn down. A pencil that has been sharpened to the nub with only a tiny bit of eraser left.

Mama's face relaxes as Aunt Sadie's tea takes effect. She closes her eyes, as if this helps her see Daddy more clearly. "His eyes were gray with a hint of blue sky mixed in," she says. "I could lose myself in those eyes and that famous McAllister smile." She sighs. "I could forgive him for almost anything, Sadie, though he didn't do much that required forgiving."

While Mama's eyes remain closed, Aunt Sadie rubs lotion into her hands. Her familiarity touches me. I always thought that Aunt Sadie would go first since she is at least fifteen years older than Mama. But I have no doubt Mama would do the same thing for her.

Minutes later, Mama is sleeping again, and Sadie motions for me to come with her. We go into the living room to talk, our voices lowered.

"It's hard to see her like this," I say.

"I know," she says to me. "The dying have work to do. It's

their job to remember the past and see the span of their lives. I've sat at enough deathbeds to know this process."

"I'm sorry I wasn't here sooner," I say. "But it doesn't seem to matter anyway."

"You mustn't take Nell's bitterness personally, sweetheart," she tells me. "You're just the closest hook for her to hang her grief coat on. That coat is ragged by now."

"You could have been a poet," I say.

She smiles. "I could have been a lot of things."

For the first time I wonder if Aunt Sadie has regrets. She was never married. Never had children. Her career was making mountain remedies, being a midwife, and stitching quilts. Not to mention making her famous blackberry spirits. She always seemed to have enough of what she needed. Did she want more? But it is Mama who holds her full attention now. Any regrets will have to wait.

"Nell's life hasn't been easy," Aunt Sadie begins again. "She did the best she could, and I know you wish she'd been different. I think she wishes she'd been different, too, but her stubbornness is what has kept her going all these years."

"I wish I understood her as you do," I say.

"It's easier for friends to see than daughters," she says. "But it's good you're here. It's never too late for some final mending."

I nod. "Do you think it will be soon?" I ask.

"I think so," she says. "Every creature knows when it's their time. Cats will go off deep in the forest to be by themselves, seeking out a spot on the rich forest floor to dig their claws into before nuzzling down."

I think of Pumpkin, who one day wandered off and just disappeared. I was outside calling him deep into the night.

"Nell wants to die where she lived her life. In this house

and in this bed that she and Joseph shared. I want to honor her wishes."

The bed Mama refuses to leave is the same one where Daddy died. It is also the bed where my Grandma McAllister passed when I was five years old. This house was hers before it was Mama's. I forget that, sometimes. A homestead has deep layers of history if it has been around a while.

Today the past feels more alive than ever. While Mama lays her burdens down, I want to believe what Aunt Sadie says about Mama's bitterness not being personal. What would a final mending look like between Mama and me? With that thought, I lean toward forgiveness.

CHAPTER SIX

Daisy

Gran opens the screen door and asks me to sit in Granny McAllister's room while she talks to Daniel and Sadie.

"What if she dies while I'm sitting there?" I ask.

"Then come get me," Gran says. "But I doubt that will happen. She's been talking a blue streak, and nothing can shut Mama up if she has something to say."

"What if she starts talking to me?" I ask.

"Then listen," Gran says. "Sometimes listening is the biggest gift you can give a person."

I follow Gran into the house and enter a room filled with the smell of blackberries and my father's liquor cabinet. Until today I have spent very little time with old people. Now they seem to be everywhere.

With Gran's encouragement, I sit in an old rocker in the corner of the smelly room. The rocker creaks against the wooden floor every time I move, so I don't move. The old lady in the bed is sleeping. She is Gran's mother, but Gran doesn't look anything like her.

"Come get me if you need me," Gran says at the door before leaving.

I need her now, but don't say it.

As soon as Gran is gone, I quietly open the window a couple of inches to let out some of the smell. For the second time today I want my mom. Everything is strange here. Everybody acts like they know me. I am Lily's girl. But the truth is, nobody knows the real me. Or the secrets I carry that haunt me.

The rocker crackles against the wooden floor, and I accidentally wake the almost-dead. The old lady opens her eyes and looks straight at me.

Startled, I look away. Should I run to get someone?

When I glance again, she holds me with her gaze. "Who are you?"

"I'm Lily's girl, Daisy."

Narrowing her eyes, she looks at me as though searching for the family resemblance. I turn so she can see my profile. She nods, content with my proof.

"What are you doing here?" She sounds like a blues singer —her voice raspy.

"I'm staying with Gran this summer while my mom travels."

"Who's your mother again?"

I start to answer, and she says, "Just kidding. I know who your mother is."

"I didn't realize dying people made jokes," I say.

A chuckle catches in her throat, followed by a cough, and the world turns serious again.

"Should I go get somebody?"

"No," she says. "I'm fine with choking to death."

I offer her a glass of water sitting on the nightstand. She takes a sip and thanks me. Veins stretch like purple snakes up the backs of her hands, and her skin is paper-thin. Brown spots cover the surface like large freckles. I remember what Gran told me before she left, about how listening can be a gift. I turn toward the old woman with renewed purpose.

"I'll listen if you feel like talking," I say.

Her gaze softens, followed by a long pause.

"My husband died a long time ago," she begins, "but today I've remembered the day we met. We talked for hours, and by that evening, I knew I would become Mrs. Joseph McAllister." She smiles and turns toward the window, as though it has opened into the past.

"He proposed over at Sadie's place," she begins again. "We were having a picnic under a giant oak." She lifts her chin as though feeling the sunlight on her face. "Are you married?" she asks me.

"No, I'm thirteen."

"Oh," she says. "Well, before I met Sadie, I didn't realize women didn't have to marry and have a mess of children if they didn't want to. Sadie lived alone, managed a piece of farmland, and learned everything she could about mountain medicine. It turns out there were all sorts of elders here in the mountains who knew about such things. Some had learned them from the Cherokee."

She closes her eyes, as if that helps her remember. When she opens them again, she asks if I'd like to hear more. I tell her yes. At this point, I am not only giving her the gift of listening, I actually want to hear more. It occurs to me that I should move closer, but I am not ready for that yet.

"The first time Joseph kissed me, my knees went wobbly," she says with a grin.

Goosebumps tingle up my arms. Do wobbly knees come before falling in love?

"When Joseph asked if I would marry him, my voice was calm when I answered yes, but my insides were shooting off fireworks like the Fourth of July."

She looks suddenly younger, as though old age is a mask she's been wearing.

"After that, Sadie and Joseph and I danced in the open field behind Sadie's house."

I smile picturing it—people I've only seen old, dancing in their youth.

"Later, Sadie told me that she knew all along that Joseph and I would be together. Sadie has a way of knowing things."

I wonder if I have this "knowing," too, but it is more like a hearing. Hearing voices from the past.

In the seconds that follow, we exchange a look, as though both aware that I will carry this family story with me for the rest of my life. A story that will remind me of who I am: the great-granddaughter of Joseph and Granny McAllister.

A black bird lands on the windowsill outside as if bearing another gift. I never notice birds in Nashville, and I suddenly wonder why. The crow looks in on us, slowly rocking its head from side to side. It flies to the back of the porch swing and perches there.

"Crows know when someone is dying," she says.

"They do?" I shiver.

"I'm ready to go," she says. "I've got one foot in the grave already." She shakes her left foot under the quilt as if pulling my leg.

"Are you afraid?" I ask.

"No," she says. "It's my reward."

"Reward?"

"Haven't you ever heard of heaven? What's your mama been teaching you?"

I shrug.

"Use words, girl. Nobody knows what those shrugs mean."

For someone who is dying, she sure is speaking her mind. At this moment, the woman everyone calls Granny McAllister seems too ornery to die. For the longest time, we sit in silence. The crow on the porch calls out before flying away.

"How many times did it call out?" she asks.

"Three times."

She appears to ponder this. "That means I only have three hours or three days before I'm dead."

I shiver again.

Then she looks toward the door. Her cheeks turn a light shade of pink. A slight smile graces her lips, and her eyes widen as though someone has just walked into the room.

"Do you see him, Daisy?" she whispers.

"See who?" My whisper matches hers.

I turn toward where she is looking. An old housecoat hangs on the back of the door, blue with small white flowers. Other than that, I see nothing.

"He's here," she whispers again, sounding like a young bride. "You see him, don't you?"

I nod, wanting to see him.

"Joseph, this is Daisy," she says.

Her eyes follow him across the small room until he is standing by her bed. Whatever she sees is real to her. Tears pool around the edges of her eyes.

Then the voices start. Overlapping snatches of conversations of their life together here in this house. They are happy here. A girl laughs. A girl Joseph calls Wildflower. When I look over at Granny McAllister, her eyes are closed, and she is smiling. Her left foot, the one foot in the grave, moves to the slow rhythm of a banjo playing.

The tune sounds familiar. Then I remember where I've heard it. It was a lullaby my mom sang to me before bed when I was younger. Now she sings it at the end of her shows as an encore. My great-grandfather, Joseph, has a bright, steady voice and sings along with his banjo, the same song I've heard my mom sing many times:

Goodnight, Irene. Goodnight, Irene. I'll see you in my dreams.

CHAPTER SEVEN

Wildflower

When I return to check on Mama and Daisy, Mama is sleeping, and Daisy has her eyes closed. She is humming something.

"What's going on?" I ask.

She stops humming and opens her eyes. "Nothing," she says, but her *nothing* is full of *something*.

"Has Mama been sleeping this whole time?"

"Not the whole time."

I wait for her to say more, but instead she hums again. I have never known Daisy to hum. It reminds me of Daddy. The rocking chair creaks on the old wooden floor, an accompaniment to the melody. The sound sparks a memory of when I found Mama sleeping in that chair after Johnny attacked me. For weeks I slept in her bed. It was the first time I realized Mama's devotion to me. I look over at her, seeking forgiveness. Both hers and mine.

This old house contains layer upon layer of McAllister

history. Stories fill the place. Those told and untold. Daniel reminded me recently of how Mama spoke fluent German and hid this fact from everyone in Katy's Ridge. Especially after Hitler rose to power. She lived in fear that she might be accused of being a Nazi sympathizer. She burned any proof of her German heritage. I hadn't remembered that at all. I look at Mama now and wonder what else I have forgotten. Probably thousands of things.

"You sure you're okay?" I ask Daisy.

She nods, and I believe her.

Meanwhile, Mama moves slightly and moans.

"Is that you, Wildflower?" she asks, her eyes closed.

I am surprised she doesn't call me *Louisa May*.

Mama never took to calling me the nickname Daddy gave me. A name I reclaimed four years ago when I turned fifty. A milestone birthday required a proclamation of some kind. So, with the help of the great State of Tennessee, I legally became Wildflower McAllister in hopes of claiming back some of the confidence I used to possess.

"Have you heard from Lily?" Mama asks, her voice sounding weaker than it was when I first arrived.

Of all her grandchildren and great-grandchildren, Lily is the one she asks after the most.

"She's on tour again, Mama."

"Where this time?"

"Scotland," I say.

"You know, your Daddy's people are from there," Mama says.

I sit on the bed and hold her hand. "Lily found some McAllisters in a cemetery near Glasgow," I tell her.

"Did you hear that, Joseph?" Mama says, looking to her left. "Lily found some McAllisters in Glasgow." I always think of Daddy living at the cemetery, not hanging out in Mama's bedroom. But perhaps he has come home to retrieve her.

I wish Bee were here. The old Bee. The not-so-busy Bee. The woman who used to stitch needlepoint bumblebees to the collars of her blouses and whose face brightened whenever she saw me. Right about now, I could use her reassurance that everything is going to be all right.

"Your daddy misses you," Mama says to me.

Being home has primed the pump for tears. If I'm not careful, I'll start gushing.

When I was a girl, Aunt Sadie told me that spirits were all over these mountains. Not just wood sprites and fairies like in the old country that Daddy used to talk about, but the souls of people who walked the land before us. Not only my family but Horatio's people, the Cherokee, who were here before any of us. Horatio was a friend of Daddy's and is married to my friend June. I remember the dream I had this morning of walking the hidden path to the cemetery. A way that was my secret as a girl. What are my secrets now? And why would Daisy be in my dream?

Mama squints toward the rocking chair as if spying a stranger in the room.

"That's Daisy, Mama. Lily's girl."

The McAllister family tree has three generations of daughters. No sons. I think of the magic threes Daddy used to talk about that were always in fairy tales. He said that whenever a three shows up, you can expect magic just around the corner. I want to believe that this dull, complicated world can have magic in it.

"Lily's girl?" Mama says, as though forgetting that Lily is grown now.

Sometimes I forget Lily is grown, too. Grown and living a

life vastly different from my own. A life so busy she barely has time to see Daisy, much less her extended family and me. At best her trips back to Katy's Ridge have been infrequent. But Lily outgrew Katy's Ridge in the womb. Spirits haunted her, too.

Not that I've been much different. After we left, it was too painful to spend any amount of time here. Too painful to remember the scandal and the shame that came from people judging Bee and me. People said hurtful things. Called us names. Without any livelihood, we didn't have a choice about whether to stay or leave. Our secret pushed us out into the bigger world.

However, Mama never wavered in her support. More than once, I underestimated her. Mama pats the bed for Daisy to sit next to her. Daisy and I trade places, me taking the rocker.

"You're Lily's girl?" Mama pats her hand.

"Yes, ma'am," Daisy says.

Her level of politeness surprises me. She never says, "ma'am." Has Katy's Ridge changed her this quickly?

"Why isn't Lily here?" Mama asks her.

"She's on tour," Daisy says.

"That's right," Mama says, closing her eyes. "Lily is visiting Joseph's family."

Within seconds, Mama is sleeping again. We leave her resting, and Daisy follows me out into the living room.

"Is she okay to be left alone?" Daisy asks.

"I think so, but we'll check on her soon," I tell her. "My sisters are coming over, too. Get ready for a lot of people."

Daisy's momentary concern fades, and she begins to hum again.

"That song sounds familiar, what is it?" I ask her.

"'Goodnight, Irene.'"

"That's right," I say, suddenly remembering the tune. "Growing up, Daddy used to sing that song at the end of the day to Mama and all us girls. Mama told me once that she wished her name had been Irene instead of Penelope."

"Her name is Penelope?"

"Well, everyone calls her Nell except for her kids, who call her 'Mama,' and her grandchildren and great-grandchildren, who call her 'Granny McAllister.'"

Daisy nods, as though filing this away in her memory.

"Mom sings that song as an encore," Daisy says.

"How did I not know that?"

"Maybe because you've never been to one of her concerts," Daisy says.

"I haven't? Yes, I have. Haven't I?"

Hundreds of times, I have watched Lily sing, but Daisy is right that I haven't been to one of her full concerts. When she sang at the Grand Ole Opry that first time, I did wait backstage. I was so nervous I thought I might lose my supper the whole time. It worried me that she might mess up in front of millions of people on television. I hate big crowds, too, and most of her concerts these days could hold the entire population of Katy's Ridge several times over. But I remind myself to apologize for the oversight next time I see her.

"Do you mind if I get my book from the car?" Daisy asks.

"Of course not," I say.

She leaves to retrieve it, her dark mood a tad lighter. Perhaps being around family—even family she doesn't know—will be right for her. Maybe being home will be good for me, too. My family is like Mama's hummingbird quilt, and I am one of the fabric squares stitched into the quilt. In Nashville, I have never quite felt a part of anything, but here in Mama's house, I seem to remember who I am.

For a few seconds, the clock on the bedside table and Daddy's pocket watch are in sync before they wander off on different paths again. I think of Mama and her life winding down like a watch. We are all watches in the process of winding down. Since I turned fifty, four years ago, I think about this fact more and more.

For years after Daddy died, Mama kept his pocket watch nearby, winding it every evening before bed like he used to. Somehow that old watch kept him alive for her. When I moved to Nashville, Mama gave me Daddy's watch, telling me that he would have wanted me to have it. Of all my possessions, Daddy's watch is one of the things I cherish the most. Out of habit, I tap the pocket of my blue jeans, feeling the watch's heartbeat against my skin.

In the kitchen, I join Sadie and Daniel. They catch me up on the mundane happenings of Katy's Ridge before Sadie excuses herself to go check on Mama.

The round table in Mama's kitchen looks smaller. A table that has graced the McAllister kitchen for as long as I can remember. It is practically a member of the family, always there to hold us together. With the renovations, the room now extends beyond where the porch used to be. Growing up, six of us sat around this same table. The two youngest, Meg and I, sat on stools that Daddy made, while my two older sisters and Mama and Daddy used the four chairs that came with the table.

Celebrations involving extended family required an extra leaf put in the table that was so heavy it took two people to lift and place it. A card table was set up in the living room for the kids. Graduating from the kid's table was a rite of passage in the McAllister family. In some ways, it still feels like an honor to sit here, even four decades later.

An orange tabby named Oscar weaves around my ankles, a distant descendant of Pumpkin, who was our cat when I was a girl. Mama's letters over the last few years always contained Oscar's latest escapades. She named him after the character on *The Odd Couple* who made messes. I imagine he doesn't know what to do without Mama fawning over him. For years she gave Daddy a hard time for feeding whatever cats showed up on the back porch, but it turns out she was the cat lover in the family.

Sadie returns and reports that Mama is still sleeping. Then Daisy sits beside me, a worn paperback in her hand.

"Iced tea?" Aunt Sadie asks. "All these life-and-death matters make a person thirsty."

We thank her, and she fills four glasses with ice cubes that she empties from the metal trays in the freezer. With the weight of the tea pitcher, her hand trembles, and I rush to help her. All this time, I haven't given a thought to what it must be like for Aunt Sadie—a woman in her nineties—to care for Mama full time. Nor have I given a thought that a glass tea pitcher might be cumbersome for her. I vow to do better.

Thankfully, Mama's decline has been quick. Just last week she was still walking around feeding her chickens and hadn't yet taken to her bed. This thought eases my guilt.

Aunt Sadie takes a boxed apple pie from the top of the refrigerator and cuts us each a slice, as though our coming grief requires food. Her hand trembles cutting it, too, and I suddenly realize that not only am I losing Mama, but someday I will also lose Aunt Sadie. At this moment, life feels not only unfair but also full of loss. Loss I'm not even sure a piece of pie can cure.

In the meantime, I never thought I'd see a store-bought pie in Mama's kitchen. As long as I can remember, she made all her pies herself and taught Lily to do the same. I was often assigned to peel the apples, since I wasn't much good for anything else.

"Do you still have Daddy's old knife?" I ask Daniel.

He pulls it from his pocket, a gift I gave him when we worked at the sawmill together twenty-five years ago.

"Your daddy could peel an entire apple in one long peel," Daniel says. "Do you remember that?"

I tell him I do, and my memory produces a dangling roll of unbroken peel almost reaching the floor, along with the smell of sliced apple.

"It took me years to finally be able to do that myself," I say. "Mama used to hate it when I practiced, leaving peels everywhere."

They laugh, but the mention of Mama causes us to go quiet. Daisy pretends to read. No pages turn. I imagine she is listening. Always. She is so much more mature than I was at thirteen. Maybe that's from being an only child and watching the grown-ups. Her childhood will be gone soon enough as it is. I wish she didn't feel the need to be so watchful.

"I can't imagine Nell not being here anymore," Aunt Sadie says.

"I can't, either," I say.

"It's going to be hard," Daniel says. He stares at his hands as though helpless to stop what is happening. Mama and Daniel have been close since Daddy died. She relied on him to do the things she couldn't do herself and repaid him with friendship.

"Nell's tired," Sadie says. "She's ready to go. Not everybody is. So that's a blessing, at least."

I think of Daddy, who was not ready to go. His life shortened by an accident. A pang of familiar guilt visits me. Guilt that if I'd listened to my secret sense and convinced him not to go, he might be sitting with us at this table. If Mama were here, she would accuse me of beating a dead horse and tell me to get over it. Guilt serves no purpose in Mama's world. Not when work needs doing.

Our conversation pauses again. Death requires pauses. Especially death that lingers in the hallway, allowing for longer goodbyes.

"How long has Mama been talking to Daddy?" I ask Sadie.

"I've sensed his presence since last night," she says. "That's why I called you this morning."

Daisy looks up from her book.

"What is it?" I ask her.

The shake of her head says *nothing*, but I know it is more than nothing. Does she sense that Daddy is here, too?

Unlike Lily and me, Daisy didn't grow up in these mountains where long-forgotten voices whisper in the wind. Daisy is a city girl, with no reason to believe in invisible things and long-silent voices with stories to tell. In all the years I've lived in Nashville, I never once heard anyone talk about death. Not to mention ghosts or spirits. Not once.

However, now I wonder if Daisy is more versed in spirits than I give her credit for. Maybe it doesn't matter where you live, but whether or not you are paying attention.

"Last night Nell started talking to her sister, too," Aunt Sadie says. "In German."

I nod. "Sometimes when I was a girl, I would overhear Mama and Aunt Chloe whispering in German here in the kitchen," I say. "It was weird to hear her speak a foreign language, but that doesn't freak me out as much as her talking to Daddy in English like he's sitting right there in the room. I got goosebumps."

"Goosebumps tell us when spirits are close," Aunt Sadie says.

She told me this when I was younger, except now it has more meaning.

Daisy rubs her arms, as though she has goosebumps, too. Aunt Sadie and I exchange a look, both of us wondering if the secret sense has passed to the latest generation.

CHAPTER EIGHT

Daisy

I turn a page of my book, not reading a word. In a roomful of people, I am good at becoming invisible.

"I've never known Nell to talk so much," my great-great Aunt Sadie says. "She's turned into a chatterbox."

You have no idea, I want to say. Nobody knows that I heard her story about meeting and marrying her beloved Joseph.

Gran agrees with Sadie. "For a woman of few words, Mama has a lot to say."

I am a person of few words, too. I wonder if I got this trait from Granny McAllister.

"Maybe Nell felt talking was a luxury she didn't have time for," Daniel says.

He catches me studying him, but he doesn't give me away.

"I'm still having a hard time believing Mama isn't going to live forever," Gran says.

Sadie agrees and pats Gran's hand. Sometimes she acts like Gran's mom.

It feels strange that the person they already miss is still a stranger to me.

"As a girl, I didn't think Mama even slept," Gran says. "She was always up before me and was the last to go to bed."

"She's making up for that now," Sadie says, tapping the kitchen table three times with her index finger as though adding exclamation points to her words.

"The blackberry spirits help," Daniel says.

Sadie lets out a brief chuckle. "Blackberry spirits could never hurt."

The laugh opens into a silence that lasts for over a minute, but it isn't an uncomfortable silence like at the dinner table with my father. At his house, I feel like Karana in *Island of the Blue Dolphins*—all alone and fending for myself, but without a wild dog to talk to like Karana.

"When are the others coming?" Gran asks.

She must be talking about her sisters. Siblings are hard for me to imagine.

Sadie looks at the kitchen clock.

"An hour from now," she says. "I think I'll go rest for a while if it's okay."

Gran and Daniel encourage her to rest.

"I'll check on Nell," Daniel says.

Sadie nods and places a hand on my shoulder as she's leaving the kitchen.

"I'm glad you're here, Daisy."

I look up at her wrinkled face and thank her.

"If Daniel's sitting with Mama, I may take Daisy to the cemetery," Gran says. "I need to get out of the house for a while."

Is going to a cemetery Gran's idea of a joke?

"Say hello to Joseph for me," Daniel says. "Unless, of

course, he's in the bedroom with Nell. In that case, I'll say hello myself."

Despite their sadness, they laugh. I've never heard anybody talk about ghosts, and I'm not sure I want to visit a graveyard.

Sadie leaves, followed by Daniel, leaving Gran and me alone in the kitchen. Gran washes the tea glasses and pie plates and leaves them to dry on a towel.

"Isn't going to the cemetery putting the cart before the horse?" I ask, repeating a phrase my cousin Nellie used earlier.

She smiles. "You have more of a sense of humor than I realized."

I stand, pleased that she has underestimated me. I return my book to my backpack before zipping it closed.

"I've been hanging out in cemeteries since I was a girl," Gran says. "You'd be surprised how peaceful it is."

As Gran gathers herself, I go out to the front porch, thinking of the crow that looked in Granny McAllister's window. Sadie's dog, Rufus, lifts his eyes at me but not his head. I sit beside him, and he moves his head to my lap. As I pet him, he softly moans his pleasure. He is not a wild dog on Karana's island, but he will do.

When Gran comes outside, Rufus gathers himself and stands at attention, though he is a bit wobbly.

"I used to walk to the cemetery from here," Gran says, "but today we'll drive since we only have an hour."

In the pickup again, we travel the roads of Gran's childhood. She tells me about the different places we pass.

"When I was a girl, I never thought anything of the distances I traveled on foot," she says. "I easily walked a mile or two to see Mary Jane. It was even farther to school, and June and Horatio's house."

She looks over at me as though I should be impressed.

"Sweeney's store was my farthest jaunt." She points to an old building boarded up on a corner with vines covering it. A white sign with faded red letters is above the door. "Sweeney's was far enough to warrant a rest, and I'd sit out front and enjoy the penny candy that Victor always gave me."

"Victor?" I ask.

"An old friend," she says. "His father owned the store."

We continue along the river, and Gran shifts down before pulling into the parking lot beside a small white church.

"We're going to church?" I ask.

"Not exactly," Gran says. "This is where my family went to church when I was a girl. We were here every Sunday until I was your age. The cemetery is behind it."

"Why did you stop going to church?" I ask.

"It's a long story," she says with a sigh.

I wait. I have plenty of time for long stories.

Gran looks over again. "You really want to hear this?"

I nod.

Her forehead creases. "Well, the long and short of it is that Preacher said I was the one in the wrong for what Johnny Monroe did to me, and that I should pray for forgiveness. I never forgave him for that. Nor did Mama. The whole family went less and less."

"Who is Johnny?"

"A boy I used to go to school with."

"What did he do?"

Gran turns off the engine and gets out of the pickup as if typing THE END on the final page of her story. The sound of hammering comes from inside the church, and she suggests we go inside. The doors are open wide, and I follow Gran. The old windows are open, too. A dull breeze blows. Heavy and warm. Honeysuckle blooms somewhere nearby.

Gran walks down the aisle like a hesitant bride. Then the voices start that she can't hear. Voices from the past. Voices all speaking at once. I cover my ears to block out the desperate prayers haunting the church, and I suddenly realize that Gran is also talking and asking if I'm okay. I uncover my ears and tell her I am, though this is far from the truth.

Thankfully, the voices stop.

Meanwhile, Gran takes a long, slow look around. "Daddy preferred an unroofed church," she says, and I ask her what she means by that.

"A place in nature," she says, "like a mountain stream or an oak grove. God was everywhere to him. Not just in a building."

I don't tell Gran that I've seldom thought about God at all.

She stops at the third row from the front of the church and looks at the long bench as though it holds a lifetime of stories. "This is the family pew," she says. "Mama, Daddy, me, and all my sisters sat in this row. Aunt Sadie always sat on the end near the aisle in case Preacher said something that made her angry and she needed to make a quick exit."

For the longest time, I stare at the bench and imagine having a big family. A family that includes a mother, father, sisters, and aunts.

"I wish I knew what goes on in that head of yours," she says.

I open my mouth, tempted to tell her about the voices,

but then close it. Hammering begins again on what Gran calls the new addition.

"Miss Mildred would have loved that shiny new pipe organ," she says as she walks past it.

I don't ask who Miss Mildred is, except that I'm pretty sure she is one of the voices that haunts this place.

The hammering continues. Gran goes to investigate, with me close behind. A young man with black hair, maybe eighteen, hammers a board on the floor. When he sees us, he puts his hammer on a ladder and approaches.

"How's your daddy?" Gran asks him.

"Good," he says with a smile.

"Daisy, this is Adam Sector. Your mom used to date his dad, Crow."

Adam wipes a hand on his overalls before shaking mine. My face grows momentarily hot.

"This is Lily's daughter," Gran says.

I study my shoes.

"Grandma June told me this morning you two were coming," he says, giving me a brief smile.

"Should have known she'd be looking for me," Gran says. "June has always had a way of seeing things before they happen."

Adam agrees. "Sorry about your mama," he says.

She thanks him.

While I soak in shyness, they talk until Gran looks at her pocket watch and says we have to go. We say our goodbyes and leave the church. When the hammering begins again, I think of the blueness of Adam's eyes and how the color goes perfectly with his black hair. Meanwhile, the graveyard stretches across a hillside above us. I wait for the voices, but it is quiet.

CHAPTER NINE

Wildflower

The church grounds are newly mown, and the smell of fresh-cut grass lightens my mood. Sometimes I wish I'd kept track of how many times I have visited this cemetery. I don't feel Daddy's presence here at all. It's like only his bones are here. His spirit seems to have more flexibility.

As usual, Daisy is quiet, the deepest of still waters. However, the blush of femininity that rose when meeting Adam has not faded. I skipped that level when I was her age. The step that contains the infatuation with boys and the sweet and harmless flirtations of youth. Johnny took that away from me.

Daisy and I walk up the hill toward the weeping willow.

"Let's go barefoot," I suggest, slipping off my sandals.

Daisy glances back at the church. The hammering continues. She slides off her shoes. The grass is soft, a plush carpet of green. Plastic flowers—faded in the sun—stick out of the dirt around a few tombstones. Otherwise, most of the gravesites are bare. I stop halfway up the hill to rest. It is steeper than the path at Mama's house. When I was younger, I could run up this hill and not think anything of it. But at fifty-four just walking up it takes more energy than I want to admit.

Daisy waits up ahead. I take note of a tombstone with the name Floyd "Doc" Lester on the front. Mama wrote to me a few years ago that he had died. Surprising myself, I spit on his grave. Nothing ever happened to him for spying on Bee and me. Or for presenting himself as a real doctor when he had no training with human beings. Sometimes spitting is the only justice a person gets.

Daisy doesn't appear interested in the scenic river below, nor in the thick oaks and maples creating ample shade or the majestic weeping willow in the center of the knoll. Perhaps graveyards are an acquired taste.

In the distance, handpicked flowers rest on the graves where the Monroes are buried. The mother was the first to go. Then the older daughter, Ruby. I attended Ruby's funeral. Her death was shocking because she was a girl my age. Ruby Monroe has been dead almost as long as Daddy, as has Ruby's brother, Johnny. Johnny is a part of my history that I don't have the luxury to forget, given he is Lily's father. His younger sister, Melody, died a decade later. At the final resting places of the Monroe clan, there are new headstones where none existed before, giving the dates of birth and death. As far as I know, the Monroe lineage has died out, so it is a mystery who might be leaving flowers or paying for engraved markers.

Up ahead, Daisy has pulled her book out of her backpack and sits against a maple tree reading.

My scalp tingles. Johnny's words from forty years ago

force their way into my mind: *Wildflower? People should call you weed. I think I'll pull this weed.* After the attack, I spent decades being that weed.

Daisy looks up from her book, giving me a piercing look, as though she has somehow heard Johnny's words. I tell Johnny to leave her alone. Leave us both in peace. But fear cuts through me. Fear that has lived inside me for decades. I try to remember a time when it never entered my mind to be scared. Or a time when I didn't worry that bad people might be watching. Daisy walks over to me. I stand taller for her, trying to shake off the fright. For her, if not for me.

"What's happened?" Daisy asks. "You look like you've seen a ghost." She seems to know more than she's saying.

"Nothing's happened," I say, when "everything" is closer to the truth.

"I heard—" She stops there.

"It's nothing," I say again.

To distract myself, I lead her up the hill to the willow tree. At Nathan's grave, I introduce Daisy to Amy's husband, who died in World War II. Amy has been a widow for three decades. Perhaps that's why she has become so disagreeable over the years. I tell Daisy that Nathan always hitched up his pants. A man so skinny his hips were practically nonexistent. A small American flag graces the soil in front of his grave. Perhaps in preparation for the Fourth of July in a few days.

Nearby, I pay my respects to Baby Beth, the sister who died the year before I was born. Leaning over, I pull several weeds that have grown up around her baby lamb marker and toss them in a pile next to the tree. I think of my job at the nursery. Planting and weeding is such a solitary job, and one of the reasons I chose it in the first place.

When we approach Daddy's grave, I smell tobacco juice

and moonshine, remembering the day Johnny defiled his tombstone. Glancing back at Johnny's new marker, I wish him the opposite of resting in peace. But this trip home isn't about Johnny. It's about saying goodbye to Mama, and maybe more. I can't shake the feeling that being here is about Daisy, too.

Standing in front of Daddy's marker, I greet him like I always do, giving him time to answer. "I brought Daisy with me," I say. "Lily's girl, your great-granddaughter."

A soft breeze rises and rustles in the willow. All of a sudden, I feel Daddy close. Aunt Sadie once promised me that the dead never leave us. Moments like these help me believe it.

However, the message that comes to me is unexpected.

Protect Daisy, Daddy says. *Keep her safe.*

The breeze drops, as if Daddy is rushing off to be with Mama again. I ponder his message, wondering if this has something to do with the sadness she carries.

Daisy's eyes find mine. "You look like him," she says.

"How do you know?" I ask. "You've never met him."

Only a handful of photographs of Daddy exist. Pictures Mama tucked away somewhere, so she wouldn't be reminded of the life she lost.

Daisy lowers her eyes and stares at the tombstone. "He was young when he died."

"Thirty-eight," I say, "younger than Lily is now."

Daisy's expression doesn't change. I doubt she thinks about death as much as I did at her age. After Daddy died, I was convinced I would die young. Taken away in an instant like him.

For the first time I notice the moss-covered area next to Daddy's grave that is reserved for Mama. All these years, I have hidden from myself that she would join him under this same willow tree.

"Did something bad happen here?" Daisy asks.

"What makes you say that?" I ask.

She doesn't answer, and I think of Daddy's message to protect her and keep her safe. As always, I question if I've imagined it. It's not like Daddy to give me messages from the grave. In fact, this is the first one I've received in forty years. But it seems an odd thing for me to imagine, too.

"How did he die?" Daisy asks.

"Lily never told you?"

"No," she says.

"That surprises me." I sit on the ground and invite Daisy to join me. "How can you know who you are without hearing the family stories?"

Daisy shrugs, a gesture that is already tiring the second day of our summer together.

"I don't know my father's family stories, either."

"I find that very sad," I say. "To answer your question, Daddy died from a sawmill accident. The men he worked with brought him home. He lived just long enough to say goodbye. Everybody in Katy's Ridge came to the funeral. I wish you could have known him."

Daisy looks toward the river. "In a way, I feel like I do."

Before I have time to ask her what she means, the gate squeaks open behind us. I jump, thinking of Johnny. My heart beats faster, remembering the past. My legs twitch, ready to run. I remind myself that Johnny has been dead for decades. His grave is just down the hill.

A tall stranger steps into the cemetery carrying a handful of wildflowers. He appears not to see us and walks in the direction of the Monroe graves.

Daisy looks at me, an eyebrow raised to ask who he is.

"No idea," I whisper.

The stranger wears blue jeans and a blue T-shirt and hiking boots. He is midforties, physically fit. Something about him feels familiar, like an actor you've seen on television before, but you can't place the face with the program.

Katy's Ridge has never collected newcomers. The stranger adds wildflowers to the Monroe graves. I wonder if he picked them down the trail at the memorial I created to mark what happened that day.

Hammering starts up again at the church and breaks the spell. I look at my pocket watch, aware that my sisters will be arriving soon. I stand, telling Daisy that we had better get back. I say goodbye to Daddy, but it feels like he's already at the house waiting.

As we walk down the hill, the man spots us. His surprise elicits a hand wave that I return. The familiarity nags at me again. He is tall and lean like the Monroes. The tilt of the head while walking seems familiar, too. Then I realize he looks like an older version of Johnny. Although this is not someone who had a hard life and stood at a crossroads spitting tobacco juice into an old peach can. This is someone who stood at a crossroads and chose a direction to go in and took it. However, my secret sense is not convinced I should trust him. There is unfinished business there. Somehow, it seems, our fates are connected.

CHAPTER TEN

Daisy

The hammering continues inside the church. Adam is much more handsome than the boys at my school with their picked-at acne and their tendency to make fun of girls. I can't believe my mom dated his father. A man named after a bird. I don't think of my mom dating anyone except my father. She should have gone with Crow.

Gran stops to wave at the stranger in the cemetery. She looks like she's seen a ghost again and gets really still. I've never seen this side of Gran. A woman with a history.

I am ready to leave this place. I nudge Gran, and she suggests we go. My relief comes out in a shrug. Then I remember what Granny McAllister said about using words instead of shrugs.

We get in Gran's pickup, and I slam the door so that it will stay shut. My father calls her truck a "bucket of bolts." He and Gran don't get along.

Gran looks over at me as if I am a bank safe she wants to

crack open but doesn't know the combination. I want to tell her things, but I don't know how.

In the meantime, Katy's Ridge is starting to grow on me. Compared to Nashville, it feels simple here. In three months, I start a new middle school, which is the opposite of simple. The school is huge. Just finding my classes will be a nightmare. It's supposed to be a decent school, but I don't know anybody there, and it means spending more time at my father's house because the new school is closer to where he lives than my mom's house. I chew on my bottom lip. I hate my dad.

"Would you like me to teach you how to drive while we're here?" Gran asks.

"Are you serious?" I ask, sitting taller in the seat.

"Dead serious," she says. "It's safer to learn on these old country roads."

"I'd like that," I say, taking a deep breath of mountain air.

"First, though, we need to get back and check on Mama," she says, "and have lunch with my sisters, but maybe afterward."

Having never been the type to jump up and down and show excitement, I hug my book to my chest, pushing my sneakers against the floorboard, braking and accelerating in my imagination. Driving means I am almost an adult. Driving means freedom.

As Gran starts the pickup, I look over as though seeing her for the first time. She isn't as affectionate as Bee is—I miss Bee—but she tries, and she has a room in her apartment for me to live when Mom is touring, so I don't have to stay at my father's house. Now she has agreed to teach me how to drive a stick shift. More than anyone, she seems to want to know me. I have plenty to tell her, but I'm not ready for that yet.

I ponder how a person might start a conversation to show their interest. I hug my book again, thinking how much I am like Karana. Even though I live in a big city, sometimes I feel like I live on a deserted island like her, and I'm doing everything I can to survive without getting killed.

"What is it like to have sisters?" I ask.

Gran looks at me as if my question has opened a little door where she can see inside. I look away and hug my book tighter.

"Well, we don't get to pick our siblings or our lack of siblings," Gran says. "My sisters could be irritating when I was a kid, but they could also be lifesavers. We're not as close now," she continues, "and I regret that. If I still lived here that might be different." Gran pauses and taps the steering wheel.

For the second time in an hour, I try to imagine having family around. My father's family lives in California, and I haven't met most of them. Now it turns out that my mom has been keeping her family a secret. Not on purpose. I think she has just been intent on not coming back here.

"Are you close to your father?" Gran asks.

My throat tightens. Here we were wading into a sweet talk, and now we're at the deep end of the pool.

"Not really," I say, resisting my inclination to shrug.

She nods, as if she can understand why.

"You've never really liked him, have you?" I ask.

"No," she says simply.

"Not many people do," I say. "He's bossy and conceited. But mom says he can also be charming sometimes."

We turn into Granny McAllister's gravel driveway

leading up the hill. Gran parks and turns off the pickup and then turns toward me.

"There's no love lost between your father and me, and I won't pretend differently," she says. "What matters is that you have a good relationship with him. I want that for you."

I lower my head, not knowing what a "good" relationship is. Whatever my father and I have, it sure doesn't feel right.

Gran looks up the hill toward the house. I wonder if her hesitation is about seeing Granny McAllister or her sisters. Or maybe both.

"If you ever need to talk about anything, I'm here," she says. Gran squeezes my hand, and to both our surprise, I squeeze back.

CHAPTER ELEVEN

Wildflower

At the house, Meg sits with Daniel on the porch swing, and Nellie sits on the step. Meg is my sister closest in age, with me being the youngest. Her hair is dyed black. She is wearing bright red nail polish with matching lipstick and looks like the Katy's Ridge version of Elizabeth Taylor. Meg used to read Hollywood magazines when she worked at Woolworths, and as a teenager, she hid romance novels in our closet and underneath our bed. Meg always knows the gossip of the rich and famous, as well as the poor and forgotten here in Katy's Ridge.

We embrace, and she tells me how much I haven't changed. I am never sure if this is a compliment.

It is hard to forget Meg's reaction to finding out about Bee and me. It was a disappointment at best. But at least she was better about it than my sister Amy, whose judgment blindsided me. Of my three sisters, Jo handled it with the most acceptance. Although part of the deal was that we never speak of it again.

Meg smells of White Shoulders. A perfume meant to attract, but that I find repelling. She greets Daisy, introducing herself as Aunt Meg. Though they have met before, it has been a while. Daisy says hello to her cousin Nellie and then leans down to pet Rufus, who drools his happiness.

"Mama still sleeping?" I ask.

Daniel says she is. It seems a luxury to see Daniel twice in one day. It reminds me of the times when we spent entire days working together at the sawmill.

Aunt Sadie steps onto the porch, closing the screen door with a delicate touch. She invites us to come inside for lunch.

Sometimes it shocks me that I am fifty-four and that Mama and Aunt Sadie are as old as they are. If we're lucky, time moves us along at a rapid pace. Lucky, that is, if we are granted longevity. Plenty of people in the graveyard weren't fortunate that way. Daddy included.

If I get to be seventy-eight, Mama's age, will Lily be the one sitting by my bedside? If so, I wonder if I will mistake her for Johnny, as Mama mistook me for Daddy. Lily looks like Johnny if the light catches her just right. I think of the stranger tending to the Monroe graves. A stranger who felt more like a ghost than a man. A stranger who earned my mistrust and dislike by merely being a Monroe.

A plate piled high with pimento cheese sandwiches cut into triangles sits on the table. The pimento cheese is Sadie's own recipe, but she is using store-bought bread. I'm not sure why these changes surprise me, except that they are parts of the past that I want to stay the same.

A guest now, I am not allowed to help, though I spent years helping prepare meals in this room. Jo and Daniel's youngest daughter, Nellie, pours glasses of iced tea. She is a different kind of beautiful than Jo was as a teenager. A wholesome beauty instead of the movie-star variety. She is competent in the kitchen, as someone might be who helps in the kitchen often. I wonder where Jo is.

I always felt more confident in Aunt Sadie's kitchen than in Mama's. I felt free to help and unjudged by my lack of skill. Mama's kitchen is more functional, and minus the bird's nests, houseplants, and river rocks of Aunt Sadie's. With the renovations, shiny new appliances are everywhere, and a large gas stove and central heating now replace the wood stove that used to live in the corner. No wood chopping is needed anymore. No need for anyone to run out to the back porch on the frostiest of mornings to grab pieces of wood.

Daisy takes a chair at the back of the round table next to me, while Meg and I talk about the new church addition and Adam Sector and how much he's grown. The latest news from the Katy's Ridge grapevine is about little Wiley Johnson —now an extra-large man in his thirties—who as a child almost drowned in Sutter's Lake and who Preacher deemed destined to do God's work. It seems Wiley is now in prison drowning in bank fraud.

Amy enters the kitchen with hellos. It is incredible how much she looks like Mama now. Amy is carrying a large Tupperware container protecting her strawberry shortcake. Her way of showing disapproval is to not look at me, and from the look of things, she definitely disapproves.

Jo enters next, as beautiful as ever, apologizing for being late, though she is right on time. Jo is approaching sixty now. My favorite sister, Jo is the one who took the most time with me when I was younger. She places a big salad and two large bags of potato chips on the table. My family could always throw together a decent meal at a moment's notice, and today is no exception.

I think of Daisy's question again, asking what it was like to have sisters. We may disagree, but the bond is there regardless. Three sisters are bounty indeed, compared to being an only child, and I think I've taken this for granted for every single one of my fifty-four years.

Everyone talks at once, exchanging news. Being with the family has always been the salve that soothed my broken places, and I realize now how much I've missed it. When Bee and I parted, I got used to living alone, but something about it never felt right.

The look on Daisy's face is of someone caught in a sudden rainstorm after a drought, not knowing whether to be delighted or angry about getting drenched. I know better than to pull her into the conversation; that will have her seeking refuge somewhere else. The tone grows quieter when sharing news about Mama, who is sleeping in her room. That Mama is not part of the kitchen gathering is well noted—the missing captain of the McAllister ship.

I remember what it was like to lose Daddy so suddenly. The hole he left in the family was a gaping wound for years. We would have gone aground if not for Mama, Aunt Sadie, and Daniel. It is hard to imagine Mama being a widow for forty years—most of my life really. I don't think it occurred to any of us that she might remarry. It might have never occurred to her, either. Daddy was her one great love. We all knew that. How could she possibly move on to someone else?

I think of Bee and hope her talk went well. While I have somewhat moved on from what caused us to leave Katy's

Ridge, Bee has not. Over the years, she has refused to even speak of it.

As for my sisters, Meg has been a widow now for five years. Cecil died of a heart attack in his chair while watching *The Waltons* on television. Cecil's daughter, Janie, Meg's step-daughter, still lives with Meg and never married. She works at the hospital in Rocky Bluff as a secretary. Amy still sews and has a shop in Harriman now, too, as well as in Rocky Bluff. She never remarried after Nathan died, perhaps following Mama's example.

Of all my sisters, I am the least settled. While Bee moved from teaching to be an administrator, I have had a series of jobs, none of which appealed to me. Working at the nursery has been the best fit so far. At least I get to spend my time outside. But even though I am in good shape for my age, it is getting harder to dig, lift, and plant.

My family gathers, and I ask about the stranger at the cemetery who was at the Monroe graves.

My sisters exchange looks, but it is Sadie who finally speaks.

"Nell didn't want you to know," she says.

Mama used to tell me everything in her letters, once even sharing her pride in her regular bowel movements, so it's hard to believe she didn't mention a newcomer to Katy's Ridge.

"Why didn't she want me to know?"

An uneasy silence settles over the kitchen, broken only by the sounds of familial chewing. It might be humorous if not so unnerving. Daisy tosses an unspoken question in my direction, and I throw her back a reassuring look. I imagine the bigness of the McAllister clan has her a bit unnerved, and these are only the elders. First, second, and third cousins are absent. That gathering would genuinely blow her mind, as the kids say these days.

"Okay, someone needs to tell me what's going on," I say. "Or at least tell me why you don't want to talk about it."

Uneasiness passes around the table like an empty butter dish.

It is Daniel who finally speaks. "That stranger you saw is Melody's son."

After turning fifty, I thought nothing would shock me anymore, but at this moment I am indeed shocked. "Melody Monroe had a son?"

"Evidently," Meg says. She and Amy look at each other as if they have talked at length about this issue.

I pause to put the latest puzzle pieces together.

"He's been here for a little over a year now," Aunt Sadie begins. "He showed up out of the blue just like Melody did that day looking for Lily. It seems he inherited the old Monroe place."

A shudder passes through my body. Melody Monroe set in motion the events that exiled me from Katy's Ridge.

"Melody never mentioned having a son when she came back that time," I say. "She acted like Lily was the last of the Monroe line."

"My mom is part of the Monroe line?" Daisy asks.

We turn in her direction. I imagine cats rushing out of bags. Has Lily never told Daisy who Lily's father was? Has Lily been so busy she hasn't given Daisy even a basic family history?

"Melody Monroe wasn't in her right mind when she came here," Aunt Sadie begins again. "She'd been drinking heavily for years. The boy was living with his father at the time."

I sit with this new information, creating a rough road map in my mind where there wasn't even a path before.

"What is he doing here?" I ask.

"Nobody knows," Meg says. "But he seems harmless enough."

"Harmless or not, why are you just now telling me?" I look around the family table.

Daniel looks at his hands. "We were being protective."

I suddenly feel tired. It seems like days since Daisy and I arrived in Katy's Ridge, and it has only been a few hours. Meanwhile, secrets are already bubbling to the surface like hot springs.

"What do you know about him?" I ask.

"He may be wealthy," Meg says. "He tore down the Monroe cabin and started over. Built a nice house in its place."

A wealthy Monroe is hard to imagine. I remember Johnny's tattered clothes and smelly breath before shaking the image away. Until this morning, I hadn't dreamed about him for years. I thought I had finally erased him.

"People rarely move to Katy's Ridge," Jo says. "It gives us something to talk about at least." She smiles at Daniel. Nellie, who has been leaning against the counter all this time, walks over to her mother and begins to braid her hair. I wonder how my life may have been different if Mama had let me touch her in this way.

"Who knows, maybe someday you'll come back to Katy's Ridge, too, Wildflower." Meg winks.

I tell her it will never happen, but somehow, even my resistance feels tired.

For one thing, Bee is my family, too, and she would never move back to Katy's Ridge. Even Nashville seems too small for her now. If not for Lily and Daisy and me, she might be living in Atlanta or Boston. A place with museums and symphonies instead of the birthplace of country music.

"How's Lily?" Meg asks me.

Lily has done things none of us imagined a McAllister would ever do—traveled the world, had a gold record, won a Grammy Award. All this in the last three years.

I glance at Daisy. "We heard from her briefly yesterday since it was Daisy's birthday."

Birthday wishes spread around the table, making Daisy blush and duck her head back into her book. It strikes me as sad that none of them knew.

I think again of Melody Monroe having a son and my family still trying to protect me from the past. I wonder at what point the past isn't an issue anymore.

"I think I'll go check on Mama," I say. Rising from the table, I rest a hand on Daisy's shoulder, telling her I'll return shortly. I need a break from my well-meaning family. I need a break from my granddaughter, too, and her unrelenting, silent intensity.

When I open the door, Mama is still sleeping. I hope she is dreaming of Daddy. Her breathing is shallow, and more color has left her face. I keep thinking that any minute she will get out of bed, put her apron on, and get busy. But it appears Mama's busyness has finally stopped. The last floor has been swept. The last of the firewood stacked. The final meal cooked.

"I love you, Mama," I whisper.

She takes a deep, raspy breath, as though she has heard me but doesn't want to come back from wherever she is.

Aunt Sadie comes in and puts an arm around my waist.

"Do you think it's okay if I get out of here for a while?" I say to her. "I need some fresh air."

She says she understands.

I have no idea where I need to go, but I make my apologies in the kitchen and tell everyone that I will be back soon. The look on Daisy's face causes me to motion for her to come along. She puts her book in her backpack, tossing it over her shoulder. We will escape together.

CHAPTER TWELVE

Daisy

Leaving the house, the mountain air smells sweet with honeysuckle. Something else is blooming that I don't know the name of.

"We're going to run the roads some," Gran says. "You okay with that?"

I nod. Not many people get to run country roads with their grandmother in a beat-up pickup that she is also going to teach me to drive. For several sweet seconds, my life feels good, and I wonder what it would be like to feel this way all the time.

"We're going to the old sawmill," Gran says.

I wonder if this is the same sawmill where my great-grandfather, Joseph McAllister, had his accident. I envision bloody saw blades and faded pools of blood still on the floor from long ago. Although I doubt Gran would take me there if it were gruesome.

The road is grown over in parts. Gran drives slow. Huge

potholes, half-filled with water, dot the bumpy dirt road. When we come to a field of wildflowers, Gran calls them by their names. Crested irises. Tiger lilies. I add these to my list of things I never knew existed. I do, however, recognize the daisies. Millions of them it seems. I always thought they were such ordinary flowers. But seeing them out like this, covering the landscape, they don't seem the least bit ordinary.

"Aren't the daisies beautiful?" Gran says. "Just like you." My face grows hot, and she tells me that she didn't mean to embarrass me. Mom tells me I'm beautiful all the time, but moms are supposed to say things like that.

"Why did you leave Katy's Ridge if it's so beautiful to you?" I ask.

"Didn't Lily ever tell you?"

"Mom never talks about this place," I say.

Gran's surprise makes me wonder why I never questioned my mom about her childhood or the place she grew up. Somehow, I got the message that she wouldn't like that. Or maybe I thought everybody had hidden family tucked away in the hills somewhere that they never saw.

Gran slows the truck to drive through a deep pothole that covers the entire road and looks like the beginning of a small lake.

"To answer your question, we left Katy's Ridge because people found out about Bee and me."

I always thought Bee and Gran just decided to move someplace bigger. Nobody could blame them for that. It never occurred to me they might have left because of a problem.

"What did they do?" I ask.

"People stopped doing business at the mill, and Bee lost

her job teaching. With both livelihoods gone, we had to leave, and Nashville made the most sense."

A single tear falls down her cheek.

"I'm sorry," I say. "No wonder Mom doesn't like coming back."

"Lily was fine with getting the hell out of Dodge," Gran says.

"Do you ever wish you'd stayed?" I ask.

Gran puts the pickup in a lower gear to get ready for the next potholes. "Leaving here was a little like leaving the best part of me behind."

"I've never felt that way about a place," I say. "But sometimes I wish I could live at my mom's and not at my father's. I'd like to have just one bedroom for a change."

Gran looks at me. "Have you told Lily that?"

"No," I say.

"I think you should tell her," she says. "To want to only live in one place doesn't sound unreasonable to me."

I don't tell Gran that I would be okay with never going back to my father's house again.

We stop in front of the sawmill.

A NO TRESPASSING sign is tacked onto the door of what looks like a large barn.

"The mill still belongs to Bee's parents," Gran says. "Several years ago, they moved to Florida and never took the time to sell it. It will belong to Bee eventually."

A rusty chain and padlock are wrapped around the door handles. I follow Gran around to a side door. A bench sits below the window.

Gran tries the door, and she acts surprised when it opens. We walk inside. She flips a light switch, but nothing happens.

"What's that smell?" I ask.

"Rotting wood," she says.

I think of Granny McAllister and try to picture her Joseph here.

A conversation from the past begins: *We need to finish this order as soon as possible,* a man says. I wonder if this is Joseph.

Another man says that his wife just went into labor and that he told her he'd be home an hour ago. After a pause, Joseph tells the man to go home, that he'll do the order himself. He isn't angry. It is an act of kindness.

The voices from the past fade.

When I look up, Gran is watching me.

"Where did you go?" she asks.

I resort to another shrug.

It is too soon to tell Gran about what I overheard. Too early to tell anyone, if I ever do.

We walk among the saws and long tables. Sunlight filters through the high windows. Thankfully, I don't hear any voices from this room concerning the accident.

"I couldn't have held this place together without Daniel," Gran says.

She looks around as if overcome with memories. I leave her and go outside and eventually end up back in the truck.

Gran returns. "Tell you what," she says. "I'll let you start the engine, and you can practice putting it into first gear."

She tosses me the keys. They jingle their importance. Meanwhile, Gran looks back at the crumbling sawmill as if she is now the one hearing conversations from the past.

CHAPTER THIRTEEN

Wildflower

When we return to the house, everyone has left, and Aunt Sadie confirms that Mama is slipping away from us. I sit next to her bed, already missing her, and longing for what could have been, instead of what was.

After Mama goes, Sadie is next in line, then my sisters and me. Heartbreak is woven into every life. All of us in the process of slipping away.

Later that evening Bee calls and Daisy and I go into the kitchen to talk to her. A lone telephone hangs on the far wall next to the pantry—evidence that the McAllisters have finally entered the current century. The phone is red and doesn't quite match the red of the old rooster clock that hangs over the new gas stove. The clock ticks as noisily as ever, keeping steady time with the day, reminding us with every moment that life is ticking away.

The long cord twists like a jump rope. Daisy talks first and tells Bee about her driving lesson. They have a closeness that I sometimes envy. When Daisy hands me the telephone, my eyes tear up from hearing Bee's voice. Even though we are no longer together, she is my dearest friend. A person who feels as much like family as Daisy does.

"How did the speech go?" I ask her.

She hesitates. "I was so nervous my voice shook, Lou. That's the part I hated. But the shaking stopped after a minute or two. And a bunch of people told me it went really well."

I tell her how proud I am of her.

"How's your mama?" she asks, concern in her voice.

Bee and Mama always got along. But with Bee's refusal to set foot in Katy's Ridge again and Mama's refusal to leave all the chores she must attend to, they haven't seen each other for years. However, in my letters to Mama, Bee always wrote a paragraph or two at the end. I often thought Mama appreciated those paragraphs more than she did the rest of the letter.

"Mama's sleeping a lot," I say. "Sadie says that's perfectly normal for—"

Seconds pass. Though hundreds of miles separate us, I can feel her presence. She knows the struggles I've had with Mama. She also knows how much I love her despite our struggles.

"She thought I was Daddy, Bee. She just kept talking to me like I was him."

"Sounds like you've had a rough day," she says, in that way that makes me feel not only heard but loved.

"I wish you were here," I say.

"I do, too," she answers, though I know this isn't true. Bee will never forgive Katy's Ridge for turning on her. On us.

I glance at Daisy sitting at the kitchen table. Even as a

baby, she appeared to be listening, as though the heavens were speaking, and she didn't want to miss a word.

My secret sense twangs like a string on Daddy's old banjo. I look at Daisy. What is my intuition trying to tell me? Is it my turn to listen? But how do you listen to someone so reluctant to speak? In the next second I wonder what happened to Daddy's banjo. I can't remember when it stopped being in the living room, where it always sat next to the woodstove.

I tell Bee that I should go. I hate that she's paying for long-distance when she doesn't make that much even as a school administrator. "I'm so glad your speech went well," I tell her.

"Take care of yourself," she tells me. "Give that mind of yours a rest."

Bee knows how much I lose sleep thinking about things. My thoughts are like a wheel stuck in the mud that keeps turning and digging itself deeper. Bee never loses sleep over anything. She is the type to close her eyes and wake eight hours later feeling refreshed. Something I'm not sure I've ever done.

We skip the *I love you* at the end of the call, though I know love is still there. After I hang up the phone, I untwist the long cord, and Daisy and I join Aunt Sadie outside on the front porch where she sits petting Rufus.

"That was Bee," I say.

Aunt Sadie nods. "How is she?"

I tell her about Bee's talk, and Sadie says how lucky the schoolchildren are to have Bee on their side. I agree and glance through Mama's bedroom window, which overlooks the porch. Daniel and Jo are with her now. The family will take turns sitting with Mama until there's no need to anymore. When Mama passes, the world will keep going like it did before. No one will even notice, except for those close to her.

When the sun drops below the highest ridge, the cicadas warm up their melodies. Nighttime ambles across the mountains. With every passing minute, the heat of the day cools. I think again of my secret sense, wondering what it sees coming that I don't.

On the porch swing, Daisy turns her head as though hearing something. Her uneasiness passes to me. Within seconds, a figure comes into view, walking up the hill. At first I think of Daddy. Then I flash on Melody Monroe, who showed up drunk in 1956, wanting to find Lily. Rufus stands. Half-blind and half-deaf, he barks, an echo of his former self.

We wait for the figure to come into view.

"It's Melody's son," Aunt Sadie says.

Even at ninety-six, she has better eyesight than most.

"What's he doing here?" I recognize the man I watched in the cemetery put fresh wildflowers on the Monroe graves. A man who looks more and more like Johnny. He carries more flowers in a mason jar. But like Rufus, I am not willing to relax just yet. This stranger is a Monroe, after all, and I have learned through experience to never trust a Monroe. In the mountains, a poison and its antidote often grow near each other, like poison ivy and witch hazel. I wonder what the cure is for this particular Monroe.

Aunt Sadie quiets old Rufus, and the stranger addresses her as the elder. He glances at me with a disarming smile. "I heard Mrs. McAllister is ailing and wanted to pay my respects," he says. After climbing the hill at a faster pace than most, he is hardly winded.

Sadie nods, motioning for me to take the flowers he

holds, which are equally disarming. The two of us meet in the middle of the porch steps.

"Wildflower McAllister," I say, by way of introduction.

"Matt Monroe."

Johnny peers at me from behind Matt Monroe's brown eyes. I flash on Johnny tossing me to the ground. A splinter of a memory. Was it only this morning that I dreamed of Johnny's blood on the gold medallion? Matt Monroe is Johnny's blood relative. Yet Lily told me years ago that Melody told her she couldn't have children, and that Lily was her only remaining relative. If so, then how does Melody have a son?

However, the look of a Monroe is unmistakable, and like Lily, Matt Monroe has had better luck with the gene pool.

"So, you're Wildflower McAllister," he says, as though he's heard stories. But what kind of stories has he heard? My forced exile from Katy's Ridge? He couldn't possibly know about what happened with Johnny, the uncle he never met, could he? I suddenly wonder how long it takes for stories to wither on the Katy's Ridge grapevine.

"How is she doing?" he asks Sadie, motioning toward the house.

"Won't be long now," Sadie says.

He lowers his head and looks at his shoes as though an actor on a stage conveying remorse. My resentment flares. Who is he to ask after Mama? And since when does a Monroe show up at our door without a motive? The Monroes have always been takers. Takers of anything or anyone they want. Johnny took me that day, and I barely survived.

"I'll put these in Nell's room," Aunt Sadie says, taking the flowers and thanking Matt Monroe for his thoughtfulness.

This seems overly generous to me. She excuses herself to go in to check on Mama, leaving Daisy and me to deal with Matt Monroe.

Seconds later, Daisy excuses herself and goes inside, too.

"Something I said?" Matt Monroe offers a brief smile.

The day has been too long for me to return the smile.

"Mind if I sit for a minute?" he asks.

Southern manners win out over my skepticism, and I motion for him to sit on the porch. For several seconds, we sit in awkward silence.

"Did you know my mother?" Matt asks, studying the knuckles on his hands.

"I did."

He waits for me to say more. I don't.

"She died here in Katy's Ridge." His eyes find mine.

My resistance collides with my resentment. More silence is the result. There are many things I won't tell Matt Monroe. For instance, Melody's body was found in almost the exact spot as her brother, Johnny's. It was ruled an accident by the sheriff in Rocky Bluff, just like Johnny's death, an odd coincidence at best. Melody had been staggering drunk the night she died, and the last time I saw her, she was following the whispers she heard in the woods. The real cause of death might just as well be those whispers.

Our family in the old country believed in fairies and tree spirits, but they would never hurt anyone like those whispers hurt Melody when she followed them that night.

"We didn't know about you," I say to Matt Monroe. "Melody never mentioned having a son. She seemed more interested in finding Lily than anything."

"Lily?"

"My daughter." He doesn't ask the next logical question,

which is why his mother might look for my daughter. But maybe he already knows the answer.

"I grew up in Louisville with my great-aunt," he says instead. "I barely knew my mother. Then when I was eleven, we got a telegram that said she had died. It said she'd fallen off a mountain or something."

"I saw her that night," I say.

"I know," he says.

I aim my distrust in his direction.

"After I moved here, I went in search of the sheriff's report, and your name was listed as the last person to see her. That's usually the prime suspect in a murder investigation, you know." I hesitate, imagining Johnny laughing from the grave.

"You think I murdered your mother?"

He grins. "Of course not." His eyes dart toward his shoes again. "It was clearly an accident."

"Did you know your mother had a drinking problem?" I ask.

"Everybody knew my mother had a drinking problem," he says.

"I was surprised she could still walk around that night," I say. "I tried to get her to turn around, but she was determined to go down that trail."

It is dusk now, and Matt Monroe shows no signs of leaving. I wish Aunt Sadie or Daisy would return.

"What brought you here?" I ask, deciding a change of subject might help.

"I inherited a hundred acres here."

"The Monroes had a hundred acres?" I think of how poor they were and that horrible little cabin and wonder why they didn't sell off some of that land and live decently.

"By the time I got here, the cabin had collapsed," he says, "but the land it was sitting on was quite beautiful."

"You don't look old enough to be retired," I say.

"Inheritance from my father. He owned property in downtown Louisville. I would have thought you already knew this. Gossip is like kudzu around here."

"Gives people something to do," I say.

He grins again.

Mama keeps a shotgun by the back door for the foxes that might threaten her henhouse. Is there another fox in our midst? Then I remember Mama pointing that shotgun at Melody. She never trusted the Monroes, either.

"Do you live here in Katy's Ridge?" he asks me.

"Not anymore," I say, feeling like we are playing a game where we ask each other questions we already know the answers to. "I live in Nashville now."

"That's quite different, I imagine."

I laugh a short laugh. "For sure."

"Do you ever miss this place?"

I pause, wondering how much truth to share with a possible fox.

"I do," I say.

"What do you miss?"

I hesitate again, questioning whether to answer him. "I miss nights like this," I begin.

"Nights where the only noise is the sound of the mountains vibrating with life. Coyotes. Owls. Foxes out and about." I narrow my eyes before offering a grin. I can be disarming, too.

Aunt Sadie steps up to the screen door and startles me, but seeing her also brings relief. "Time for you to come," she says.

The game Matt Monroe and I are playing ends in a tie.

He offers his condolences and walks back down the hill.

Aunt Sadie waits on me at the door. "I've called Meg and Amy. You ready?" she asks.

Emotion catches in my throat, a lump impossible to swallow. "Is anybody ever ready?"

"No," Sadie says, lowering her eyes, and we walk into Mama's room to say our final goodbyes.

CHAPTER FOURTEEN

Daisy

Gran sits by her mother's bedside. Gran's sisters are here, too, along with Daniel. Periodically different neighbors and people from the church walk up the hill and squeeze into the room and then leave again. It feels like a small, crowded airport where Granny McAllister's flight has been called, and the plane is ready for takeoff. Destination unknown.

I stand by the window, waiting like everyone else. After a few moments, the radio frequencies of the past align, and I hear two voices. The voices are a much younger Granny McAllister and her beloved Joseph. It must be a time early in their marriage. The conversation fades in and out, then suddenly becomes clear as though happening now.

You need to promise me something, Joseph says, sounding serious.

What do you mean? She sounds young, almost playful.

Exactly what I said, Nell.

Why do you do this, Joseph? Why do you always make a big deal out of everything?

Because it is a big deal. I need you to tell me that you understand what I'm about to say to you.

The voices pause, and I imagine a young Granny McAllister rolling her eyes.

Okay, out with it, she says, but she isn't angry.

If anything ever happens to me—

She stops him, telling him not to be silly. But her voice finally grows serious, too. She is the one asking for promises now. Promises that nothing will ever happen to him.

You must hear what I am about to say. I imagine Joseph making her sit as they look into each other's eyes.

In front of the boulder in the back, I buried a metal box.

Why would you bury something in the backyard?

Because I want to keep it safe. There are people in Katy's Ridge that I don't trust.

You're scaring me, Joseph.

I'm not trying to scare you, he says. *I'm trying to tell you something important.*

She grows silent.

The metal box I buried contains everything my daddy left us. If anything ever happens to me—

Nothing is ever going to happen to you, Joseph McAllister. I won't allow it!

The voices fade.

But I wonder if Granny McAllister kept that promise. I overheard my mom tell my father once that she grew up poor. If Granny McAllister had dug up the metal box, wouldn't that have changed things?

Later that night I am told to go to bed, but I can't sleep thinking of buried treasure by the big boulder in the backyard, as well as Granny McAllister dying in the next room.

CHAPTER FIFTEEN

Wildflower

The house is quiet without Mama in it. It has been three days since she died. During a passing thunderstorm in the middle of the night, the house moaned with the wind as though grieving her loss, too. For decades she cleaned and dusted every inch of this place, and I imagine she knew where every cobweb was known to hide. This old house was used to her touch, both gentle and harsh.

In the waiting time before the funeral, Daisy has been reading Daddy's books: Shakespeare sonnets, the Bible, Mark Twain, and others. She is also working on a project in the back of the house requiring a shovel. I have no idea what she is up to, but I hope she buries the melancholy that has descended on her in the last few months.

After Mama died, I was able to reach Lily by telephone to tell her the news. When she mentioned postponing her concert dates, I told her Mama wouldn't mind her not coming home for her funeral on account of Mama being so proud. She wouldn't want Lily to miss a moment of her success.

I find Aunt Sadie sitting on the porch, staring out into the forest and seeming to remember every conversation she and Mama had while sitting in this same spot. They were sisters-in-law and best friends for all these many years. I can't imagine her loss. Nor, I guess, can she imagine mine.

Gravel crunches in the driveway, and Jo blows the horn of her Buick to tell us it is time to go to the church. Aunt Sadie sits in front with Jo, while Daisy sits with Nellie in the back seat. Daniel and I ride over in my pickup. It is altogether strange to be going to church without Mama with us. Who will complain about how hot the church is? Who will straighten our clothes, even though we are past middle age? Who will caution us about the dangers in the world? Mama was Mama. She was not perfect. Not even close. But her presence will be missed.

Walking from the parking lot, I approach the small, white Baptist church that I attended throughout my childhood. The doors are wide open on this warm summer day. Because of the renovations, the church smells of old and new lumber. People wait out front before going inside, where it is guaranteed to be at least ten degrees hotter.

People turn, their eyes following me as I approach the church. Then their eyes turn to someone standing near the door. When I see Bee, tears come, but I refuse to let them fall and water the grapevine any more than I already have.

"I didn't know you were coming." I lower my voice, as well as my eyes, not wanting to tempt the tears.

"I didn't want to," she confesses, "but how could I not? It's your mother, Lou."

I want to squeeze her hand but don't. She wouldn't want

me to. She wouldn't want me to do anything to create a wave in this tiny pond. Instead I thank her for coming.

Within seconds, Daisy arrives with Aunt Sadie, Jo, and Daniel. When Daisy sees Bee, she offers a rare smile and hugs her.

"I didn't know you were coming," Daisy says.

"I didn't think I was until the last minute." Bee looks nervous, the way I feel.

"Daggers from every direction," Daniel says, looking around. "I'd like to withdraw my membership from the human race, please." I have always appreciated Daniel's loyalty.

"Shall we do this?" I ask.

We turn and walk inside. Do all these people want to pay their respects, or are they here for the sideshow? While I love Katy's Ridge, and my family is here, I would prefer not to deal with the small-mindedness of a few people. One of them, my sister Amy, our harshest critic, refuses to look at Bee. At least Meg greeted her with a nod.

Bee takes a seat in the back row. I want to insist she join us, but then think better of it. We walk up front where the family is to sit. The packed church inhales to receive us. I think of other funerals I've attended here: Ruby Monroe. Daddy. Nathan. Melody Monroe. Now Mama.

I study the people around me—country people in their Sunday clothes. They speak in whispers, as though not wanting to disturb the person in the open casket. The lump in my throat returns.

Please, God, let my tears hold off until after the service.

A few people, bearing no daggers, shake my hand and offer condolences.

After everyone has taken their seats, Daisy leans in to my

shoulder. "You look beautiful," she whispers as though a dollop of sweetness might help the sourness in life.

I tell her she does, too, which is true. Amy made her a dress for the occasion in two days, and it is lovely. While Amy's views can be ugly, she sure makes pretty clothes.

Soft organ music begins to play. An older preacher with gray Elvis sideburns steps up in front of Mama. Mama wrote about Preacher Bill in her letters. He is still the "new" preacher even though he has been here a decade. Thin and wrinkled, Preacher Bill looks like he would be more at home on a tractor than in a pulpit. The congregation quiets, and I pull a tissue from the pocket of my dress to have handy in case of what Mama always called my waterworks. The preacher welcomes everyone and then announces the first hymn, which has me fumbling for a hymnal that Daisy and I share. "Shall We Gather at the River" was always one of Mama's favorite hymns. We can actually see the Tennessee River from here, and after a hard rain, we can even smell it.

Aunt Sadie and I exchange a look while singing about God's celestial shore. It occurs to me that we are singing at Mama's funeral. Can a person become an orphan at fifty-four years of age? Yet, in a way, I felt orphaned after Daddy died, Mama's grief seemingly separating us forever.

We sing another verse, and another, always coming back to the refrain and to the river. The beautiful, the beautiful river. A picture of how life continues to flow along even after the people we love pass away.

With Lily McAllister as her mother, people often ask if Daisy can sing, too. If she has any talents, they are not visible. She pretends to sing, emitting no sound. I hope Daisy doesn't have regrets someday like I do. Regrets that her relationship with Lily wasn't more. Something deeper. Richer. Closer. The hymn ends.

Outside, a car skids to a stop on the gravel. Heads turn toward the high windows that face the parking lot. Heels click on the concrete sidewalk. Someone is late. Even Preacher Bill pauses to see who it is since all heads have now turned toward the back of the room. A woman steps into view, followed by a collective gasp.

"Sorry, everyone."

Lily stands in the back of the small church. She seems to sparkle against the gray backdrop of the foyer, grandly different from anyone else attending. *Worldly* is the word that comes to me. Her dangling silver earrings match the silver bangles around her wrists. She wears a long, flowing black skirt, black heels, and a gray blouse. Her long brown hair is touched with blond tints. She is not one of us, but at the same time, she is.

Everyone on the family bench scoots down to allow room for the sparkling woman walking down the aisle. I stand. Lily gives me a kiss on the cheek and then steps past me. She does the same with Daisy and then sits between us, putting her sizeable glittery purse under the pew.

All this time Preacher Bill has waited, his thin lips revealing a slight smile despite the gravitas of Mama's funeral. It is not every day that an international singing sensation attends the small Katy's Ridge Baptist Church. The full church flutters like a flock of birds about to take off from an open field. It takes several minutes for the deceased to regain the full attention of the crowd.

Lily, Daisy, and I hold hands. A united force. Three generations of McAllister women, saying goodbye to a fourth. I imagine the entire maternal line. Unbroken. All the generations holding hands, today back to ancient times.

Preacher Bill reads a Bible verse from the book of Matthew that he says Mama picked out for the occasion: "Consider the lilies of the field, how they grow: they neither toil nor spin; and yet I say to you that even Solomon in all his glory was not arrayed like one of these."

This was actually Daddy's favorite verse. He told me once that it was one of the reasons he nicknamed me Wildflower. That same verse is why I named my daughter Lily. Hearing it again causes an ache in my chest, as though Mama has sent me a love letter from the grave.

Tears rush down my cheek, and I quickly wipe them away. Meanwhile, Mama is in the wooden box in front of the altar. This reality keeps hitting me like the clang of a church bell. Preacher Bill invites people up to the pulpit to tell stories about Mama. They come up one by one, occasionally glancing down at Mama in repose in her simple white coffin, and often over at Lily, the McAllisters' shining star. I can't imagine what it is like to carry the weight of all that admiration. I wonder if this is why she always looks so tired.

The stories tell of how generous Mama was with whatever she had, and what a good cook she was. Whenever the church had potlucks, her food always ran out first, someone says, and there was often a line. People laugh. Several mention her banana pudding. I also hear about how stubborn she could be as if it was an endearing trait. Several older folks say how hard it was on her after her husband died, and how she raised four daughters on her own.

All four of those daughters and their families sit in the first two pews on the right side of the church, facing Mama.

After a steady stream of people shares memories, the preacher asks the family to say a few words.

Taking a deep breath, I stand. It was decided earlier that I would speak for the family, and I question now why I agreed to do this. I gently touch Mama's casket on the way to the lectern. I glance inside the box at the woman made-up at the funeral home. She looks nothing like herself. Mama never wore lipstick or eyeshadow. Looking out at the full church, tears threaten again. A river of tears as we gather to say goodbye to Mama.

My hands tremble, and I fold them in front of me. "Mama would love that you all are here," I begin. "She'd be embarrassed by the attention, that's for sure. I know I would—"

Tension fills the room like a hive of bees starting to stir. Tension buzzing with judgment. Some of those gathered give me an eyeful of evil. Defiance straightens my backbone. I search for friendly faces.

"Mama would be very grateful for the honor you pay her by being here." I challenge myself to stay strong.

"I like to think Mama is with Daddy now," I begin again. "A few days ago, when I first arrived back in Katy's Ridge, Mama saw me and thought I was Daddy coming to take her home. I don't think I've ever seen her so happy."

Emotion cracks open my words, and my voice shakes. I apologize to the friendly faces. The tissue I hold is in a tight white ball and would be useless if any tears began to fall. Through the open doors of the church, I glimpse Daddy's willow tree in the distance. I imagine Mama and Daddy standing together under that tree, reunited. I let out a soft gasp, pulling in tears at the same time.

"Family meant everything to Mama," I begin again. "She

was very proud of her children, grandchildren, and great-grandchildren, as well as her son-in-law." I glance at Daniel.

I pause, wondering what else I should say. From the back row, Bee beams me courage.

"The McAllister clan is grieving today," I say. Then I thank Aunt Sadie for being so kind to Mama for all these years and for taking care of her at the end. Sadie lowers her head, and her body quakes with silent tears. Daisy, sitting closest, puts an arm around her, and then Lily puts an arm around Daisy.

Finally I send Lily a questioning look, inviting her to sing. She nods her okay and then stands and walks to the front, where we hug. She whispers, "Good job," before I return to the pew and sit next to Daisy.

While I have seen Lily sing hundreds of times, somehow this time feels different. We are saying goodbye to the matriarch of the McAllister clan. A woman some of us feared. A woman all of us respected.

Lily steps out from behind the lectern and closer to the crowd. She clears her throat and then closes her eyes, as though flipping through a songbook in her mind. Then the tiredness and jetlag Lily wore into the church appear to fade away. Without opening her eyes, she lifts her head and begins to sing a song I've heard before. A song that typically is sung fast, but she is singing it slow. The slowness of the fast tune makes the words seem more meaningful. Lily's rich voice fills the church, which is hear-a-pin-drop silent. Goosebumps climb my arms, and my resistant tears begin to flow.

"Some bright morning when this life is over, I'll fly away," Lily sings. "To that home on God's celestial shore, I'll fly away." When she begins the chorus, her voice reaches for the rafters, and the congregation has more tear-filled eyes than dry ones. I hope Mama can hear Lily's song. It would mean so much to her.

"I'll fly away, oh glory, I'll fly away, in the morning. When I die, Hallelujah by and by, I'll fly away."

Boxes of tissues pass down the pews like offering plates. By the time Lily finishes, I am ready to fly away, too.

CHAPTER SIXTEEN

Daisy

As Gran is speaking in the church, I notice how beautiful she is. Not in a glamorous way like my mom or my great-aunt Jo, but in a down-to-earth way. Her black dress is plain on her thin frame, and she wears a sprig of wildflowers in her long hair. I turn to look at Bee in the back row. She winks at me and puts a tissue to her eyes.

Scanning the crowd, I narrow my eyes at the people who refuse to look at Gran.

Some people are just stupid, I decide. If they really knew Gran, they wouldn't act this way.

At the other end of the long bench sits Nellie, who gives me a grieved smile. We have spent more time together in the last few days, whenever I am not in the backyard digging. I never even knew I had a second cousin. Her father is my great-uncle. He told me I could call him Daniel. He and Gran are like best friends. He uses a cane because of an injury he got in World War II. I also had a great-uncle named Nathan, who died in the same war. His wife is my great-aunt, Amy. It isn't easy to keep all the sisters and husbands and kids straight. But after a while, it starts to make sense and fit together.

My great-aunt Amy made the dress I'm wearing. I've never actually known anyone who made a dress from scratch. She looked at a teen magazine and found one to recreate. It has layers to it that make the top look flowy. I borrowed a pair of Nellie's church shoes to wear with it since we wear the same size.

It seems incredible that all these relatives resulted from two people getting married and having children. For the first time in my life I feel like I am part of something bigger. Something I never even knew existed. A week ago, I had no idea that two hours east of Nashville, I had a huge extended family.

After my mom starts to sing, everything changes. The sneers and judgments fade into the background. This happens a lot with her singing, especially her slow songs, and I like how she's singing this one unhurried. To have a famous mom isn't always easy. The hardest part is sharing her with her fans. Sometimes I would just like to have her to myself.

Tissues pass down the row. When Mom finishes singing, the room is silent, as if everyone is holding their breath. This is followed by a giant exhale. Then Mom's high heels click on the wooden floors as she comes back to the bench. Gran pats Mom's arm and thanks her.

The old minister talks more about how Granny McAllister is in a better place. When Mom holds my hand, I realize how much I have missed her. This year has been her busiest touring year yet. She looks tired, and not just from jetlag.

With the service finally over, people file out of the church. Several people come to tell my mom how much they liked her song and how much Granny McAllister would have liked it, too. Gran takes my hand, and we leave Mom with the crowd outside the church and find a shady spot under a tree near the parking lot.

In the distance, Mom signs the front of several funeral service programs as people ask for her autograph.

"What happens next?" I ask Gran.

"Most of these people will leave," she begins. "Then Mama's casket will be driven to the back of the cemetery and carried to where she will be buried. After that, there's another little ceremony at the gravesite, mostly family."

I decide that funerals are exhausting.

"You okay? I know this was your first." Gran turns toward the graveyard as though remembering her first, too.

I nod.

"It's harder because she was a close relative of yours," Gran says.

Close? I want to say. I feel like I just met her.

Mom breaks away from the crowd and finds us under the tree. "Sorry about that," she says, giving me a hug. "How are you holding up, Mama?" she asks Gran.

"I've been better," Gran says.

"How was the song?" Mom asks.

"Gorgeous," Gran says. "You outdid yourself, honey, and that's saying something."

Mom smiles. Every now and again, I realize how close they are, as well as how much I've missed her.

"How long can you stay?" Gran asks her as if she has missed her, too.

"I'm not sure, Mama. I'll make a phone call when we get back to the house."

Gran tosses me a glance. Neither of us has much hope that Mom will stick around. I'm surprised she even came to the funeral. Gran excuses herself to check on how things are going with the next phase of the funeral, as if realizing I might need time alone with Mom.

"Sorry your summer vacation got upended," Mom says to me. "I imagine Katy's Ridge is the last place you'd like to be."

"I don't mind it," I say. "It's simpler here."

She looks at me as though I've surprised her. "Has your gran told you how long you'll stay?"

"Not yet," I say.

"Well, hopefully it won't be much longer." She looks around like she has already been here long enough, and it has only been an hour.

"Were you close to Granny McAllister?" I ask.

Mom looks at me all curious. "Of course I was. She was my grandmother."

I nod, wondering why she didn't bring me here more often if she was so close to her grandmother.

"People grieve in different ways," she says, looking toward the cemetery. Then she sighs, seeming to realize how tired she is. "Granny was very good to me," she begins again, her voice softer. "She taught me how to cook and watched out for me. And after we moved to Nashville, she sent me letters every week asking me how I was, how school was going, and later how my singing career was going. I now regret that I didn't write her back more often."

My feet shuffle like they are ready to go. I hate to see my mom sad.

"How are you, sweetheart?" she asks, putting an arm around me.

I want to duck away, but at the same time, I enjoy her touch. Sometimes I do this when she calls me when she is away, too. I pretend I am totally uninterested in what she has to say, while at the same time, I am hungry to hear her voice.

I pause to answer her question. I don't know how I am. I am here. That's about all I know. Then I shrug.

"You're such an enigma," she says.

My feet go quiet.

"A what?"

"A great mystery."

She smiles, and I catch myself smiling back. I guess I like thinking of myself as a mystery.

Looking at my hands, I notice dirt under a couple of my fingernails. Everyone has been so distracted by Granny McAllister's death, nobody has seen me digging for buried treasure in the backyard. I know there is probably no real treasure there, but the mystery of what might be hidden has given me something to do.

"Do you think there's a heaven?" I ask, surprising myself with the question.

Mom looks surprised, too.

"I'd like to think so," she says.

"Do you think Gran believes in heaven?"

"You need to ask her, Daisy, but I imagine so."

She smiles at me as though I have become even more mysterious.

"Do you have to go back?" I ask, already knowing the answer.

She hugs me and sighs. "I wish I could stay, but I have

people counting on me," she says, as though even she knows how lame this answer is, when I count on her, too.

Gran returns and says that everyone will be walking to the gravesite now. Mom takes my hand, and we enter the old cemetery that contains a whole slew of the family I never knew I had. All of a sudden, this feels like a buried treasure of a different kind.

CHAPTER SEVENTEEN

Wildflower

Mourners walk up the hill to the gravesite. It is a much smaller group than there was inside. Bee is talking to someone in the church. I wonder if she is making herself scarce on purpose. Aunt Sadie rides up with Mama's casket in a truck that belongs to Silas, an old friend of Daddy's. He and Daddy were the same age, and I try to imagine what Daddy would look like if he hadn't died forty years ago in a sawmill accident. He'd be an old man now. Seventy-eight years of age. My thoughts progress, and I wonder how life would be different if Daddy hadn't gone to work that day, or if the saw blade hadn't cut so deep. Would Lily even exist? Or Daisy? I forget who told me life could turn on a dime. Probably Aunt Sadie. In some ways, I feel like that dime hasn't stopped spinning for forty years.

Lily and Daisy walk behind me, holding hands. When I glance at Daisy, hints of her teenage glumness remain, but not nearly as much as when she rode in my pickup to Katy's Ridge three days ago. I still want to talk to Lily. Surely she has noticed the change, too.

The solemn procession advances up the hill while Lily and Daisy join me. Bee is somewhere behind us. I hate that she doesn't want to walk with us. It was ridiculous not to hug her when I saw her at the church. Everyone hugs at funerals. All of us happy to be among the living. But I knew she wouldn't want us to. She has spent a lifetime trying to not draw attention to herself; that's why speaking at that conference was so hard for her.

At this moment, grief feels like an old friend. A friend I met when Daddy died, and that stuck around for years. Leaving Katy's Ridge was a different kind of grief. It wasn't the loss of a person, but the loss of a place that was my home. I hate to admit how tender the scar still is. I glance back to find Bee. I am braver than her. If left up to me, I would have held her hand through the entire service. To hell with small-minded people. But I wasn't about to disrespect her wishes. I will invite her to come to Mama's house after the service and spend some time with Lily and Daisy and me, but I don't know if she will even do that.

We catch up with Daniel, cane in hand, walking up the hill. Until a few years ago, he had shrapnel in his leg from the war and chewed aspirin like they were peppermints. But then he had an operation at the Veterans Affairs hospital in Nashville and now only has a faint limp with the help of his cane.

June Sector waits at the top of the hill. I didn't see her in the church. As with Mama and me, June and I have not missed a month of exchanging letters. She checked in on

Mama for me and looks after Aunt Sadie, too. Although neither of them would admit to needing to be looked after.

June holds a handful of lilies from her yard to put on Mama's grave. If anyone knows firsthand what it is like to be an outsider in Katy's Ridge, it is June and her husband, Horatio. Even in this day and age, marriage between a white woman and a Cherokee man invites all sorts of disapproval. June helped me survive as a young mother, and I relied on her friendship. Lily and I take turns hugging her. Before her attention turns to me, her gaze lingers on Daisy as if seeing something unexpected.

"I just couldn't deal with the crowd," she says to me, offering an apology.

I tell her that I understand.

As we approach the gravesite, I notice the hole dug into the earth under the willow tree, right next to Daddy. I swallow a sob. My sister Jo and I exchange a look, as though remembering when she came to retrieve me after Daddy died. Losing him seemed unbearable that first year and evolved into something I could survive. I turn and look at the river. A scene that has changed very little except for trees that have grown taller.

In the distance, Matt Monroe stands close to his family's graves. A surge of resentment surprises me, as though he is the latest Monroe to spit on Daddy's grave. I don't want a Monroe anywhere near my parents' graves. If an apple doesn't fall far from the tree, I suspect Matt Monroe may very well be worm-infested.

Preacher Bill begins to speak again, words I don't even hear. Grief blurs the rest of the ceremony. While losing Mama is something I always knew would happen, I still can't believe she is gone. June lays the lilies on top of Mama's grave, and Bee adds a bouquet of wildflowers, something I wish I'd thought to do as well. Lily takes one of my hands, and Daisy the other. In the distance, I hear the faint sounds of Daddy's banjo riding in on the summer breeze. He plays the same soulful tune Lily sang in the church. *When I die, Hallelujah by and by, I'll fly away.*

CHAPTER EIGHTEEN

Daisy

We stand beside Bee's car in the church parking lot saying our goodbyes. Everyone has left except us. Aunt Sadie went back with Daniel and Jo, and Mom left earlier in her rental car to go back to Granny McAllister's and get a little rest.

"Can you come by the house?" Gran asks Bee.

"I'd better get back," she says. "I'm worn out from all those looks."

Gran and Bee have not touched once, and I wonder if it is hard for them to act like they don't care for each other. Bee puts a soft hand on my cheek. "Good seeing you, sweetheart."

"Good seeing you, too." We embrace.

"How about I take you out to dinner when you get back to Nashville?" she asks. "It can be a late birthday celebration."

I tell her I'd like that, and then she turns to Gran.

"Sorry about your mama, Lou." Her words are soft.

"I hope you know how much she loved you," Gran says to her.

The edges of Bee's eyes turn red, and she nods.

"Call me later?" Bee says to her.

Gran nods.

Before leaving, Bee whispers in my ear, "Take care of your Gran, okay?"

I tell her I will, though I have no idea what that might look like. Gran doesn't seem to need taking care of, but maybe she needs people more than she lets on.

Bee gets into her car and waves before driving away. Gran's shoulders drop as if a sad day just got more miserable.

"Shall we go home?" she asks me.

For a moment I wonder if she is talking about Nashville, but I have never known Gran to call Nashville home.

We are silent on the short ride, and I even forget to pay attention to her shifting gears. For days now, there have been no driving lessons. When Gran enters the driveway, Mom's rental car sits in the other parking space. We find Mom napping on the couch, and Aunt Sadie having a cup of tea in the kitchen. Gran and Sadie talk about the service while my eye wanders to the boulder outside that is taller than the chicken coop. Having never dug a hole with a shovel before, I had no idea how hard it was. My thoughts drift to things dead and buried.

Mom comes into the kitchen, and before I have time to talk myself out of it, I hug her.

"What's gotten into you?" she says, giving me a squeeze.

My face warms, and I wonder the same.

"Sadie says I can stay over at her house tonight," Mom says to me. "You want to go over and help me air the place out? She says it's been sitting empty for months."

"You're not going straight back?" I ask.

"Not planning to," she says, "but I've got to make some calls." She asks Sadie if the phone line is still hooked up, and Sadie says it is.

I try to imagine my mom growing up in this kitchen and can't. She seems too big to be contained within these walls. While Mom and Gran talk, I put my things in my backpack. Within minutes, we get in Mom's rental car and drive over to Sadie's farm. I am learning my way around Katy's Ridge now, and we drive out past the elementary school and beyond to a road that leads to a lake.

Sadie's place is called a farm, but it doesn't look like one. There are no animals anymore, but it does have a barn and a big white farmhouse. A considerable porch is attached, and there is a big welcoming front door. Mom looks at the place like she remembers a lifetime of visits and has missed this place.

"Can you believe Sadie never locks her door out here?" she says, not waiting for an answer.

She steps inside and starts opening doors and windows and inviting in the fresh air. I never realized before that air could have different smells. Fresh air smells like trees and light and is totally different from the air in Nashville.

"I've always loved this house," Mom says. She checks the cabinets to see what food might be there. I like that she seems to be settling in and catch myself daydreaming about what it might be like to have her around for a while.

Mom tosses me a rag and asks me to dust the countertops, and then she finds a box of Lipton tea bags to make iced tea. When I finish dusting, I fill two glasses with ice from the freezer. With drinks in hand, we go outside on the porch. The day is heating up, as Gran likes to say, but there is a promise of a breeze once the sun goes behind the mountain in an hour or so. I am getting to know the rhythms here, too, the rhythms of the simple mountain days.

As I sit in the swing, Mom lounges in a chair nearby. Porch swings are as plentiful as honeysuckle here in the mountains. This swing has a lonesome melody all its own.

Mom asks me how I'm doing, and I say I'm fine. She lets it go at that.

"Do you think the song at the funeral went over okay?" she asks.

I'm always surprised when she asks questions like this. It's like she's just starting out instead of someone who has sung all over the world. "It was smart to sing it slow," I say.

She smiles. "Emmylou does that sometimes, to surprise folks. I think it's very effective."

"It was," I say, thinking about the time I met Emmylou Harris, who was not only beautiful but incredibly nice.

"How have you been getting along with Mama?" she asks. "This is the most time you've spent with her when she wasn't working, right?"

"I like her," I say.

She laughs. "Well, you should. She's your gran."

"She said I could call her Wildflower if I ever get tired of calling her Gran," I say.

"Did she?" She yawns.

"Were you two close when you were my age?"

She looks at me as though I've asked something peculiar.

"We were very close," she says. "I guess that was part of the problem."

I ask her what she means.

She cocks her head, as though the motion helps her think. "Well, I was just a different person than Mama," she begins. "I needed an adventure. She would have been fine living in these mountains her whole life, but I was suffocating here." She looks around as if the wide-open space of Sadie's valley is not nearly wide enough.

"Why do you never talk about your father?" I ask.

Her face registers surprise. "I never knew him," she says. "Did Mama bring him up?"

"No," I say. "It's just that—"

I pause, aware that this is already more than Mom and I usually talk. By now, she is often busy with something. Something that involves work, not me. But it seems Katy's Ridge has slowed her down, too. If she's not careful, she may start to relax.

"It doesn't matter," I say.

Mom nods, and then takes a big breath as though relieved I have dropped the subject. We sit in silence for several seconds while the porch swing moans a lonely tune. How is it that I can miss my mom even when we're sitting across from each other?

"What have you been doing while you're here?" she asks.

"Different things," I say.

"Yeah?" She yawns again.

"Gran says she's going to teach me how to mosey while I'm here." I don't mention she has also promised to teach me how to drive.

Mom smiles. "You'll probably be good at moseying," she says. "It's in your blood, after all."

I wonder if it is in my mom's blood, too, but maybe she's had a transfusion.

"I still can't believe Granny is gone," she says, more to herself than to me.

"When she was dying, she told me the story of how she met Joseph," I say.

"She did? I thought she was out of it there at the end."

"She was that, too," I say. "But one time she woke up when it was only me in the room, and she told me this long story about how they met."

"I don't think I've heard that story," she says.

"Gran says that family stories are really important," I say.

"Does she?" She raises an eyebrow.

I stop the porch swing, and the world gets quiet. "Can you tell me about your father?" I ask, my curiosity returning.

Her shoulders drop, as if she has already climbed one mountain today and I am asking her to climb another. "Is this something you need to know right this second?"

I shrug and then challenge myself to use words. "Since I've been here I've realized that I have all this family I never knew I had."

She sighs and finishes her iced tea. "Fair enough. What do you want to know?"

"Now that I know a little about Joseph, my great-grandfather on the McAllister side, I'd like to know about my great-grandfather on the other side. Like what was his name?"

"His name was Arthur Monroe, and your grandfather was Johnny Monroe," she says. "Trust me. He wasn't a nice guy."

"What do you mean?" I say, pushing off the porch swing with my toes.

Her eyes narrow, and she looks over at me like she is creating a list of reasons why this is a bad idea. How bad a guy was my grandfather? Did he murder people? Rob banks?

I am aware that at any moment, my mom might wander into the kitchen to find the coffeepot. Instead she finally says the words she's been debating:

"Johnny Monroe forced himself on Mama, and I was the result."

I gasp and let this news settle in. "Did he go to jail for it?"

"No. He died a week later from a fall down a mountain."

I gasp a second time.

"Why didn't you tell me?" I ask.

"It's not something I usually tell people," she says. "Your father doesn't even know."

It occurs to me that I now know what the word dumbfounded means.

"It took me years to get the truth out of Mama," she begins again. "Now I wish I'd left it alone."

The porch swing sings its sad song. A song that somehow feels appropriate given what I've just heard.

"When I was your age, Johnny's sister came to visit, and I talked to her a few times," she begins. "Her name was Melody. She told me that my father, Johnny, wasn't all bad. Nobody is, I guess."

She pauses and takes a long sip of air while I contemplate another family member I never knew I had.

"You said *was*. What happened to her?"

"Well, she fell down the same mountain. Died in almost the very spot as her brother. It was eerie. Before that, she had heard these whispers coming from the bottom of that ravine, and it was almost like her brother—my daddy—was calling her to join him."

I gasp for the third time in my life, and she nods as if she understands.

"Welcome to Katy's Ridge," she says, as if this is what I get for being curious about the mysterious ways of mountain people.

"A guy came to the house before the funeral and introduced himself as a Monroe. Gran turned as white as a sheet," I say.

"A Monroe came to the house?" she says, sounding slightly alarmed. "Do you remember his name?"

"No, but I think he said he was Melody's son."

Mom sits straighter. "Melody's son?" Her brow wrinkles the way it does when she's thinking. "Was he just visiting?"

"No, I think he lives here."

"Your gran must be having conniptions," she says.

I wonder what conniptions are.

"Granny McAllister died right after that," I say, "and Gran hasn't brought it up again."

We sit in silence, as though collecting these revelations in a folder marked, *FAMILY SECRETS*. I think of my own secret that I don't want her to ever find out about.

The telephone rings in the kitchen.

"I'd better get that," she says. "I gave my agent this number."

Seconds later, I hear her talking to someone but can't tell what she's saying. I realize how fast my heart is beating at the thought of my mom leaving again so soon. When it comes to her career, she can't seem to say no to anything. I take a deep breath to calm it while the porch swing sings along.

After Mom gets off the phone, she comes back outside and tells me that she has to give a radio interview over the telephone in an hour. I follow her into the kitchen while she finds the coffeepot and coffee grounds and puts it on.

"Fortification," she says, suddenly looking tired again.

Then she asks if I'm hungry and says she can fix me something if I want. I tell her I'm fine. In the meantime, the smell of coffee fills the room. Mom pours some in a cup with yellow flowers along the edge. She always drinks her coffee black and strong.

The telephone rings again, and Mom is what she calls *on.* As she talks, she is more animated and smiles nonstop, as if the people on the radio can see her as well as hear her. I listen to her talk about her music and her fans and realize again how different she is from most moms. People think her life is all golden records and glowing fans, but there is a downside, too. She is always working. Always composing, practicing, or talking about her job to radio stations and for magazine articles. I wonder if this is the price of being someone different. I think of one of the songs she wrote, about wearing golden handcuffs. The lyrics talk about how beautiful they are, and how she's looked all over but can't seem to find the key to unlock them. I imagine she is wearing those golden handcuffs now.

CHAPTER NINETEEN

Wildflower

The next morning I drive to Sadie's to pick up Daisy. I am taking her to June's house, something we arranged last night at dinner.

"Mom's got another telephone interview," Daisy says, meeting me at the door. We go to the kitchen, where Lily is on the phone telling someone about her first appearance at the Grand Ole Opry. She winks at me. Bee and I were there that night. We were in charge of keeping four-year-old Daisy occupied. Daisy wore a yellow dress that Amy made, and Bee embroidered a white daisy etched in green on the collar. It is hard to see that little girl now. Though she has always been quiet, her seriousness seems more recent. I leave Lily a note on the kitchen counter telling her that she is welcome to join us later if she wants.

When I open the door to the pickup, I toss my keys to Daisy. She gives an uncharacteristic squeal. I laugh, despite my grief. We buried Mama yesterday. Yet throwing a set of car keys to a thirteen-year-old elicits unhindered joy. Further proof that life goes on.

Daisy goes to the driver's side and slides in while I settle into the passenger side. With the keys in the ignition, Daisy places her hands on the steering wheel in the two o'clock and ten o'clock positions. She pauses, as though pulling from her brain the things I taught her the other day.

I glance toward the house. "Maybe don't tell your mom yet about the driving lessons," I say.

Daisy agrees. She puts her foot on the clutch, makes sure it is in park, and then turns on the engine. The pickup sputters its consent.

As taught, Daisy checks the rearview and side mirrors and slowly lets up on the clutch while pressing the gas. We jerk forward. The engine dies.

She huffs. Her face colors.

"Everybody does that when they're learning," I say. "You'll get the hang of it."

Daisy starts the truck again. We jerk forward. It dies again as soon as she puts on the gas. She glances toward the house. I coach her on how to find the spot between letting off on the clutch and pressing on the gas pedal. Letting go and moving on. Letting go and moving on. A task I am not so good at myself. Eventually, she finds it. We cruise along at the breakneck speed of fifteen miles per hour. I encourage her to speed up a bit and put it into third gear. She does. I then encourage her to relax her hands. Color returns to her white knuckles.

"June is Adam's grandmother," I say. "The Adam you met at the church the other day?"

"He'll be there?" She looks at me, and we swerve toward the ditch. I urge her to pay better attention. She brakes, the truck dies, we start over. Being a grandmother requires more patience than I realized.

The pickup strains forward in first gear until it screams for relief.

"Put it in second now," I say, trying to remain calm.

She does as told, and then grinds my old truck into third. I offer a silent apology to the pickup. It strains with Daisy's indecision about whether to go into fourth.

"You're doing great," I say, deciding to err on the side of encouragement. "Since we're going to turn soon, just slow down a little and keep it in third."

The decision makes Daisy's foot, and the pickup, relax. I wish I could do the same. She slows at the turn onto the road and the pickup heaves and jerks until I feel like my teeth might rattle out of my head. I direct Daisy to shift down, but we haven't had that lesson yet, and the pickup dies again on the dirt road. A road we luckily have to ourselves.

"Sorry," she says, lowering her head.

"No big deal," I say. "When Daddy was teaching me to drive his old truck, I jerked us all over these mountain roads. I'm surprised we didn't get whiplash."

"Really?" she says.

"At some point, it will be easy, Daisy. I promise."

I was twelve when Daddy first taught me. Unlike Daisy, whose legs are already longer than mine, I could barely reach the pedals. But I started begging him to teach me when I was eleven. Perhaps I somehow knew that he wasn't going to be around when I was older. Or maybe I just wanted to be like Meg, who Daddy had been teaching that year, too. Daisy starts the truck and begins again. So much of life is about stalling out and beginning again.

"That's June's house at the end of the road," I say. "Just park in front."

Daisy does as I tell her, ending in another abrupt stop. We exchange a look that might have us laughing if Mama wasn't with Daddy under the willow tree. Two other pickups are out front. We approach the house, a log cabin with a big porch and wooden rockers lining the front. It overlooks a valley with the mountains rising in the distance.

"I've always loved this spot," I say to Daisy. "When I was pregnant, I would come up here, and we'd have picnics. June's husband, Horatio, is Cherokee. He and June are two of the nicest people you'll ever meet. She'll read your fortune if you want her to."

"She tells fortunes?"

"For as long as I've known her," I say. "She predicted your mama being a famous singer even before Lily had sung a note."

June also knew that Crow and Lily wouldn't end up together, just like she knew that her daughter Pearl, Lily's best friend growing up, would end up living someplace far away. She is in California now, living in San Diego. I wonder what she might predict for Daisy.

June steps outside onto the porch, her gray hair in a long braid. She wears an apron over her clothes like Mama always did. Next to her stands Horatio, his long hair in a twist, too. When I step onto the porch, they hug me like I am their long-lost relative finally come home.

"Good to see you, Miss Wildflower," Horatio says. "So sorry about your mama."

Horatio has called me Wildflower since Daddy first gave me the nickname. He must be in his seventies now, but his hair is black as a piece of coal.

"June said it was a lovely service," he says.

I agree. Was that only yesterday? Horatio has never stepped foot inside the church in Katy's Ridge, and I didn't expect him to start with Mama.

"Still got that good luck charm I gave you?" he asks.

Knowing I would probably see him, I brought the star ruby with me, though it usually stays in my jewelry box these days. I take the small pouch from my pocket to show him.

Daisy stands in the yard, watching our reunion. I introduce her.

"Apple cider is in the kitchen," June says, motioning for her to join us. "There's catching up to do." She smiles back at Daisy and adds, "Catching up and getting acquainted."

We follow June into the spotless small house. It hasn't changed since the last time I was here. Small wood carvings grace the mantel above the chimney: birds, foxes, and little black bears—a mama and two cubs. Colorful blankets cover the furniture in the living room, and the scent of cinnamon and apples makes the place smell heavenly. I think of Lily and wonder if she is finally off the telephone. I hope she joins us.

When we walk into the kitchen, Adam is there, as well as Crow, who, unlike his father, has a few streaks of gray in his black hair. He must be forty now. I introduce him to Daisy.

"I used to be in love with your mama," Crow says to her.

June gives her son a playful slap. "Since when are you so forward," she says to him.

"You remember Adam," I say to Daisy.

She lowers her eyes, giving away what I deem a seedling crush.

"Crow and Adam came by for lunch," June says. "They're on a break from working at the church."

She offers to fix us lunch, too, but I tell her that we're fine.

Crow stands and takes his dishes to the sink. Adam follows his father's lead, but not before aiming a dimpled smile in Daisy's direction.

"Well, we need to get back to work," Crow says. "Nice to meet you," he says to Daisy.

I imagine what it would have been like for Daisy to have had Crow as a father instead of Jerry. But that would have required Lily to stay in Katy's Ridge, and she had bigger plans.

June hugs her son and grandson, and Horatio walks them outside. Daisy's expression borders on a frown. This is confusing to me. Is it hard for her to see such a close-knit family when hers has been in tatters most of her life?

We go out back and sit at a picnic table that Horatio made. June brings apple cider and homemade gingersnaps. Daisy and I help carry the glasses, napkins, and small plates. Birds chirp and flit between bird feeders made from various-sized gourds hanging in trees or on poles. White beehives line one side of the property. If I lived here, I would want to eat outside all the time. I taste a gingersnap and sip cider, and my taste buds become wide awake.

"How are you doing since your mama passed?" June asks me.

I tell her I've been better, and it strikes me anew that Mama isn't at the house waiting for me to come home. Only June would ask me how I'm doing and really want to know. In Nashville, I haven't found a best friend or even the beginnings of one, unless you count Bee.

Looking out over the mountains, unexpected contentment falls over me. I question why I ever left this place. My mind wanders to how my life might have been different if I hadn't moved. From somewhere deep inside, a sudden longing rises in search of what could have been. But then, my heart heavy, I remember exactly why I left.

"I told Daisy about you telling fortunes," I say to June.

"I do," June says. "You want me to read yours, Daisy?"

Daisy hesitates, her look admonishing me for putting her on the spot.

"You can do mine first," I say to June. "Then, Daisy will know what to expect." I wink at Daisy, who doesn't smile back.

June goes back into the house to retrieve her fortune-telling cards.

"Don't you worry that she's putting ideas into your head?" Daisy asks.

"June's not like that," I say. "She doesn't tell me I'm going to meet a tall, dark stranger or anything."

Daisy looks away. "I wish Mom had come with us."

"I do, too." I can only imagine what it's like for Daisy to have Lily gone all the time. "Maybe she'll surprise us and stay for a while," I add.

"She's been like this forever, though," Daisy says. "I'm not sure she could change if she wanted to."

"She hasn't always been like this, Daisy."

Her look says she disagrees.

June returns to the picnic table with an old deck of tarot cards. Well worn, the pictures are dull and the edges ragged. My fortune involves significant changes. Unexpected twists and turns. I thank June and tell Daisy it is her turn.

After shuffling the cards again, June puts them on the table, letting Daisy cut the deck. Daisy watches with noted curiosity as June places four cards faceup on the table. June pauses and stares at the spread for several seconds.

"What is it?" I ask.

She looks at me. Her eyes apologize. "Family darkness," she says.

"Mama's death?" I ask.

"Further back." She doesn't look up from the cards. "A ghost from the past."

"A ghost?" Daisy looks intently at the cards as though trying to see what June sees.

"An old pattern," June begins. "Something unresolved that needs to be dealt with in this generation." She looks at Daisy and then at me as if making a secret connection. Her eyes widen.

"What does it mean?" I ask, looking from June to Daisy.

June pauses as if debating how much to say. "A darkness needs to be confronted and witnessed. Once you do, it will lift."

June's lips tighten, as if unwilling to let more words pass. Horatio steps out on the back porch, as though summoned. She looks at him, and a silent message passes.

"June, can you help me a minute?" he asks.

June swoops up the cards, returning them to the deck. She excuses herself and goes with Horatio into the house, taking the cards with her and putting them in the pocket of her apron.

Daisy and I exchange a confused look.

"That was weird," I say. "I've never seen June act like that."

"What are we supposed to do?" Daisy asks.

"I have no idea," I say.

When June returns, her apron is off, and she apologizes

for being in the house for so long. "Horatio was trying to fix our old furnace and needed a hand," she says.

But something doesn't feel right. June never lies to me, but right now, she is hiding something.

As though starting over, she asks Daisy about her school, her interests. She asks me how Aunt Sadie is taking the loss of Mama. We don't talk about the cards again, yet they are ever-present in my mind. Something strange has happened, and I have no idea what it is.

On the drive back, Daisy and I are quiet. I wish now that I hadn't suggested she have her fortune read. I saw it as something fun to do, but it turned into something serious. When we arrive at Aunt Sadie's house, we find Lily folding clothes and putting them in her suitcase on the bed. Daisy's gloominess intensifies.

"Where are you going?" she asks Lily.

"They've rescheduled the concerts I missed," Lily says.

"I thought you were going to stay awhile." Daisy's voice weakens.

"Sorry, honey. It can't be helped." Lily tucks a white slip into the suitcase, along with several pairs of pantyhose.

"Can I talk to you?" I ask Lily, who at the moment seems more like a stranger than kin.

Lily momentarily looks up. "Sure, Mama."

I give Daisy a reassuring look before she leaves the room.

The smell of a cedar haunts Aunt Sadie's bedroom. A closet she added sometime in the late sixties.

"How was June?" Lily arranges the clothes in her suitcase with the precision of someone who has packed a thousand times.

"Fine," I say, not going into the fiasco of the fortune-telling.

"What do you want to talk to me about?" She counts underwear and socks.

I look at the child I carried inside me for the hardest nine months of my life. A child who is now approaching middle age. My love for her was instantaneous. A saving grace for a terrifying circumstance. I have often thought that our love for each other saved us both. However, at this moment, I feel disappointed in her. I bite my lip to silence the part of me that speaks her mind. The part that received Mama's wrath more than once. The part that may have even driven Bee away. Despite knowing better, nothing stops the words that want to come.

"I can't believe you used to love to linger," I say to her.

"Mama, don't start." Her voice is low.

I think of patterns passing. Family darkness. My silence causes Lily to finally look up. Does she know how unusual it is for me to keep silent? I close the door to ensure Daisy won't overhear. If I don't tell Lily, no one will.

"What is it?" she asks, now concerned more than irritated. "Are you okay?"

"Honey, I'm worried about Daisy," I say. "I think she may be in trouble."

"What kind of trouble?" Her sudden attention reminds me of how much she loves Daisy.

"I'm not sure."

My answer causes her to frown as though she was looking for a reason to stay behind, but my uncertainty is too vague. Lily returns to her suitcase and folds her nightgown into a small square of fabric. I see the girl she used to be, focused on moving on. Going to the next city, the next country, the next pin on the map.

"Please stop and listen to me for a minute," I say, my voice giving away my frustration. Frustration not only at Lily for not taking this seriously, but also for my inability to figure out what the actual problem is. June's cards confirm something is going on. Something serious enough that June couldn't bring herself to say more.

Lily sighs before sitting on the end of the bed.

"Sorry, Mama. I'm listening."

I hesitate, my thoughts like chickens in the yard that refuse to gather. "When Daisy arrived, she seemed different. Withdrawn. Closed."

"She's always been that way," Lily says.

"No, she hasn't," I say. "She's always been quiet, but not sullen and sad."

"She's a teenager," Lily says. "Teenagers are always sullen."

"You weren't," I say.

"I would have been if I'd known it was an option." When I look at her, I see a woman possessing more than a little bit of Mama's stubbornness.

"It's more than being a teenager," I say. "She listens to everything and everybody as if her life depends on it. She's always studying people, and disappears into every crowd, and hides behind a book."

"Maybe it's because she's an only child," Lily says. "They're always more grown-up than people with lots of siblings. They relate more to their parents and other grown-ups than their peers."

Lily sounds like she has read up on this.

"Well, that makes sense, but I swear it's something deeper." *Something darker,* I want to say.

"Oh, Mama. You see shadows where there's nothing but light. Why are you bringing this up right before I'm leaving?"

"What other option do I have? You're always leaving. If

Mama hadn't died, I wouldn't even have the opportunity now."

"Don't start," she repeats with a sigh.

"I'm not trying to start anything, sweetheart, I'm trying to protect Daisy."

"Protect her from what?" Lily raises her head, and our eyes meet.

I pause and lower my voice. "I don't even know."

Lily stands and goes back to her suitcase and the pile of neatly folded clothes on the bed. Is it my imagination, or does she tend to run away from hard things? Her first inclination after she found out about Bee and me was to run away, too.

"Well, when you figure it out, let me know," she says. For an instant, Lily looks like Johnny. I almost expect her to spit tobacco juice at me.

"What's her relationship like with her father?" I ask.

Lily stops again. "Why would you ask that?"

"I don't know," I say. "Daisy sure doesn't like to go over there."

"What did she say?" Lily stands straighter, a doe alerted to something in the forest.

I search my memory. "I get the impression that Daisy hates his new wife."

"Well, I do, too, but that doesn't make me sullen."

"I never liked him," I say, regretting my words the second they leave my mouth.

"That's not news, Mama," Lily snaps. "Tell me something I don't know."

We exchange another look. It isn't like Lily to snap at me. And it isn't like me to channel Mama, either, sharing my judgments with whoever will listen.

"You've been pushing the river your entire life," I say, my voice softening. "Don't you ever get tired from all that pushing?"

Lily walks over to me. She has Johnny's intense eyes. Eyes that penetrate and won't let you escape. But I am convinced that she is the one that isn't seeing right now. She places a hand on each of my shoulders. I have to resist brushing them away. "Feel free to talk to Daisy and ask her what's going on."

"Why don't you?" I ask, my frustration growing again.

"I can, but I don't have much time. I have a flight out of Nashville tonight."

Since when are you an absent mother? I want to say.

Instead I close my lips, so the words don't escape. More than once, I've said something I regretted. Something that I couldn't go back and retrieve before it did its damage.

On the way outside, I pass Aunt Sadie's old walking stick and fedora hanging on a hook by the door. The past is everywhere. When I was Daisy's age, Aunt Sadie and I sat on this very swing as I confessed what Johnny did to me. Her words were like a healing balm on a raw wound. She told me I didn't do anything wrong, and she was the first person to know I might be carrying Johnny's child. I realized recently that Sadie was only fifty when I had Lily, two years younger than I am now, and I already thought she was old.

I join Daisy on the porch swing. The swing squeaks loudly, crying out for grease. Greasing things was always Daddy's job. After he died, there seemed to be crying hinges everywhere. Daisy chews on a fingernail, pretending to read. What Lily and I talked about, she isn't ready to hear.

"I thought that maybe we could stay in Katy's Ridge for the rest of the summer," I say. "I've got all sorts of vacation time saved up, and it might do both of us good to get out of Nashville for a while."

Daisy looks up at me as though I've extended her driving lessons indefinitely.

"So it's okay with you?" I ask.

She nods, and her shoulders relax. A burden somehow lifted.

CHAPTER TWENTY

Daisy

Gran and I sit on Sadie's front porch overlooking the valley surrounded by mountains. A bed of wildflowers waves in the breeze below the porch. Small birds hover among the blossoms, a light hum accompanying their flight. They dip and dive at one another and hover over the flowers.

"Those are hummingbirds," Gran says.

"Hummingbirds," I repeat. Another thing I never knew existed, like honeysuckle, lavender, and tree frogs the size of quarters that come out after a rainstorm.

The screen door opens, and Mom rolls her sizeable black suitcase onto the porch. When I was younger, seeing this suitcase made me automatically cry, and though I don't weep anymore, a familiar heaviness sweeps in on the breeze.

"Well, if it isn't my two favorite people in the whole world," Mom says with a smile.

I imagine Gran and I both know she means it, but

somehow it isn't enough. Spending time with people is how you know you matter to them. Spending time and listening. I'm not sure Mom has ever been good at either. Like the hummingbirds, she flits from flower to flower, her songs the nectar for strangers.

"Will you let us know you arrived safely?" Gran asks my mom.

"Of course," she says. "I'll call you sometime tomorrow."

Mom will do as she says. She will call the house and say something sweet to me like how great it was to spend time together, which will make her absence hurt even more. I get up from the swing and roll her cumbersome suitcase down the steps and along the rocky walkway toward the rental car. In a way, I wish I could go with her, not that she has ever asked me along.

Mom hugs Gran on the front porch and then walks down the stone path behind me. Together we lift her suitcase into the trunk. I want to beg her to stay, but I know it won't do any good. It will just make her feel worse for leaving when she feels she has to.

A makeshift valet, I open the car door for her. Gran joins me, and we stand at the end of the walkway and wave as Mom drives away. As the dirt rises and falls, Gran squeezes me, as though she knows what it's like to be left behind.

Shortly after, we close up Aunt Sadie's house and return to Granny McAllister's. When we arrive, we find boxes stacked by the front door full of Sadie's things. We find her in the kitchen packing up herbs and tinctures in small bottles. Her eyes are red. A small pile of tissues graces the kitchen counter.

"I thought I'd go back home, so you and Daisy can have

more room," she says, as though she already knows that we are spending the rest of the summer.

"There's no need for that," Gran says. "This is your home, too."

Aunt Sadie pauses. "Truth is, Wildflower, I came to help Nell. I've missed my place. Rufus has, too."

She pats her dog, whose panting smile confirms he would be happy anywhere, as long as Sadie is there. Rufus and I have become friends. He won't chase a ball anymore, but if I throw a stick, he wanders over and sniffs it as if humoring me.

Gran thanks Sadie again for her excellent job of taking care of Mama. Sadie pulls another tissue from the box on the kitchen table, wiping away fresh tears. I have never been around so much crying as I have since Granny McAllister died. At first it bothered me, but now it reminds me of one of those fast-moving summer thunderstorms that come almost every afternoon. They are scary at the time, but nobody gets hurt, and the air smells cleaner afterward.

"I still can't believe Mama is gone," Gran says to Sadie.

Aunt Sadie agrees, and her eyes redden again.

"You sure you'll be okay all alone?" Gran asks.

"Of course," she says. "I've lived alone most of my life. It's people that challenge me." She offers a brief smile.

Gran and I help Sadie finish packing, and then we load her things into the back of the pickup before the three of us, and Rufus, return to Sadie's and help her unpack.

IN THE MIDDLE of the night, I call out, a dream pushing me awake. Gran rushes into the room, asking if I'm all right. My summer nightgown is drenched with sweat. I am sleeping in what was Gran's bedroom when she was a girl. The same bedroom Aunt Sadie stayed in while she nursed Granny McAllister.

"I had nightmares when I was your age, too," Gran says. "Do you want to talk about it?"

I sit up in bed to shake away the dream.

"A man was in the house creeping around in the shadows," I begin. "Except it wasn't this house. It was in Nashville. My father's house." Gran hands me the small glass of water on the nightstand. I take a sip.

"You're safe here," Gran says. "I'm here, and Daniel is just across the road. Only a phone call away."

"Tell me about Johnny Monroe," I say, an odd request given it's the middle of the night.

Gran hesitates. "Did Lily say something?"

I nod, remembering what Mom told me.

Gran sighs. "Why don't we talk on the porch in the morning."

I agree, and she stays a little longer before suggesting that I try to get more sleep.

When I wake the next morning, Gran has breakfast made. Within an hour, we are sitting in two rockers on the porch. Gran's coffee sits on the table between us, steam rising. The smell makes me miss my mom. The mountains are still foggy, and the morning sun is only beginning to break through the trees.

Gran angles her rocker so that we face each other. I question if I really want to know what she has to say.

"This is a family story I never thought I'd tell you." Her words are clear, as though she has been practicing what she is going to say. "Daddy had died the year before. I had just turned thirteen. I was on my way to the cemetery because it was the anniversary of his death."

I try to imagine Gran at thirteen. My age. I think of the dream again—the man in the shadows.

"Johnny was always crass with girls, even my sisters," she continues. "One day, he was up at the cemetery and had been drinking. He was more brazen than usual. I told him to leave me alone. But he chased me down the path behind the cemetery, and finally caught me."

Gran pauses. My imagination fills in the rest.

"Daniel and Mama found me in the woods later that night and brought me home."

We sit in silence, my thoughts traveling the hills. I don't know whether to feel angry or sad. Right now, I feel both. "I'm sorry," I say finally.

"I am, too," Gran says. "For years I thought it was my fault. But what I've learned from my fifty years of living is that sometimes bad things happen, and you didn't do a single thing to deserve it or bring it on."

Gran's words sink in deep.

Something catches in my throat, making it difficult to swallow.

"You know you can tell me anything, right?" Her words are soft.

Not this, I want to say.

"Anything," she repeats.

A tear slides down my cheek. I stand. "I'm supposed to meet Nellie at the bottom of the hill. We're taking a walk by the river."

"Anything," she says a third time.

I wipe the tears as quickly as they come.

Gran lowers her eyes as if to offer me privacy. "We McAllisters have never liked to be seen crying, but sometimes it's the best thing you can do," she says.

"I've got to go." I leave the porch and walk down the hill. Before I know it, I am running. Running from the man in the shadows. Running like Gran down the path in the back of the cemetery. Running to escape. All the while, running to embrace the words I desperately needed to hear: *Sometimes bad things happen, and you didn't do a single thing to deserve it or bring it on.*

CHAPTER TWENTY-ONE

Wildflower

A broom sits in the corner of the front porch where Mama left it. Suddenly her absence makes my chest ache. With Daisy gone, and the house empty, I move from Mama's rocker to the top porch step where I used to sit as a girl waiting for Daddy to come home. In a way, that girl is still waiting.

Telling Daisy about Johnny reminds me of the shame I carried after it happened and still do. Shame that feels perfectly preserved, like taking off the lid to a jar of Mama's strawberry jam. Even years later, it is as fresh as the day it was sealed.

Pushing down feelings is the McAllister way. Yet Mama's death has invited new grief. With the thought of returning to Nashville, my homesickness returns, an echo of the feelings I had when we first moved away. In those days, I doubled over aching for the mountains where I was born. Not only for the people I left behind, but for the land spread out before me now. The forest. The contour of the land. The ease of the river. The birds. Chipmunks and squirrels. The deer grazing in the valley. Everything.

Endings are a part of life as often as beginnings. Mama is gone to be with Daddy. I am home again. But only for a brief time.

A car pulls up the gravel driveway, unseen but not unheard. The last thing I want to deal with right now is another person. It is probably someone paying their condolences. Doing what they think is right instead of what a person might need. From the sound of the gravel, it is a heavier car. I blow my nose with a used tissue in my pocket. I stand but then sit again, fantasizing about hiding in the house, locking the doors. But the notion of southern hospitality has been bred into me like the McAllisters' blue eyes.

A woman comes into view, laboring up the hill. A woman with some heft to her. I squint to make out her features, searching for recognition.

"Is that you, Wildflower?" the woman calls from below.

I recognize the voice of Mary Jane, my childhood friend, but don't recognize her.

Our friendship didn't last after Lily was born, her mother seemingly afraid that my bad luck might rub off on her daughter. At least that's the story I heard.

Mary Jane labors up the path in front of her. As she approaches, I stand again, feeling my past catch up with me. She stops a few feet from the steps.

Despite her breathlessness, a smile erupts. "Wildflower?"

I return the smile.

As the most agile between us, I approach, and we embrace. I didn't realize how short Mary Jane was when we were kids. Now, more than fully grown, she is all of five feet.

Though her body has changed, her voice has remained youthful.

"What are you doing here?" I ask.

"I heard about your mama." Her expression drifts from buoyant to sad.

"You came all the way from Arkansas to give your condolences?" I ask.

"Well, no, I'm also visiting Victor."

"Victor's here?"

Victor is Mary Jane's older brother. How have I not thought about him for all these years? Victor, who for weeks after the attack sent me peppermint lifesavers by way of Meg, calling them courage pills, prescribing them three times a day. Victor, who would have gladly been Lily's stepfather if I had only been willing to marry him. A man everyone liked. Every dog in the county seemed to like him, too.

"You don't know?" Mary Jane asks.

"Know what?" I imagine Victor dead and gone, Mary Jane visiting his grave somewhere in the cemetery, and me not even knowing about it. Dead from some mysterious disease that only takes the kindest of people. Renewed sadness comes, mixed with a sudden regret that I never thanked him properly.

"Victor lives in Katy's Ridge now," Mary Jane says.

"He does?" My words come out in a whoosh of relief. Relief that I don't have to add one more person to the list of all I grieve. Then I wonder why Mama never mentioned Victor's return in her letters. That would be big news. Nor did she mention Matt Monroe. I always thought she told me everything, but it turns out she was selective.

Mary Jane lowers her purse to the ground, as if no longer willing to carry it. "Victor built a big house over where we used to live," she begins. "Well, it's a second home, really, or actually it's his third."

Mary Jane never could resist bragging.

Meanwhile, I can't imagine even one home, having lived in apartments for so many years. I invite her inside for a glass of tea, but she doesn't budge. Nor does she seem to want to sit for a while on the porch. I decide to sit again on the top step. We are eye level.

"How are your parents?" I ask.

She rests a hand on a generous hip.

"Mama's still around, living in Little Rock, but Daddy died two summers ago."

I tell her how sorry I am. "I liked your father," I add.

"He was such a cutup," she says. "Do you know what his final wish was?"

"No idea," I say.

"For us to go to granddaddy's yard and dig up that leg he lost in the first world war—the one buried with all the family pets? He wanted us to put it in his coffin."

Mary Jane giggles like the girl she used to be, and I catch the giggles like a summer cold. The laughter, after so many tears, lightens my grief.

"We found two cat skeletons right beside his leg bone," Mary Jane continues, "so we threw them into his casket, too. Daddy always did like cats."

We laugh like we used to as girls. At this moment, I forgive her for abandoning me when I needed her most, but then I wonder if I am too generous. Friends who betray friends are nearly impossible to trust again unless they fess up to their betrayal.

"Remember that time Cecil Appleby nearly ran over us

when we were rolling in laughter down by the mailboxes?" she says.

"Do you remember what we were laughing at?" I ask.

She says she doesn't. We think for a while.

"Oh, I think it was something about Johnny being a boil on my backside," I say, "and me wanting to lance it."

I start to laugh again, but with the mention of Johnny, Mary Jane goes quiet, as though I have broken an unspoken rule by mentioning this part of the past.

She clears her throat, and I feel a sudden chill.

"I'm staying with Victor while I'm here," she says. "I'll tell him you asked after him."

I thank her, perplexed by her sudden change. "Tell Victor I appreciated all those peppermint lifesavers," I say.

Her eyes dart her discomfort. She picks up her purse, ready to leave, but then pauses.

"Why don't you come up and have dinner with Victor and me tonight?" Mary Jane says.

I hesitate, not knowing if I can get through an entire dinner with Mary Jane's moods. But I'd love to see Victor.

"Do you mind if I bring my granddaughter, Daisy?" I ask. "She's staying with me this summer."

"Sure, bring her along," she says. "It will be like old times, the three of us. Plus Daisy." She turns to leave and then stops again.

"By the way, Victor never married," she says. "Never found anyone good enough, I guess."

For a moment, she seems to be playing matchmaker. Has Mary Jane forgotten about Bee? Or maybe she never knew. Her family moved to Little Rock after Mary Jane graduated from high school. I'm not sure the Katy's Ridge grapevine extends that far west.

The sun directly overhead, sweat forms on Mary Jane's forehead. She gives me directions to Victor's house that I don't need, and we say our goodbyes. After she leaves, the thought of seeing Victor again causes me to smile. Here in the mountains, it is said that if you don't like the weather, wait five minutes and it will change. Minutes ago, I was engulfed in sadness. Now, a reunion is planned. A reunion with what is, and what could have been.

CHAPTER TWENTY-TWO

Daisy

Tall grasses lead to a small sandy beach by the river. Nellie leads the way. Something about this place feels familiar, though I've never been here. Voices fade in and out from an earlier time. My mom and Gran are talking. Gran is telling her about Bee. Are they why this place feels familiar? I push their voices away, determined to spend the time with Nellie. The river current pulses gently against the land. The water looks more brown than blue and smells fishy.

"How did you know about this path?" I ask Nellie.

"From exploring," she says.

"Exploring?"

"Don't you ever explore?" Nellie looks at me as though I am not from around here and am altogether strange. An inhabitant from another planet, perhaps. Someone unfamiliar with human ways.

"Sometimes Bee and I go to museums and things," I say.

She nods, her expression softening. "That counts."

Nellie is easy. Uncomplicated. I don't have to worry that she only likes me because of who my mother is.

"I wish my hair were curly like yours," she says.

"Your hair is beautiful," I say.

"Don't be silly." Nellie tosses a stick into the water, watching the current take it away.

"Do you like living here?" I ask.

"Don't know anyplace else," she says. "I've been to Nashville. It's exciting and all, but I'm not sure I could live there."

She tosses another stick in the river. I imagine she could do this all day. Sending sticks downriver on a journey that she sees no need in making herself.

"What do you do if you want to see a movie?" I ask.

"We go to Harriman. It's not that far. They've got a mall with a movie duplex." She pauses to toss another stick. "I have all sorts of cousins who drive. It's easy to catch a ride. Or sometimes Mama and Daddy will go, too. We saw *E.T.* recently."

We sit together on the small beach, the sun behind us, while I try to imagine Daniel, Jo, and Nellie seated in a dark movie theater watching E.T. phone home. It isn't easy.

"It's just a different way of life out here," I say, imitating Nellie's southern accent. Trying it on to see how it fits. I quickly decide it doesn't. "I'm not saying it's bad," I add in my usual voice, a much watered-down version of the southern dialect.

"A lot of kids can hardly wait to get out of Katy's Ridge," she says. "I'm not blaming them. This place can be boring as dirt sometimes. It just works for me."

"What will you do after you graduate?" I ask.

Personally, I hate that question because I have no idea.

I'm not like Mom, who has undeniable talent. Unless reading lots of books counts for anything.

"I want to get married." Nellie says this with a dreamy smile before tossing another stick in the river.

Getting married is not something I aspire to. But if I do, I will keep the McAllister name like Mom did. She refused to be a Rooney like my dad. She said Lily Rooney sounded like something you would order at an Italian restaurant. After I was born, she insisted that my last name be McAllister on my birth certificate, too, and thankfully, my father went along with it.

"You have a boyfriend yet?" Nellie asks.

"No," I say. "You?"

She blushes.

"You know Adam Sector?"

We are sitting side by side; otherwise, Nellie might notice my surprise. "I met him the other day," I say, trying to sound indifferent.

"We've been eyeing each other since we were kids." Nellie nudges me with her shoulder and then smiles. I wonder if she has written *Mrs. Adam Sector* a zillion times. The only things I write into the night are secrets and cuss words in my diary.

Nellie and I sit in silence, the ample shade adding a hint of coolness to the summer day. Nellie's ease is about as foreign to me as her life here in Katy's Ridge. Could I be content staying in one place the rest of my life? Content with marrying the boy I went to school with who will build me a house one day while we create children together? I think I would always question if there was something better out there for me, more exciting or more adventurous.

Something rustles in the underbrush, and Nellie touches

my arm, pointing toward the tall grasses a few yards away. At first I don't see anything, but finally I notice the fox inching up to a small rabbit on a rock. My eyes widen when I realize that the rabbit is about to become the fox's lunch. In the next instant Nellie claps her hands and scares the fox, who darts away as the rabbit hops into the tall brush.

"You don't see stuff like that in the city," I say, smiling my relief.

"Well, we've got foxes, rabbits, possums, bobcats, and bears, among other things."

"We had mice in our kitchen once," I say.

Nellie laughs.

"Have you had your first kiss yet?"

Though we're the same age, she seems much younger. I shrug, darting away from the question like the fox.

"Have you?" I ask.

"Not yet," she says, blushing again.

I imagine her thinking of handsome Adam and their kid-filled house that he built himself. With renewed awareness, I decide my life is totally screwed up.

"Your father seems nice," I say, changing the subject.

"He's a war hero, but he doesn't tell anybody about that," she says. "He even has a medal the Army gave him for saving a bunch of people. He was trying to save my Uncle Nathan, too, who was in the same outfit, but he couldn't . . ." Her voice trails off.

"Gran showed me Nathan's grave in the cemetery," I say.

Nellie nods. "What's your father like?"

"Nothing like yours," I say, thinking my father wouldn't get a medal for anything unless making money and random creepiness qualified.

Nellie turns to me as though I am a dark cloud sitting

next to her, and a silver lining is called for. "Well, it must be exciting to have a mother in the country music business." Her smile practically glows.

"It has its moments," I say.

Nellie's glow dulls as she looks at me. "Daisy, I don't think you are very happy."

"Sure, I'm happy," I say, working up a snarl.

She stands, tossing a final stick into the river that bobs along with the current.

"Well, I'd better go help Mama with supper." She brushes the sand off her hands.

We walk back to the mailboxes in silence. I want to apologize for being me but say nothing. In Nellie's generous way, she smiles and tells me it was nice to get to know me a little better.

As she crosses the road, I wonder why I am so different and see dark clouds instead of rainbows, as the poster in my third-grade classroom admonished. I begin my trek up the hill. Next to Gran's pickup is a large, light yellow Cadillac with fins on the back. It is odd to see such a big car in such a small driveway. A short, roundish woman is coming down the path as I am going up. She stops and smiles at me.

"You must be Daisy," she says, slightly out of breath. "I'm an old friend of your grandmother's."

Offering a moist, wimpy handshake, she tells me that she will see me later tonight. She waves as gravity aids her descent.

As I approach the house, Gran sits on the steps of the porch. She looks tired, or maybe sad, or perhaps both. She stands and hugs me.

"You okay?" she asks.

I choose words instead of a shrug. "I've been better."

She nods as though she knows the feeling.

"Let's go inside, and I'll fix you a snack," she says. "We've been invited out to dinner, and it's going to be later than usual."

"Who was that?" I ask.

"A friend who deserted me a long time ago."

"And we're having dinner with her?"

"Her and her brother, Victor. He's the one I want to see," Gran says. "He didn't desert me at all."

"Good to know," I say.

We walk into the house, the screen door slamming at my heels, and I imagine all those sticks Nellie threw into the river, slowly making their way to the sea.

CHAPTER TWENTY-THREE

Wildflower

Thunder rumbles.

The sun hides behind the growing dark clouds. The wind dashes through the trees, announcing what is to come. During the summer months, afternoon thunderstorms are frequent here in the Tennessee mountains.

Daisy and I sit on the porch as the skies open. The deluge of rain hammers out a staccato melody on the tin roof. We are protected by the porch, yet part of the storm.

"I found some things in Mama's closet that she saved for me," I say, raising my voice to be heard over the storm.

I take from my pocket my rabbit's foot keychain and hand it to her. "I thought I'd lost this forever. It's supposed to be good luck."

Daisy studies the rabbit's foot, holding it as if she could use some luck. She then closes her eyes and squeezes it for maybe an extra dose.

Thunder rumbles again, and the storm intensifies. A gully

washer, Mama would call it. The rain will run off the mountain, cutting into the land, making new streams. Daisy watches while holding on to the rabbit's foot.

"You can keep that," I say.

She thanks me.

"There's a secret path that leads to the back of the cemetery," I say. "I'll show it to you while you're here if you want me to."

"A secret path?"

I nod.

"There used to be an old rickety footbridge that stretched across a ravine. I carried that rabbit's foot for good luck to get safely across."

"You did?"

I nod. "Mountain people often use charms for luck," I begin again. "Daddy had a lucky silver dollar that he always carried in his pocket. Horatio gave me the star ruby, and Daniel still carries a buckeye."

She studies the rabbit's foot before tucking it into her shorts pocket.

"Mama had saved this for me, too." I hand Daisy a photograph of Lily and me when Lily was a baby.

"Is that Mom?" she asks, studying the image.

I nod. I look awkward holding Lily, and young enough to still play with dolls instead of hold a baby of my own.

"I didn't realize you were so young when you had Mom," Daisy says, looking at me.

"I was your age."

A thunderclap makes us jump in unison, as if God himself is making a comment. The rain surges and then begins to slow.

"What was Mom like when she was growing up?" Daisy asks.

I welcome her question. "Incredibly curious and always hungry." I laugh. "Mama took care of the hunger part, but it was a full-time job answering her questions."

"I'm different from her," Daisy says.

"Yes, you are," I say, "and that's not a bad thing."

Within ten minutes the rain has stopped, but with the trees dripping, it sounds like it is still raining. Checking Daddy's watch, I tell Daisy that we need to get ready for our dinner out. "You may want to wash under your fingernails," I say.

Daisy closes her hands as if hiding the evidence of her digging.

"We're walking, by the way."

"Walking?" she asks, probably disappointed that the pickup keys will not be tossed in her direction.

"It will be dark by the time we head home. I'll grab a couple of Mama's flashlights off the back porch. Walking at night is really peaceful," I continue. "It will be good for us."

Daisy doesn't look convinced.

An hour later, we leave the house without locking the door. As far as I know, the only time this house was locked was after Johnny broke in and my sister Amy shot him. Shortly before, Johnny had left a note threatening me for telling what he did. We figured he would come back to make good on his threat. Sure enough, he did. Thankfully, Amy is a better shot than Mama and my other sisters.

Life, it seems, is divided into two parts. The years before Johnny and the years after. The *before* years were when my life felt open and safe. The *after* years, closed and locked. But I am ready to be free again.

When we reach the road, we take a left. When I was a girl, I could have walked blindfolded to find Mary Jane's house. I look forward to seeing what Victor has done with the old place. In the twilight, Daisy and I are silent. The day has already held too many words. The cicadas are in full voice, and the tree frogs add bass notes to their song. The forest is dense with humidity from the earlier rain.

When we approach, we see Mary Jane's Cadillac in the driveway, alongside a new Jeep. Victor has done well for himself. The brand-new house is almost too fancy for Katy's Ridge. When I was a girl, the Sweeney house was the biggest in our small mountain community. For a while, it was the only house with a telephone. Sweeney's Country Store was a cornerstone in the community. We saved our pennies to buy candy there when we picked up flour and sugar for Mama. After his father retired, Victor ran the store for years before moving to Arkansas and evidently making his fortune.

When Victor opens the door, I am surprised to see a gray-headed man. He is only two years older, but I seem to have come face-to-face with my own aging process. However, he has the same caring eyes of his youth, and I find myself hoping that life has been kind to him.

Pleasantries abound. I introduce Daisy. Victor offers me a glass of white wine, Daisy lemonade. Mary Jane announces that Victor has prepared the entire meal, then tells the story of how the only person allowed in her kitchen is Roberta, her black cook. Mary Jane can be counted on to embellish things. Somehow, Victor was never like his sister and never flaunted the Sweeney wealth.

We sit at the large dining room table, and I think back to the meals I had with Mary Jane's family when we were girls. My thoughts jump to Mary Jane's father, who is now—in death—reunited with the leg he lost in the war, as well as several house cats.

Around Mama's table, everyone talked at once, and not a single plate was without a chip. But the food was always delicious. At Mary Jane's, it was the opposite. The food tasted like cardboard covered with tasteless gravy but was served on perfect china plates. Tonight, the décor is no exception. The table contains matching china in an oriental pattern, polished silver, and crystal goblets for iced tea. Unlike his mother, however, Victor is a surprisingly good cook.

Daisy glances in my direction. The only time she seems halfway comfortable is when she has dirt under her fingernails or when she is reading. I give her a reassuring look in return.

"I'm sorry I didn't make it to your mother's funeral," Victor says to me. "I was out of town until late yesterday."

I tell him no apologies are needed and that it was a beautiful service.

"Everybody's talking about Lily singing. That must have been very special." He smiles at Daisy, who focuses her interest on a crystal saltshaker. But at least her fingernails are free of dirt.

"Yes, it was exceptional," I say.

Mary Jane finishes her wine in one gulp; light sparkles off her many rings as she pours herself another glass.

"Do you miss Nashville?" Victor asks Daisy.

"Not at all," Daisy says, the answer so decisive it makes him chuckle.

"A woman who knows her mind." He lifts his wineglass in a salute.

Daisy offers her first smile of the evening, so brief I question if I imagined it.

Victor seems intent on making her feel welcome, and I appreciate his efforts.

"What's it like to be staying in your mother's house again?" he asks me.

"It's strange," I say. "Especially now, without Mama there." Tears threaten to come, and I take a sip of wine instead. I don't usually drink, and I never have wine with a meal. In fact, I could write my complete knowledge of different wines on the top of a cork.

"I imagine it is strange." Victor touches my hand on the table, an action that doesn't escape Daisy's observation.

When I talk to Bee later, I will tell her about seeing Victor again. Bee always liked Victor. He was her prize student. She always believed he would do great things.

Mary Jane finishes a second glass of wine and becomes more animated, telling stories of the past. Stories about her clothes and different birthday parties that "everyone" attended. Parties I clearly wasn't invited to, like her Sweet Sixteen. My exclusion may have had something to do with me having a three-year-old at the time.

Meanwhile, Daisy hides a yawn behind her napkin.

Not all childhood friends make sense as adults. Victor is the exception. If I had married him when he asked, my life would have played out in a totally different way. How rare it is for a man to be willing to take on a young mother with a small child? I find myself grateful all over again, and also convinced that it would have never worked, no matter how kind a man he was.

Victor and I wash dishes by hand in his massive kitchen with floor-to-ceiling windows facing into the forest. Daisy watches us while pretending to read a book pulled from

Victor's oak bookshelves in the living room. A book by C. S. Lewis about different types of love.

Minutes later, we say our goodbyes, promising to get together again soon.

"Are you sure I can't drive you home?" he asks at the door. "Happy to."

Daisy looks at me with pleading eyes. Not only does she want a ride, but I imagine she also wants me to convince our host to let her drive.

"It's such a beautiful evening to walk," I say. "It's not something I get to do living in Nashville."

With a smile, he says he understands, and I am sure he does.

Daisy and I walk down the road, our footsteps echoing into the night. Daisy is quiet, which doesn't alarm me. I imagine she is thinking about the evening. Our flashlights steady, we illuminate the way ahead of us like headlights of the car she hopes to drive someday.

As before, night noises surround us. Something scurries by the side of the road. Maybe a possum or a raccoon. I wonder how many times I've walked this same road in darkness. When I was a girl, it was with Daddy. Other times, with Mama and my sisters in different combinations. As a girl, I never would have imagined that on an evening in the future, I would be walking with my granddaughter along this familiar road. That I have a granddaughter at all is sometimes startling.

"I need to tell you something." Daisy's words come out of the darkness like a car from out of nowhere.

My secret sense drops into my gut, as though it already knows what's coming. "I'm listening," I say.

We keep walking, and I wonder if we should stop. But

somehow it seems that the walking and the darkness are necessary components to any confession.

"Promise you won't hate me?"

"I could never hate you, Daisy. Never."

"Promise me?"

"I promise."

With my left hand, since my right is holding the flashlight, I cross my heart and hope to die, but this promise won't require a death. It will be easy to keep.

We continue another hundred yards, maybe more. Long enough for me to wonder if Daisy has said all she needs to say. It reminds me of the few times I confessed to friends about Bee. It was agonizing, not knowing if I would lose the friendship for being honest. Telling myself that if I did lose it, I didn't need that person in my life anyway. Not if they couldn't accept this part of me. But it was hard. To trust someone with our secrets is the biggest of big deals.

"I promise, Daisy," I say again, wanting to prime the pump, wanting the secret to spill out of her, because then she won't be alone.

We continue walking. When Daisy finally speaks, her words are softer than I expect.

"My father comes into my room at night when I stay with him."

"What?" I say, my voice a screaming whisper.

My flashlight drops on the road, the light bouncing into the trees before becoming still again. I take Daisy into my arms. At first she stiffens, but then she slowly allows the embrace. I imagine ice melting. A princess locked in a castle tower. A secret keeping her prisoner. My tower is forty years older than Daisy's, but it is a fortress I know well. Not because my father climbed into bed with me, but because

Johnny Monroe didn't give me a choice. Different, yet the same.

Darkness embraces us.

In the moments that follow, I hold Daisy the way I wish Mama had held me after it happened. I hold her the way Aunt Sadie did. All we need is one person willing to hold us. One person who will see our shame and love us anyway. Perhaps even love us more.

Daisy in my arms, I tell her everything will be all right, not knowing if it will. I tell her that she is safe. I tell her that she is loved. It is only then that the tower walls gently tumble and Daisy begins to weep.

CHAPTER TWENTY-FOUR

Daisy

Gran's strong embrace protects me as I empty myself of tears.

"Did I say that, or just think it?" I say into the darkness.

"You said it," she says. "And I'm glad you did."

"You believe me?" I ask.

"Of course I believe you," she says.

I think of the river, the ripples gently lapping against the bank. New tears come in on the next wave.

She believes me.

My father told me no one would.

Blowing my nose into Gran's bandana, which appears magically from her pocket, I feel somehow lighter.

"Shall we go back to the house and talk?" She leans over to retrieve her flashlight.

I agree, feeling like my life has forever changed with the telling of one secret. Is it too late to take it back?

While I had no intention of telling Gran, something

about walking through the darkness invited it. Voices walked with us. Voices of family. Ancestors. A chorus of footsteps marching through time. Footsteps of a clan named McAllister.

Not quite full, the moon watches us as we walk up the hill toward the house. I smell what I now know is jasmine, thanks to Gran educating me. Last week, I couldn't have told you three names of trees. Or even two names of birds. But after a few days in the mountains, I now know what honeysuckle is, as well as hummingbirds and chickadees. Cardinals and blue jays. Trees called redbuds and maples. Weeping willows, dogwoods, and oaks. Thanks to Nellie, I also know the subtle difference between mountain laurel and rhododendron. The smaller leaves and blossoms are mountain laurel. The bigger leaves and flowers are rhododendron. They bloom at different times in the spring. Mountain laurels are always first.

The porch light up ahead, I think of my mom somewhere on tour in another country. Far away. Unreachable. More than ever, I wish she were here. At the same time, I vowed to never tell her. My father told me it would hurt her. Break her heart. He also said she would never believe me. I wonder if this is true.

Now that the secret is out, I feel empty and light at the same time. Until I spoke it, I never realized how heavy it was to carry around, like my purple backpack filled with unneeded textbooks.

Gran turns on lights in the house. I follow her into the kitchen, the informal meeting room of all things McAllister.

"Hot cocoa?" she asks.

I nod, feeling suddenly naked in front of her. Exposed. Something keeps me anchored to the floor, even though I want to run away. Ever since I arrived this summer, I have pushed Gran away, but what I now realize is that I need her to stay close.

Gran mixes the milk and cocoa on the stove, adding a spoonful of sugar. I think of Mary Poppins helping the medicine go down. But Gran is not magical, only an ordinary grandmother. Although I have underestimated her gentleness and her love for me.

We sit at the table with our hot cocoa. I stir and blow the top to cool it.

"You did the right thing," Gran says, putting her hand on mine. "Now that it's out in the open, we need to figure out what to do about it."

Out in the open. The words feel dangerous.

"We're going to do something about it?" I ask, not realizing action was an option.

"Of course," she says. "Your father doesn't get to get away with this."

"But . . ."

She waits for more, but I don't have words, only a thousand regrets.

"He's my father," I say.

"Yes, he is," Gran says. "But he has committed a crime against you."

"A crime?" I ask, my voice soft. "I don't want him to get in trouble," I add, even softer.

The confusion on Gran's face mirrors how I feel.

"Daisy, we have to tell the authorities."

"No, I don't want that," I say.

Words flow out of me that I never intended to tell anyone. I tell her I don't want my father to get into trouble, and I don't want Mom to have to come home from her tour again. I tell Gran that I'll be okay. That he hasn't really done anything yet. That he just lays there and whispers to me. That he only touches my arms and face. That he probably won't do more.

Gran's eyes reveal deep sadness. My confession may be the most I've ever said to her at one time.

"Daisy," she says, her voice full of tenderness, "we've got to tell someone so that he will stop."

"If we tell someone he will stop?" For some reason, this never occurred to me.

"Yes, of course," Gran says, her eyes softening to match her voice.

"I didn't tell you to get him in trouble," I say again.

Gran holds her head as though a puzzle just got harder to solve. "It's almost midnight," she says. "We should try to get some sleep and talk about this tomorrow. Is that okay with you?"

I nod.

We get ready for bed. I wonder how Gran can sleep in the bed her mother died in a few nights ago, even with clean sheets.

Before I turn out the light, Gran comes into my room and sits on my side of the bed. She asks me to look into her eyes.

"I'm glad you told me, Daisy. This secret is way too much for you to carry all on your own. At thirteen, your only job in life is to be a kid."

Weariness settles around her eyes, replacing the sadness. I realize this isn't easy for her, either.

"The most important thing," she begins again, "is knowing that you didn't do anything wrong. Hear me?"

I wonder if this is true. Gran looks at me as if waiting for an answer. "I hear you," I say, though I'm not sure I believe it.

"Now, get some sleep," Gran says. "Rest assured that you did the right thing."

I've never seen this side of Gran. The part that is more like Bee. Forceful and loving.

She tucks me in as though I am three instead of thirteen. Then she kisses me on the forehead.

"I love you, Daisy."

I tell her I love her, too, and I realize that I mean it. She turns out the light. The darkness is immediate and substantial. I imagine my father in jail, and my mom so heartbroken she can't sing.

What have I done? I say to myself, as regrets crawl under the covers with me.

CHAPTER TWENTY-FIVE

Wildflower

Early the next morning I put on Mama's housecoat and go into the kitchen to call Daniel. I know he has been up for at least an hour. I have barely slept, thinking through the options of how to keep Daisy safe.

He answers the phone in the kitchen. I can hear Jo making his breakfast. He's wearing his I-haven't-had-my-coffee-yet voice.

"Something's happened, Daniel. I need your help."

He clears his throat. "Just tell me what you want me to do."

"Meet me at the mailboxes to talk in thirty minutes?"

He says he will.

Daisy is still sleeping. Thankfully, she did not swear me to secrecy about what she told me, although keeping someone safe is more important than any secret.

When I make it to the mailboxes, Daniel is already waiting. I tell him what Daisy told me, and his shock comes out in anger. He offers to kill the bastard. I entertain the idea of Jerry's demise before telling him my plan.

"We need him to know that Daisy isn't alone," I say. "That she has people looking after her. That he has to stop."

His brow crumpled, Daniel nods in agreement. I remember the time Mary Jane and I went to him and told him that Johnny was scaring us. Within minutes we were on our way to the Monroe cabin to confront Johnny. Daniel didn't hesitate then, and he doesn't hesitate now. I tell him I'm not sure what I'll do next but that I'll keep him posted.

Then I go back to the house and call June and ask her if I can come over. I tell her it's important, and that I need to talk to Horatio, too. She says she will put the coffee on.

My final call of the morning is to Bee. Hearing her answer the telephone calms me. I picture her sitting at the kitchen table in the small house we used to live in together. Then I tell her what Daisy told me. Her reaction is swift. She asks what we should do, and I hear her searching for tissues. Whenever Bee gets angry, tears always follow.

"She doesn't want Jerry to get in trouble," I say.

"But we have to tell the authorities," Bee says. "She's just a child. She doesn't get to decide."

"I think she's already starting to regret she told me," I say.

"Well, I'm so glad she did," Bee says. "How long has it been going on?"

"Sounds like months," I say. "I keep thinking that it's good that nothing's happened yet, but the fact that Jerry is even going into her room—"

"I know," Bee says. "Bad stuff has happened, just not the worst."

Bee sighs, and for several seconds, we are silent on the phone, trying to think of what to do, thinking of Daisy.

My hands begin to shake holding the phone. Until now, I hadn't realized how absolutely furious I am.

"I never liked Jerry," I say between gritted teeth, not that she needs reminding. "What do you do when your granddaughter confides that someone is hurting her, and then insists that they not get into trouble?"

"You protect her," Bee says. "You do what's right, and hope she forgives you. Let me check around and find out what the protocol is for things like this."

We agree to talk later. Before we end our call, Bee asks if I am okay.

"Not really," I say, "but I'm going over to June's as soon as we get off the phone." I don't tell Bee of my plan. It isn't really fully formed yet, and I imagine she wouldn't go along with it anyway.

"I'm so glad Daisy is with you this summer," Bee says. "I like how far away you are from Jerry."

I agree.

After we say our goodbyes, I leave a note for Daisy on the kitchen table with June's telephone number, telling her to call when she gets up. Knowing her usual sleeping patterns, I will probably be home before that happens. I go back to Mama's room to get dressed. Not only am I dealing with Mama's death, but now, I must face a genuine threat to Daisy. The only thing I know for sure is that I can't drop this bombshell on Lily when she's so far away. For now, it is my dilemma to deal with, and action is required.

Thirty minutes later, I am sitting in June's kitchen. We wait for Horatio to return from working with the beehives. In the meantime, June pours me a cup of coffee and gives me a biscuit with butter and honey. The biscuits aren't as good as Mama's but close to it, and the honey is marvelous. Until that moment, I hadn't realized I was hungry.

"You sounded so worried over the phone," June says. "What's happened?"

"Should we wait for Horatio?"

She looks out the back window. "He might be busy for a while."

I hesitate. The words are hard to even contemplate, much less say. "Daisy told me something when we were walking home last night," I say.

June's expression darkens, as though she already knows what I might say.

"I saw something in the cards," she says.

"What did you see?" I remember how June suddenly stopped reading Daisy's fortune.

"It was something dark," June says. "A pattern from the past."

I lower my voice. "Her father is coming into her room at night."

June winces and damns Jerry to hell. I repeat her sentiments.

"Do you know what I realized last night?" I ask. "That Daisy is the same age I was when Johnny attacked me."

Our eyes meet. "Is this coincidence or fate?" I ask her.

"It's like an echo of what happened before," June says.

"So history is repeating itself, but with a different twist?"

June nods. We look at each other as though we have just figured out that two plus two equals four.

"But maybe it's also an opportunity to set it right," June says. "So that it never happens again."

"How?" I am genuinely curious. If I had known how to set

things right so that this wouldn't happen to Daisy, I would have done it a long time ago.

"It's like putting a stick in the bike spokes," she says. "You do everything you can to stop the pattern."

I wish I understood.

Horatio walks into the kitchen. "Good morning, Miss Wildflower."

I return his good morning, even though I'm not so sure it is. While he makes himself a cup of coffee, I think about what June said. How do you break a pattern you didn't even know existed?

When Horatio joins us at the table, June tells him what has happened. His dark eyes appear to become even darker.

"Round up three men, Miss Wildflower. I can be one of them. A predator needs to know he is being watched. He needs to be sent a message."

"I was thinking the same thing, Horatio. Jerry needs to know that Daisy isn't alone. There's strength in numbers, right?"

Horatio nods.

"I've already talked to Daniel," I say. "He's willing to do anything we need."

But who will be the third? I think of Victor. Victor stood up for me even after Mary Jane abandoned me. But would he be willing to confront Jerry? It is a lot to ask of anyone.

"Daisy won't like this plan," I say.

"But Daisy is the prey, Miss Wildflower, as you were with Johnny Monroe. Children must never be prey."

Horatio reminds me of Daddy sometimes. An honorable man.

"I'll talk to Victor," I say.

I stand to leave, and June hugs me. "Daisy is fortunate to

have you," she says.

"Is she?" I ask, already wishing I had done more when I first noticed how she had changed.

"She is fortunate," June repeats. She holds me by both shoulders, looking into my eyes like she did when I was a young mother and overwhelmed. I take a deep breath.

"Do not underestimate how important this is," she says. "What you do at this moment will affect seven generations forward, and seven generations back. Actions taken today will heal old wounds and prevent new wounds."

"You're scaring me," I say with an uneasy smile.

June laughs a short laugh. "Well, I don't mean to. It's just that people don't realize how one choice can change everything."

I tell her that I understand.

When I arrive at Victor's, it is nine o'clock, and he is finishing breakfast. He invites me in and asks if he can fix me something to eat. I decline but join him at the table.

"I didn't expect to see you so soon," he says. "Everything okay?"

"I need your help, Victor."

"Of course," he says, sitting forward in his chair.

I tell him that what I am about to say to him must be kept in confidence. He assures me that Mary Jane is still asleep in the guest room. We carry our two coffees and sit on his porch in two large wicker chairs for further privacy.

I tell him why I'm there.

"You can count me in," he says. "We can take Mary Jane's Caddy. It's big enough to carry all of us."

"But don't tell her why," I say, thinking of the Katy's Ridge grapevine.

He agrees.

As expected, Daisy is still asleep when I return. I let her sleep. Despite my fatigue, I pull together the plan, calling everyone to arrange that we meet at eleven A.M. tomorrow so we can be in Nashville after lunch.

By early afternoon, Daisy is up and pretending that what she said last night never happened. After she eats, she disappears into the backyard. Physical exertion is probably the best thing for her right now. Meanwhile, I am preoccupied with my plan.

My sister Amy knocks on the front door and follows me into the kitchen. I am surprised to see her. Amy isn't the type to just drop by to chat; that would be more like Meg. She makes herself a glass of iced tea and sits at the table.

"Word's gotten around about what you intend to do," she says. Her thin lips form an almost perfect line.

Within seconds I realize that I have underestimated the Katy's Ridge grapevine.

"Who told you about this?" I ask, hands on my hips, standing at the kitchen sink. Victor would never tell someone about our plan. Nor would Daniel or Horatio.

"What does it matter," she says with a huff.

"It matters to me," I say. "This is about Daisy, my granddaughter, your great-niece."

"I haven't told anyone else," she says, and I wonder if this is true.

"Who told you?" I ask a second time.

She hesitates before confirming that it was Mary Jane who overheard Victor and me on the front porch.

"She must have been hiding in the bushes to overhear us," I say.

Amy scoffs. "You're so naïve, Louisa May."

I know she is using my old name on purpose to irritate

me. I wonder what she means about me being naïve. Not that I have any inclination to invite her thoughts.

"You need to keep your nose out of it," she says, sounding just like Mama. "This is none of your business."

"My granddaughter is none of my business?" I stand taller, feeling the full measure of my feistiness. "I am not in the mood for your holier-than-thou act, Amy." An act that seems to increase in intensity the older she gets.

"How do you know she's even telling the truth?" Amy taps her foot, but I refuse to be blindsided again. "Girls her age are prone to exaggeration, you know. You don't want to go accusing an innocent man."

My temper rises like the first tiny bubbles in a pot that promises to build to a rolling boil.

"I believe her," I say, my voice just above a seethe.

"You could get in a lot of trouble for this," she says with another toe tap.

"What do you propose I do?" I ask, wondering what caused Amy to turn into this person. Even Mama could be open-minded if an occasion called for it.

"Let sleeping dogs lie," she says.

"Well, that mangy dog in Nashville isn't sleeping. He's got his paws on Daisy."

We stare at each other. I remember how guilty Amy felt after Johnny because she didn't say anything about what he had done to her.

"If you had told me about Johnny, I might not have been hurt," I say to her.

She narrows her eyes and then crosses her arms.

"It will sort itself out without your help," her words clipped.

I wonder if my other sisters feel the same as Amy about

confronting Jerry. Not Jo; she is more like Daniel. As for Meg, unless the news story has made it to Hollywood, I doubt she has an opinion about it.

Amy stands as if to reason with me, not knowing that her argument is making me even firmer in my position. She repeats what she has already said. It's all I can do not to slap her.

"If women don't protect girls, Amy, what hope do we have?"

"You won't be able to go back and undo this," she says. "Jerry is a prominent man. He has a lot of power. He could do things to you."

I slam the dish towel on the counter, refusing to say aloud the words I want to say. Words guaranteed to hurt her. Words telling her it's a good thing she never had children if she were going to turn a blind eye.

"Just stay out of it," I tell her. Disappointment undergirds my anger. "And don't spread this around. Tell Mary Jane not to spread it around, either." I pause, thinking how odd it is that Amy is the one Mary Jane told. "By the way, since when are you and Mary Jane friends?"

"She came into my shop this morning," Amy says, looking away.

"Well, this is none of her business, and it's none of yours, either."

She turns to leave. "This is a mistake," she says. "Just wait and see."

Her threat sounds like a curse and gets the desired effect. Within seconds, doubts creep into my resolve. Doubts that warn me that I am doing the wrong thing. Doubts that insist that it won't matter anyway and that somehow Daisy will be the one to pay for it.

CHAPTER TWENTY-SIX

Daisy

When I hide my shovel under the back porch, I hear voices coming from the kitchen. Who is talking to Gran? I wash my hands at the outdoor spigot, proud of the territory I covered today. I have mapped out the area in front of the boulder as a grid. Every day I dig a foot down before covering it back up if I don't find anything. Joseph McAllister wouldn't have buried something deeper than that, considering he was telling his wife to dig it up if anything happened to him.

When I go into the kitchen, Gran's sister Amy is leaving. Gran's cheeks are red like she just ran a sprint.

"I need to talk to you about something," she says. Gran sits at the table, and I join her.

I remember my confession the night before, and my face warms. I wish now I'd kept my mouth shut.

"I need you to trust me," Gran says.

My shoulders edge toward my ears. "Trust you about what?"

"With what I'm about to tell you."

My heart races toward the door, but the rest of me stays put.

"We're going to Nashville tomorrow," Gran says.

"Why?"

"At no time will you be in any danger," she says. "I promise you. This is all about getting you safe again."

"What have you done, Gran?" I ask, even though I don't really want to know. My right knee jiggles the way it does whenever I have a big test at school.

"We will only be in Nashville for the afternoon," Gran says, "and then we'll come straight back here."

"What are we doing there?" I ask.

"Let me worry about that," Gran says.

My insides get as jittery as my leg.

"I'll make a deal with you," she says thoughtfully. "If you trust me and go along with my plan, I'll let you drive the pickup every day for the next two weeks."

My knee stops shaking. My insides calm. Turns out I am a sucker for a carrot dangling in front of me, if the carrot is learning how to drive.

"Agreed," I say.

THE NEXT MORNING Gran and I get into the pickup. As part of trusting her, I am not to ask questions. All I know is that we are going to Nashville. To my surprise, we go back to where we had dinner a couple of nights ago. The Jeep and the giant Cadillac are still in the driveway. It feels like a hundred years have passed since we were here, even though it was just the other night.

Victor comes out and gives us a wave. Gran thanks him for helping us, and I don't even know what he is helping us with. We get into the massive Cadillac the color of the filling of a chocolate eclair. It reeks of heavy perfume. Instantly, the three of us lower the windows to let in the fresh air.

Gran makes me sit between her and Victor, saying we have more people to pick up.

"More people?" I ask.

She nods. Gran has put her hair up in a French braid like she does when she wants to look good. She wears a flowery blouse with her best jeans.

I remind myself that trusting her means I get to drive the pickup every day for the next two weeks. I would rob a bank for that, maybe even embezzle money, if I even knew what that meant.

Victor smells of aftershave and coffee. His aftershave competes with the perfume in the car. The perfume wins. Less than a minute later, we pull up in my Great-Uncle Daniel's driveway. He comes out and gets in the back seat. Nellie waves from the porch. Something is up, and nobody is talking.

Victor drives to the Sectors' place. Gran's friend Horatio gets in the back seat with Daniel. I am relieved Adam isn't coming, too.

We drive out of Katy's Ridge and through the dying small town of Rocky Bluff and then get on the interstate. Windows go up, but the perfume smell has barely faded. The others talk. I listen to determine our destination. When I feel uneasy, I focus on the dangling carrot with car keys at the end.

We take the main exit to downtown Nashville. It is busy, but we manage to find a parking place on the street. I recognize where we are now. We are close to where my father works. My back stiffens. I turn to Gran with a look that says, *Surely we are not going to see my father.*

"Trust me," she says.

The five of us get out of the car and walk past my father's Mercedes in the parking lot. I haven't been to my father's office in years. Inside the grand foyer, I realize how important he is. He is a record producer in Nashville. I've been to Mom's agent's office, and it is nothing like this. In the lobby, my father's name is in gold lettering. His office is on the top floor of the building—the entire top floor. Gran pushes the button to call the elevator.

A fluttering starts in my chest that reminds me of the hummingbirds flitting around Aunt Sadie's wildflowers in the front of her house. But the hummingbird in my chest isn't seeking nectar; it's trapped in a building and desperately trying to get out.

"Wait," I say to Gran. "We can't do this. You need to call this whole thing off."

"Trust me," Gran repeats. Her look is one of pure determination.

An army of old men, along with my grandmother, steps into the elevator. They hold the door open for me, but my legs won't move. I am frozen in the lobby. Gran steps out of the elevator and takes my hand, guiding me inside. Daniel pushes the elevator button. The elevator dings with each floor, my fear rising to new heights. We are going to my father's office.

On the sixth ding, the door opens, and we enter a large hallway leading to an office. My father's name is painted on the glass door. Once we get inside, we approach a woman sitting at a desk. She reminds me of a younger version of my latest stepmom, who was also his secretary before they got married.

"We're here to see Jerry," Gran says to her, checking her pocket watch as if we have an appointment.

The woman rolls her desk chair back to get the full view of us. "What is this about?" she asks.

"Tell him his daughter, Daisy, is here to see him," Gran says.

"He's in a meeting." The secretary looks down at her desk as though she is not a very good liar.

"We're not leaving until we see him," Victor says, now standing next to Gran. Daniel and Horatio step forward, too. It never occurred to me that someday, a quartet of senior citizens would have my back. I stand straighter, realizing I am not alone.

The secretary pauses and then looks at me. "Is it important?" she asks.

I tell her it is. She picks up the phone and tells my father that I am waiting to see him.

When he opens the door, his smile fades as soon as he sees Gran.

"What's going on?" he asks me. "Are you okay? Who are these people?" He and Gran exchange looks. I almost expect them to hiss or growl at each other.

"We need to talk to you, Jerry," Gran says.

"What about?" my father asks.

"You'll probably want some privacy," Daniel says, motioning for us to go into his office.

My father hesitates but then tells his secretary to hold his calls. We follow him inside, and he closes the door. When I walk past him, he narrows his eyes at me as if I will live to regret inconveniencing him.

Gold records grace the walls, framed and mounted, most of them my mom's. He sits behind his large wooden desk in a black leather chair. My mouth feels like I've been chewing cotton balls, and my right leg is gearing up for a rumba. The only thing that comforts me is that Gran is here, along with her geriatric posse.

"I'm busy. You need to tell me what this is about and then leave," my father says to me.

"I never liked you, Jerry," Gran begins. "I never understood what Lily saw in you, though I think you took advantage of her innocence when she was first starting out."

"You collected a bunch of country rednecks in my office to tell me this?" My father sits taller in his chair.

Gran walks behind his desk, causing him to swivel.

Even though Gran is tiny compared to him, he lets her speak. Maybe because he thinks this is the quickest way to get her out of his office.

I sit back in my chair, my mouth opening with the revelation that my gran has become a superhero. She tells him that she knows what he is doing and that he has to stop, and that if he doesn't, she will contact the authorities. Meanwhile, my father's threats echo in my mind. Threats that I would break my mom's heart. Threats that if I ever told I would pay. I can't help but wonder what this moment will cost me.

"I see you've been caught up in one of Daisy's lies." He sounds calm. "Don't be embarrassed, Lou. I've been caught up in them, too. Haven't I, Daisy?" He looks at me, and the hummingbirds inside my chest threaten to throw up all over his desk.

"I've been fooled by her just like you have," he begins

again, his voice smooth. "Too bad you got these men involved, too. All of you are wasting a perfectly good day for no reason." He pauses and clears his throat, glancing at me to make sure I'm watching. "You see, Daisy has been a pathological liar since she was a young girl. Lily and I even got her into therapy at one point."

"That's not true," Gran says. "Daisy is one of the most truthful people I have ever known."

My father accuses Gran of being gullible. "Didn't Lily tell you about the counseling sessions?"

"Well, yes, she did, but they weren't about Daisy lying."

Lowering my head, I think back to the therapy sessions I was made to attend when I was in third grade. Therapy sessions that were supposed to make me more sociable. As far as I knew, they had nothing to do with lying. At one point, the therapist had me drawing turtles and talking about what it would be like to come out of my shell. Did I have a lying problem, too? Like all kids, I told white lies to keep myself out of trouble. But was it more than that? The room blurs with the beginnings of tears.

Horatio stands. I realize again how tall he is, even taller than my father. He dwarfs Gran, who is still standing by the desk. When he speaks, his voice is deep and resonates like a bass line walking alongside a melody.

"I know a liar when I see one, and it's not Daisy." Horatio looks straight at my father.

Then Daniel stands, too, as well as Victor.

"It will take a while for the authorities to investigate," Daniel says. "But we are going to make sure that Daisy is safe."

Victor speaks next: "I've done business in Nashville, and I know a couple of judges," he says. "By the time we're finished with you, you'll be ruined. Now tell your daughter that you're sorry for calling her a liar."

Gran and the old men stand around me like giant oaks. I tell myself not to cry.

Daniel reinforces Victor's request: "You need to apologize to your daughter for calling her a liar."

Horatio crosses his arms, looking even more intimidating. No one would ever know this gentleman carves statues of mother bears with her cubs.

"Bee has already called social services," Gran says.

My father laughs. "You're the pervert, not me," he says to Gran with a smile. "You think they'll believe *you*?"

At this moment, I hate my father even more.

"Besides," he begins, "even if what Daisy says is true, you've got no proof. It's her word against mine."

"But I do have proof," I say.

Everyone turns to look at me, including my father. His gaze warns me to keep my mouth shut or else. But what is the *or else*? *Or else* everything will change? *Or else* my mother will realize again that she made a mistake by marrying him? *Or else* he will finally have to admit he did something wrong? Even I know that he will never do that.

"How do you have proof, Daisy?" Gran asks.

"I kept all the dates in a notebook," I begin. It was Karana, in *Island of the Blue Dolphins,* who gave me this idea. She marked all the days that she was deserted on the island on a rock. "I also made tape recordings with the tape recorder I got two Christmases ago. I have at least a dozen recordings of him saying things to me that he shouldn't have been saying."

The air in the room shifts, as though all the permanently sealed windows in the high-rise have opened, and a mountain breeze has been let in. My father stands, saying that he will no longer tolerate my lies. But the air has left his balloon. He shoves his way past Victor and Horatio. When he leaves his office, I exhale, not even realizing I had been holding my breath. Gran applauds and walks over and puts an arm around me.

"Do you really have proof?" she asks.

I tell her I do.

"I'm so proud of you," she says. "You were brilliant to make recordings."

"I'm proud of you, too," I say. "And I didn't lie."

"I never doubted that you were telling the truth," she says.

Daniel, Horatio, and Victor agree.

With my father gone, the confrontation over, I sit and lower my head. Tears come like an unexpected afternoon thunderstorm. Gran pulls a chair close and holds my hands, telling me how brave I am. However, I don't feel brave at all. It wouldn't be like my father to let this go so easily. The war has just begun.

CHAPTER TWENTY-SEVEN

Wildflower

Lily returns to the States after her tour. She telephones to tell Daisy and me that her plane has just landed and she is driving back to Katy's Ridge. I decided not to tell her anything about Jerry until her return, and I worry about how she will take the news.

Meanwhile, in the ten days since we confronted Daisy's father, I am getting glimpses of the real Daisy. She is talking more, and I even heard her laughing with Nellie yesterday.

Mama's American flag hangs from the front porch in honor of the Fourth of July. Earlier we picked up Aunt Sadie and brought her back to Mama's house. Keeping my promise, I let Daisy drive us to and from. Now, we all sit on the front porch waiting for Lily.

Sadie sits in Mama's rocker, staring out into the distance, as though deep in thought. Old Rufus, as always, sits at her feet. With so much going on with Daisy, I sometimes forget how much Aunt Sadie might be grieving Mama, and how much I am grieving her as well. Two huge events have marked the summer of 1982: Mama's death and Daisy's secret coming to light.

A car pulls into the gravel driveway, and Daisy runs down the hill to meet Lily. They emerge in the distance, both smiling. A few years ago, Lily's career took off like a runaway train. A train I am not so sure she knows how to exit. With Lily and Daisy, time together is the issue, not an absence of love and caring. However, I have no idea how Lily is going to react to what Daisy and I need to tell her. According to Bee, many children are not believed, and this can be incredibly damaging, even worse than the abuse.

Daisy carries Lily's overnight bag into the house, while Aunt Sadie and I hug our world traveler, welcoming her home. When she removes her sunglasses, I take note of the dark circles under her eyes. *Be careful what you wish for,* Mama used to say, meaning dreams have their dark side just like everything else.

With Lily's arrival, we sit on the porch. Later, we will walk across the street to Daniel's house for a family barbecue. But right now, it is just the four of us. Mama's broom stands next to the door, reminding us of her absence.

Daisy comes outside carrying a glass of iced tea for her mom. She lets the screen door slap at her heels like I used to do as a girl, an act that drove Mama crazy. Nostalgia floats in on the warm summer breeze, honoring all those arrivals and departures. Thresholds crossed.

Lily and Daisy sit on the porch swing as I lean against one of the posts. I told Lily yesterday on the phone that we had something to talk about when she got here. *Nothing terrible,* I said, which was a lie, but it made no sense for her to worry in advance.

"Okay, I'm here. Tell me what's going on," Lily says.

Sadie, Daisy, and I exchange a look as though wondering who will do the talking. When we got home from Nashville that day, I went over to Aunt Sadie's and told her all about it. That evening, she delivered bottles from a special batch of her prized blackberry spirits to Daniel, Victor, and Horatio. Sadie seemed to think that a man like Jerry wouldn't admit defeat so readily and predicted that more was coming. I hope she is wrong.

Lily's long earrings sparkle in the early-afternoon sun. Even in jeans, she seems somehow more glamorous than the rest of us. I still remember her on this porch as a girl, singing Daddy's favorite songs, the whole family teary-eyed with wonder. Lily has a gift. A gift that she has put out into the world. Not many people honor their gifts, though some do, and those are usually people I admire. Yet from observing Lily, I know that being admired isn't easy, either.

Meanwhile, Aunt Sadie is quieter than usual, and I wonder if she is spending too much time alone. We exchange looks, but the silent message she sends is that it is Daisy who needs our attention, not her. Daisy and Aunt Sadie have been spending more time together, and that may be part of the change in Daisy. If I had to call it something, I would call it a blossoming.

"Are you the spokesperson for this little meeting?" Lily asks me.

I tell her I am. Daisy sends me a grateful look.

"Then tell me," Lily says.

"First of all, there's nothing to worry about," I begin. "Nobody has died. Nobody is hurt or sick."

"Well, that's good." Her laugh dies quickly when we don't join in.

"My friends and I took care of it," I begin. "But I need to tell you what happened."

"Something happened?" she says. "You said it wasn't anything bad."

"We didn't want to disturb you on your tour," Sadie says.

Last night I lost sleep deciding how we might tell Lily, and now those thoughts have flown out of my head.

"Are you in trouble?" Lily looks at Daisy, who lowers her eyes, as though courage is needed and she can't seem to find where she last put it.

"No, Daisy isn't in trouble," I say. "But Jerry is."

"Jerry?" Her voice makes a crescendo.

I take a deep breath, asking God for courage, and I wonder if this means that we are on speaking terms again. Then I tell Lily everything, including how I rounded up three good men to go with me to Nashville and confront Jerry. I tell her about Jerry calling Daisy a liar, and how Daisy kept a record and recordings of the incidents.

Lily's eyes widen as the story unfolds and then fill with tears. When I finish, she wraps her arms around Daisy. The two of them hold each other and cry. Lily says over and over how sorry she is, that she had no idea. Within seconds, my fear that Lily might not believe Daisy evaporates. She has done the right thing, the essential thing, which is to believe.

Instead of mother and daughter, they look like sisters sitting there, their heads touching and tears falling. At this moment, it feels like what happened with Johnny was a disguised blessing if this many years later, we can be here for Daisy. Aunt Sadie nods and rocks as though she is in the midst of a prayer meeting and the Holy Spirit is visiting. I find myself getting teary-eyed, too, but then realize the story is far from finished.

"We need to decide what to do next," I say.

Lily turns to me, as though just now realizing this song has another verse.

"Bee spent an entire afternoon on the phone with an attorney," I begin. "Even though Daisy has proof, the lawyer didn't think it was wise to take it to court because of the damage the exposure might do to Daisy. Even more damage than a custody case might do. So we were basically left with no good answers," I conclude.

Daisy wipes tears with the bottom of her shirt, and Lily puts her arm around her.

"We'll get through this," she says to Daisy.

Meanwhile, I hold on to the promise of healing seven generations forward and seven generations back that June told me about. I want to believe that as a family, we can recover.

"The McAllister women have always made the best of the hand life dealt us, as have most women," Aunt Sadie says.

I think of Mama again, and her hard life of always plowing to the end of the row. We need time to grieve before continuing to plow.

"Never underestimate the McAllister women," I say. "We're sturdy stock." Although at this moment I don't feel sturdy at all.

"I'm going to take some time off," Lily says. "Nashville can live without me for a few weeks. Okay if I stay here with you?" she asks Daisy.

Daisy smiles, though I imagine we're both wondering if this will really happen.

June spoke of it as a pattern repeating from the past until

someone dares to break it. Like putting a stick in the spoke of a moving bicycle tire. Daisy survived the crash. Now, these mountains can help her heal.

CHAPTER TWENTY-EIGHT

Daisy

My mom keeps looking at me as if I am a baby bird that has prematurely fallen from its nest, and she is somehow responsible. I tell her I am going for a walk. She offers to go with me, but I tell her I need to be alone.

"Are you sure?" she asks.

I tell her that I am sure.

The truth is, I need a break from all the attention. I want to dig for treasure, and this is one secret I want to keep to myself. Pretending to take a walk, I descend the hill and turn right at the mailboxes. Then I circle back through the woods, the house in sight the entire time.

Gran and Mom are on the front porch having a second cup of coffee. They are talking, probably about me, but I can't hear them. I imagine they won't go into the backyard for anything. At least, this is my hope. Later this afternoon the family is gathering for the Fourth of July at Nellie's, which promises to be overwhelming. Gran says it will be my chance to meet all my cousins, firsts and seconds. I wonder if I should take paper and pencil and take notes on my abundance of family. This is the opposite of living on an island alone like Karana, and I suddenly understand what a loss this was for her.

In the back is the large boulder that is bigger than the chicken coop. I use a smaller rock as a stepping-stone and climb up from behind. From the kitchen window, only the top half of the boulder can be seen, as well as the forest up above. While I'm digging, no one will even know I am there unless they walk around the side of the house.

For now, I sit on top of the rock overlooking the small barn to my left and the chicken coop to my right. In front of me is the back of Granny McAllister's house. Within seconds I hear the voice of a young Wildflower talking to her friend Mary Jane about Wildflower's father. I am relieved when the voices fade.

Welcoming the quiet, I take a deep breath, suddenly realizing how worried I was that Mom might not believe me. Or that she might blame me or be angry at me. But my mom has been none of those. If anything, she seems to blame herself. I don't want that, either. I just want this whole thing to be over.

I've been digging for days, and so far I haven't found anything except an old kitchen fork and a quarter. It's not like I have a treasure map with a big *X* marking the spot. All that Joseph McAllister said was that he had buried some important things near the boulder. It's big, and that's a lot of space.

It rained last night, and the boulder has a small puddle in one of its crevices that a bee is drinking from. From here I can see where I've already dug. Sections stretch out below me like hopscotch squares. Five of them, for five different digs. The moss helps me hide what I have done. It comes up in sheets, and I return it once I finish, like a rug in a movie covering a secret trapdoor. I didn't realize I was strong enough to dig a hole. I'm not that athletic. But there is something about doing it that feels good. I am getting stronger.

I think of Joseph McAllister, my great-grandfather, and ask his spirit to tell me where he hid the metal box with the McAllister treasure. I wait for a response and get nothing. I wonder again why Granny McAllister didn't dig up the gold coins and make her life more comfortable. I guess there is a chance she did and just didn't tell anyone, and that all this digging will be for nothing. Yet, somehow, I am okay with that, too.

There is little proof of a windfall, given the state of things before Mom paid for the renovation of the place. I overheard her on the telephone, talking to contractors. They were surprised that the old house hadn't fallen down around Granny McAllister. You wouldn't know that by looking at it now, though. It seems almost totally new.

After climbing off the boulder, I go and get the shovel under the porch, along with the old pair of thick garden gloves I found in the back of Gran's pickup. I imagine Gran digs holes all the time working for the plant nursery. She is strong for an old woman. I pull up the big pieces of moss and lay them to the side and cut out a new square, marking the space. Then I dig around the roots and rocks and loosen the soil. After a few minutes, I am sweating like crazy. I am about six inches down, not deep enough to even bury a baby bird. With big stabs, I let the tip of the shovel explore, listening for anything that sounds like metal hitting metal. Nothing. I go down another six inches then finally give up on this square of the grid.

"What are you doing?"

Nellie's voice makes me jump. She carries a basket to gather eggs and walks over to me. She looks down at my hopscotch squares, and at the hole.

"You digging your way to China?" She laughs.

My brain rushes for a reasonable explanation of why I'm digging holes in Granny McAllister's backyard.

"I just needed some exercise," I tell her. "Gran says I don't get outside enough." Neither statement is true.

"So, you're digging holes just to have something to do?"

I nod and smile as though waiting for her to recognize my brilliance. She rolls her eyes instead.

"You're weird sometimes, Daisy." She walks toward the coop. "I've got to see what the chickens have left. Mama wants to make deviled eggs for the picnic, and our chickens had a lackluster performance today. They don't like the heat. You like deviled eggs? I love them."

I imagine a permanently perky Nellie married to Adam Sector and rustling up eggs from her own chickens someday. Eggs she will feed several children of different ages who all look like Adam.

"Hey, do you mind not telling anybody about what I'm doing?" I lean against the shovel, trying to downplay the importance of my request.

"Sure," she says, as if she can understand why I might want to keep my digging a secret.

Nellie isn't really the type to go digging for treasure, not unless a river runs through it. Her biggest secret is probably a *Brides* magazine buried underneath the sweaters in her sweater drawer.

While waiting on Nellie to gather eggs, I look up into the trees, sunlight sparkling among the limbs. Until now, I never noticed that places could be this beautiful. Seconds later, a banjo picks out a slow song, its melody as pretty as the place. I imagine my great-grandfather sitting on the back porch playing for me while I dig.

Nellie waves before leaving, and I hope she doesn't tell Mom and Gran that she just saw me in the backyard. This might prompt them to come see what I am doing.

With Nellie gone, I scatter the dirt back over the hole, spread it out and then stamp it down, and cover it again with moss. I think of the grid I have mapped out in my mind. If I do one square a day, I will have the entire area covered in ten more days. That will take more sneaking around, but I think it is doable.

"Daisy?" I hear my mom call from the front porch. "You need to come get ready for the picnic."

I can't remember her ever calling me to come home before. In Nashville, I am seldom outside. I don't yell back because I don't want her to be able to track me down. I hide the shovel and gloves under the porch again. An orange cat sits on an old wooden chair nearby. Did he hear the banjo, too?

I pet him. "Are you missing Granny McAllister?" I ask.

He leans into my touch.

"The humans get all the attention when someone dies, and the pets go unnoticed," I say.

He purrs.

"My mom is calling me, but I'll be back later." His meow sounds sad, as though resigned to being alone.

"I promise." I rub his ears to seal the promise.

Mom calls again.

Making as little noise as possible, I set off through the woods again. I arrive at the bottom of the driveway and then come up the hill huffing and puffing from all the running. It feels good to run, though. The only running I ever do at home is during PE, and I never get to enjoy it because I'm trying not to look stupid.

"Where have you been?" Mom asks.

"Just around," I say.

"Why are your knees covered in mud?"

I look down, the evidence of my treasure hunting in full view.

"I fell, but I'm okay." I seem to be setting a record for lying today.

Mom tells me to wash up, that we are about to go over to Daniel's for the Fourth of July picnic. I answer with a "yes ma'am" that causes her to smile. My newfound manners have surprised even me and have accidentally drawn more attention to myself.

In the meantime, I imagine finding the metal box full of McAllister treasure and presenting it to her. She will laugh about how well I hid my secret from her. Then, since Mom is always searching for new song ideas, she will probably write one about digging for buried treasure and the surprises that come. I can almost hear it now.

My hands ache from digging, and I go inside to take a shower and put on clean clothes. When I am in the backyard, I feel like a detective, or maybe an explorer. This is precisely something Karana might do if she was trapped in Katy's Ridge instead of on the island with the blue dolphins. When we read the book in my English class last spring, my teacher, Miss Nelson, asked us what we thought that Karana learned about herself during her time on the deserted island. Maybe that is a good question for me, too.

The digging isn't only about unearthing the treasure, but something more profound. Maybe I am discovering things I never knew about myself. Like how sneaky I can be, and also how much I enjoy being outside and putting my hands in the dirt, even if it is just to dig a hole and then cover it up again. I never thought about what I might learn from all the digging. It seems related to all this family I never knew I had. Treasure of a different sort.

CHAPTER TWENTY-NINE

Wildflower

The Fourth of July barbecue is at Daniel and Jo's, as it is every year, though I haven't attended in ages. My sisters are here, as well as their spouses, kids, and grandkids. I estimate forty people, maybe more. All my family is together again, this time without Mama.

Aunt Sadie goes into the house to help Jo, and Lily introduces Daisy to her different cousins. It is good to see Lily in Katy's Ridge again, and even better to see her with Daisy. I see resilience in Daisy I never knew she had. She is taking off more on her own. Exploring the woods, learning the roads. I wonder if all that digging out by the boulder has anything to do with it. She doesn't know I know about that, but I like to see her occupied in a physical activity instead of with a book. Not that I have a problem with books. But there is something to be said for fresh air, too.

As a girl, I dug all kinds of holes, created forts, climbed trees, and built treehouses, mostly with my boy cousins.

Mama was none the wiser. Or maybe she knew all along, too. It occurs to me that I may not have known Mama at all.

It is warm and humid. A typical summer day in the south. Daniel stands in the backyard at the barbecue pit under the shade of the maple trees. He waves when he sees me. His three-year-old grandson, Matthew, hugs his knees, looking up as if Daniel is one of those giant redwoods in California I've seen pictures of. When I approach, Daniel asks me how Daisy is.

"We told Lily an hour or so ago," I say.

His eyebrows lift. "How'd she take it?"

"Better than I thought, though I suspect her anger is coming in on a slow train like mine did. At first the news is sobering and tragic, but then you get mad."

He nods. "I invited Victor, Horatio, and June to the cook-out, too."

"I'm glad," I say. In truth, they feel like family, too.

Danny, Jo and Daniel's son, approaches with his younger wife, Louise. It is hard to believe he is middle-aged. She keeps a protective arm on her enormous pregnant belly, and a smile doesn't leave her face. The three-year-old belongs to her, too. What must it be like to be pregnant and happy about it? Even my overzealous imagination has trouble envisioning that.

June and Horatio walk up the hill, having just arrived. June carries a casserole dish and juggles it as we hug.

"How did your talk go with Lily?" she asks.

"So far, so good," I say. "Lily said all the right things."

"I bet Daisy is glad that's over," she says. "At least the telling part. As you know, this is a dragon with a long tail. Many parts to slay."

Horatio stands nearby and nods. June is right. It has taken

me decades to get over the long tail of what Johnny did to me. I wonder if I am fully over it now. I think of Matt Monroe, from the same family of dragons. I feel a twist in my gut.

"Thank you again for coming with us," I say to Horatio.

"You're welcome, Miss Wildflower. If you need me again, just let me know."

They walk over to the picnic tables to put down June's casserole dish. We will have time to visit later. Grabbing a soda from the ice-filled cooler, I find a lawn chair and sit, family and friends gathered around me. We speak of simple things. The weather. The kids. The jobs. It is a relief from the seriousness of the earlier conversation with Lily and Daisy. Yet life has a way of becoming serious for all of us, whether we speak of it at a family picnic or not.

My nephew Bolt, Jo and Daniel's oldest son, was named after Daddy, but the nickname given to him as a boy has stuck with him forever. Bolt is here with his wife and three teenage sons and their various girlfriends. Nellie stands on the porch, along with Adam Sector and Daisy. Of the three, Nellie is the only one talking.

Nat, my sister Amy's son and my favorite nephew, comes over to say hello. He looks just like his father, Nathan, who is celebrating the Fourth of July in the cemetery with Daddy. Nat is an English teacher at Rocky Bluff High School. His wife, Sally, is in the house with Jo, and his four kids—ranging in age from five to fifteen—are scattered among the crowd.

Amy's daughter Lizzie, who was obnoxious as a child, is in a cluster of the family standing near the picnic tables, a dog at her side. Unmarried, Lizzie works as a dental hygienist in Harriman. Every year I receive a Christmas card that includes an Olan Mills photograph of her with her current dog.

My sister Meg waves from the steps of the house. She is there with Janie, Cecil's daughter from his previous marriage, who is still as nondescript as ever.

Tired of sitting, I walk to the back of Daniel's property near his old barn. In the distance, Daniel, Victor, and Horatio stand under a giant maple tree. Heroes, in my mind. I wonder if they are talking about our Nashville trip. For all we know, we have disturbed a hornet's nest.

Victor salutes me with a bottle of beer. I bow my head in his direction. Sometimes I wish I was attracted to him. It would make life easier, for sure. But it is our friendship that I hope to develop from here on if he is willing.

As evening falls, a bonfire is lit near the barn—our version of fireworks. Music plays from a distant radio. Laughter erupts at different times from different groupings, but within minutes, everyone has gathered to watch the fire. Lily and Daisy pull up lawn chairs next to mine. It is so unusual to have us all in one place, I find myself trying to memorize the scene. I didn't think to bring my camera with me when Mama took ill and certainly didn't mean to stay longer than a day or two.

I catch Daisy studying me, and with a glance, I ask her how she is. She shrugs, followed by the faintest of smiles. But even her shrug seems somehow lighter. Sitting by the fire, Lily appears to relax, though her attention has not left Daisy. Behind the smile, I imagine she is thinking about what to do next.

Meanwhile, Meg escorts Aunt Sadie to a chair in front of the fire. Our eyes meet, and she offers a reassuring smile.

All is well, she tells me, *even though it may not seem that way for a while.*

I want to believe her.

The fire crackles, the smoke rising to the heavens like prayers. For centuries, our ancestors have gathered in front of mesmerizing fires. We are simply the latest. Shadows of flames illuminate the barn, dancing across the old boards like the first black-and-white films without sound—the human story dancing across the screen.

I think again of that night, so many years ago, when Jo was giving birth to Bolt, and I was pregnant and next in line. Terrified, I went into that barn to escape Jo's cries. Mama noticed I was gone and came and found me. When she walked into that barn with her lantern fully lit, shadows flickered against the inside boards. The light played tricks, and I thought Mama was the gold Mary. In times of trouble, everyone needs an angel to call on. Real or imagined.

I look over at Daisy, who stares into the fire. History repeats itself until we break the patterns, June said. I wonder what pattern I need to break now. Then I think of Mama gone to be with Daddy and wonder if they are watching. Life is brief and full of loss. But I am convinced that we are observed from the shadows by those who came before.

"I think I'll go home," I say to Lily and Daisy. "It's been a big day." I stand. They say they understand. Earlier, we told the truth to one another about hard things. We survived. A quiet revolution ensued.

After several goodbyes, I walk down the hill, letting go of the warmth of the fire, the warmth of family. The world gets quiet again. My eyes adjust to the new darkness. I have walked this path thousands of times. My heart has memorized each step. As the moon reaches toward fullness, I appreciate the light it provides. I also thank the gold Mary for not deserting me.

Crossing the road, I continue up the driveway and the dirt path beyond. The Redbud Sisters gather to my left in the dark. I wave. I imagine them waving back. When I smell jasmine, I know exactly where I am. It was afternoon when we left, and I wish I'd thought to leave a light on in the house. If Mama had been here, she would have remembered, but the house will be filled with light soon enough.

The moon winks at me through the trees. When your parents are gone, it is easy to feel next in line. I stop on the path, my secret sense giving me a nudge. I listen for footsteps. I hear nothing except night sounds. Night sounds that Daddy taught us never to fear.

Then I get a whiff of Daddy's pipe tobacco. I tell myself that I should have skipped Aunt Sadie's blackberry spirits when toasting our country's independence. But as I begin to walk again, footsteps join mine. Mama always chided me for my overactive imagination, and while Daddy believed in spirits, it wouldn't be like him to haunt a place, but here he is.

"Daddy?" My voice sounds small like I am a girl again.

"Wildflower?" Daddy says from the darkness.

Tears fill my eyes. Stranger things have happened in these mountains, I tell myself. Aunt Sadie has been talking to spirits for years.

"Are you in heaven?" I ask him.

"Something like," he says.

"Something like?"

He chuckles. "You were always so full of questions."

I always thought it was Lily who was that way, but maybe she got it from me. Then I remember all those questions I used to ask Daddy to ask God when I would sit on his grave. Questions like, *Why does lightning strike old dead trees?*

Daddy chuckles. "Because they call the lightning to them to help them go," he says.

"They call it? Like they ask for the lightning's help?"

Silence follows. Perhaps it is a daydream instead of a night one. But I have felt Daddy's presence more than once since I've been back in Katy's Ridge.

"Let me see you," I whisper.

For nearly forty years, the one thing I've wished for when I've blown out a birthday candle is to see Daddy again. I can't believe it has been that long.

"I can't do that," he says, sounding as disappointed as I feel.

"I still miss you," I say.

"I know you do," he says softly. "But I'm right here. I've been here the whole time."

My tears fall in earnest.

Nearing the house, I feel his presence walk away from me in the night. "Is Mama with you?" I call after him.

He begins to whistle, and the tune fades with each step.

Moonlight sprinkles across the porch steps to light my way. I open the door and walk inside, announcing to the old house that I am home.

CHAPTER THIRTY

Daisy

At the barbecue, Nellie hovered around Adam, but it was me he kept looking at around the edges of the conversation. Nellie isn't clueless, but she possesses a stubborn version of hope. I can't imagine being that way. Not that it matters. Adam is much older than me—seventeen—and I'll be leaving soon to go back to school in Nashville.

Mom announced at the picnic yesterday that she plans to stay in Katy's Ridge for a few days. Last night I overheard her talking to her agent on the phone. Her last words to him were: *I'm doing it. Figure it out.* We haven't talked about my father, but I can tell she's thinking about it by the way she looks at me.

We stayed at Sadie's house last night, and when Gran picked me up this morning for my driving lesson, Mom was still sleeping. Gran says Mom's been overdoing it for years and to let her sleep. But I wonder how long it will last before

Mom feels like she has to get back to work and not upset her fans.

I question if I will ever see my father again and if I even want to. I've gone over what happened in his office a hundred times. The memory causes me to cringe, and also feel proud. People stood up for me and told my father his behavior was unacceptable. I can't imagine what will happen now.

I park the pickup at Granny McAllister's house, and Gran congratulates me on a good job.

"I'm not ready to go inside just yet, you want to take a walk?" she asks.

I tell her yes, even though I planned to dig at the boulder in the back when Gran got busy doing other things. Lately, she's been making lots of phone calls to get Granny McAllister's affairs in order.

Gran pulls out her pocket watch to note the time, and I remember the owner of the watch playing his banjo for Granny McAllister before she died. After the funeral, when Gran showed me some photographs she found, I had proof that I didn't imagine Joseph. It was him.

We walk along the road at first, but then we stop in front of a small boulder and a twisted tree.

"When I was a girl, I was the only one who used this path," she says. "Nobody in my family even knew it was here."

"What kind of tree is that?" I ask.

"It's a dogwood," Gran says. "Its branches are twisted like that because all its life it's been reaching for sunlight."

When I look up, I see other trees, all with branches reaching toward the sky, worshipping the sun.

"This is the secret path that I told you about. It leads to

the back of the cemetery," Gran says. "I used to go and visit Daddy up there every other day, sometimes more."

I follow her into the thick forest. The path she follows disappears in places, but she keeps going as if she could find her way blindfolded. Gran is quieter than usual. The deeper we go into the woods, the deeper she appears to go into her thoughts.

We stop at a little bridge. I get out the rabbit's foot she gave me, and it makes her smile.

"Daniel and Nathan built this new footbridge the year your mama was born," Gran says.

Voices from the past confirm her statement. Two men talk about a third, and I hear Wildflower's voice, too.

Where could he be hiding? a man asks.

Then Wildflower evidently sees something shiny in the ravine, and they take off to find it. I hear their breathing deepen as they work their way down to the stream, and then I hear Wildflower scream. The voices from the past fade. I return to the present day without Gran even knowing I was gone.

"For a time, you could hear whispers coming from down there," Gran says, looking into the ravine.

"Whispers?" I look where she is looking. Of all I have heard already, there were no whispers.

Dizziness forces me to clutch the railing. I didn't realize how high up we are.

"You okay?" Gran asks. She places her hand on mine, and I feel instantly better.

"What were the whispers about?" I ask.

"It was after Johnny died," she says. "You could hear them here on the footbridge. It was creepy. Of course, it could have just been the wind and the water talking to each other," she continues. "But Lily heard it very strongly, and Johnny's sister could hear it, too."

"Mom could hear the whispers?"

For the first time I wonder if Mom might hear voices, too. I think again of buried treasure. What is hidden inside me that is like my mom that I never realized I had?

"For years Lily wanted desperately to know who her father was," Gran continues. "In a way, I guess he was telling her."

Goosebumps come. Something that seems to happen often here in the mountains.

"I think those whispers drove Johnny's sister mad," Gran says. "Melody fell and died here, too. It was strange. And sad," she concludes.

"For a small mountain community, it sure seems a lot of people die here under suspicious circumstances," I say.

"Well, only those two."

"But your father?"

"That was an accident," she says. "Well, all of them were accidents, I guess."

I begin to take notes in my mind again. Johnny Monroe was my mother's father, my grandfather. He was not a nice guy and died from a fall before my mom was born. He fell from this bridge. His sister fell from here, too, after hearing whispers coming from below. I clutch the rail harder, looking into the ravine. Death is everywhere, it seems, but also life.

"It's called the secret sense, by the way," Gran says.

"What?"

"That thing you have where you can see and hear things that nobody else can. Sadie calls that the secret sense."

"It has a name?"

Gran nods. "It's a gift. Believe it or not, you're lucky to have it."

"Lucky?" Not once have I thought it was lucky to hear voices.

"I have it a little bit if only I'd listen to it," Gran continues. "Other than hearing those whispers, I'm not sure about Lily. My mama didn't have it, either. But Sadie does. You two should talk."

I nod, thinking maybe we should.

"What I wanted to show you is just over here," Gran says.

Ahead is an open area filled with wildflowers. Gran sits on a bench that looks like something Horatio made for her. I sit next to Gran. Here in the mountains, she is different. Here in the mountains, I can see why her father nicknamed her Wildflower. She blooms.

For the longest time, we sit in silence, like we're in church and the mountains are ministering to us. Inside the silence is more silence. I think about how hearing voices from the past has a name. It is called the secret sense, though the secret sense is also more than voices. But the secret sense can actually be something good. Something that other people in my family have and that passed down to me as an inheritance.

"I brought you here for a reason," Gran says. "I consider this place sacred because this is where my life changed forever."

I look around, trying to imagine anything bad happening here.

"I dug up wildflowers all over the mountain and replanted them here, and collected seeds from others," Gran says. "Tiger lilies mainly. Hundreds of them. I set up those cairns, too, and Horatio made the bench for me."

In one area of the wildflower beds are rock statues placed in a circle.

"At first I created this as a way to not let Johnny win," Gran begins. "He made me afraid to be here in the forest by myself, so I decided to make something beautiful out of something ugly." She pauses, and her voice softens. "But I also think I created this place because this is where I first saw the gold Mary."

"The gold Mary?"

Gran pauses again.

"She was hovering in that tree over there," Gran says, her voice softer still. "She was the most beautiful thing I've ever seen. Like an angel surrounded by sunlight, and the look on her face was pure love."

Gran pauses again, and her eyes glisten with new tears. "In those moments with her, I felt totally safe and loved."

I try to imagine what I might have done. Maybe I would have planted hundreds of flowers, too. Then I remember one of Mom's early songs.

"Mom wrote a song with a gold Mary in it," I say.

Gran's surprise opens, and she blooms even more.

"The second album," I say.

"Do you remember the words?" she asks.

I think back to the lyrics. "It's something about coming home, and a gold angel watching from a giant oak on a moonlit night."

Gran lowers her head. "She *did* remember."

A new breeze sweeps through the tops of the trees.

"Mom told me once that she can only write songs about things that have touched her heart in some way."

Gran stays quiet for so long I ask if she's okay. She says she is, and I believe her. What surprises me, even more, is that I feel okay, too. How is it possible that my life is a total mess, and I feel okay?

"Can I confess something to you?" Gran asks. She looks at me as if she's been holding back saying this for days and even now wonders if she should speak it. I know what it's like to confess. I tell her to tell me.

"Lately, I've wished that I'd handled what happened with Johnny better. If I had, maybe this wouldn't have happened to you."

I pause. "I don't think that's how things work, Gran."

"How do you know?" she asks.

I shrug. I don't know.

Another long silence follows.

"People didn't talk about things back when I was a girl," Gran says.

"People don't talk about things *now*," I say.

She looks at me like I could be right. "For the longest time, I thought Mama blamed me for what happened. You know you're not to blame, don't you?"

I try on the words like a brand-new outfit, testing to see if they fit: *You are not to blame*. But deep down, I don't believe it. I must have done something wrong. I must have asked for it somehow.

Gran turns to me as if she's heard my thoughts.

"Daisy McAllister, you did nothing to deserve what happened to you. You didn't do anything wrong. Do you hear me?"

I close my eyes, finding Gran's belief in me almost unbearable. For once, I wish the voices from the past would come and rescue me from the present. But I hear nothing other than the soft sounds of the forest.

"Can I tell you another secret?" Gran asks.

I tell her she can.

"I've often wondered if the gold Mary comes for us when we die," Gran begins again. "Not the grim reaper, like those awful cartoons, but a loving mother, full of light."

"I think other people who love us might come, too," I say. "When I was sitting in Granny McAllister's bedroom before she died, I saw Joseph."

"You saw Daddy?" She turns to me, smiling.

"Clear as day."

"Did he say anything to you?" Gran asks.

"He didn't, but he looked right at me. He knew I was there."

Gran looks up into the trees, crying and smiling at the same time. "Did he say anything to Mama?"

"He sang to her," I say.

"What did he sing?" She stands as though she might float into the top of the trees herself.

"'Goodnight, Irene,'" I say.

She laughs. "Mama always loved that song."

Gran starts to sing. Her voice is not anything like my mom's. It isn't bad or good, and when she invites me to join in, I do. While we sing, two butterflies circle our heads as if enjoying the tune.

After we finish, she sits on the bench again and takes my hand.

"Thank you for telling me about Daddy," she says.

"Thank you for showing me this place," I say.

At this moment, I feel safe and loved. My shoulders relax, followed by an unexpected rush of fear.

CHAPTER THIRTY-ONE

Wildflower

On the way home, I breathe deeply, feeling cleansed by the tears I shed in the forest. It's not like me to cry so freely. But tears don't scare Daisy as they do me. She also doesn't mind silence, though it's fertile ground for me to wonder what she's thinking. Considering all the secrets that have come to light lately, she seems remarkably fine. Resilient.

A faint whistle rides the breeze.

"You hear that?" I ask.

Daisy nods.

"Daddy used to whistle everywhere he went," I say.

"Maybe you're conjuring him up."

"Then why would you hear him, too?" I ask, amazed that neither of us is spooked. Here in the mountains, spirits roam the hills freely. Or at least it seems that way.

Daisy is smart like Lily was at thirteen. Yet it's a different kind of smart. The secret sense is awakening in her. A tea bag dropped into hot water, the flavor just now releasing.

We pass the gnarled dogwood and the big stone that mark the entrance to the path. A man steps out of the briars wearing a straw hat and carrying a bucket. He startles us, and I say my favorite cuss word. It is Melody Monroe's son, Matt. He smiles and holds up his pail.

"Blackberries," he says. "There's a huge patch in that clearing over there."

I nod, not returning the smile. I wonder if Matt has any idea how close he is to the last place I saw his mother alive. Or how close he is to the ravine she fell into and died.

He tips his hat to Daisy. I realize they have no idea that they are cousins. Hiding my fluster, I tell Daisy that we need to get going and wish Matt good luck with his blackberries. I can't seem to shake my distrust.

Daisy and I walk along the road and then turn at the mailboxes to go up the hill. Mary Jane's Cadillac is in the driveway next to my pickup. She is listening to an oldies station on the radio, her hand out the window holding a cigarette and moving to the rhythm of the Bee Gees who are *Stayin' Alive*.

"I've been waiting for you." The music drops, as does the cigarette to the ground as she gets out of the car.

I tell Daisy I'll meet her at the house and she goes on ahead.

Mary Jane crushes the cigarette under her shoe, releasing a smoldering, bitter smell. She looks up the hill as if to make sure Daisy is not within hearing distance.

"I can't believe that stunt you pulled in Nashville," she says, her words smoldering and bitter as well.

"Victor told you?" I ask, finding the possibility hard to believe.

"No, Victor didn't say a word. It's getting around the grapevine."

It occurs to me that Mary Jane is the one who started this particular vine, based on what my sister Amy said when she huffed her way up this hill to confront me. I find it interesting as well as alarming that it's the women who come to put me in my place, not the men. Men have actually been helpful.

I begin telling her that it is none of her business until she interrupts.

"It is definitely my business if you involve my brother in it."

"Victor is old enough to make his own decisions," I say.

"Victor doesn't have a clear mind where you're concerned." She crosses her arms.

"When I saw him the other night he seemed clear-minded," I say, fighting the temptation to cross my arms, too.

"Wake up, Louisa May," she says, spitting out the words as if they are meant to hurt me. "He's been in love with you since we were kids."

Mary Jane straightens the collar of her blouse, as though briefly remembering decorum.

"You're like a magnet when it comes to trouble," she begins again, putting her hands on her hefty hips. "Mama told me that a long time ago." She pauses long enough to point her finger at me. "You need to leave Victor alone. Don't encourage him. You'll bring his life down to your level."

"Victor is a grown man," I say. "What he does with his life isn't your concern."

"Are you forgetting what you are?" Her lips purse as if

she's eaten something bitter. "You ruined Bee's life, and now you want to ruin Victor's?"

My face warms, and I unwittingly make a fist. "Well, at least I don't have to wonder what you think anymore," I say.

Mary Jane huffs. She returns to her car and turns on the engine, the fumes from her exhaust adding to the toxic mix. "Stay away from Victor," she warns out the window.

As she backs down the hill, I narrow my eyes at her and then spit in the dirt. For years I looked up to Mary Jane and her sophisticated family. They were everything the McAllisters were not. But nothing is ever what it seems. I always knew that Victor was in love with me, but why is that my fault? And why am I to blame for Bee and me falling in love? Most importantly, who appointed Mary Jane judge and jury? Certainly not me.

Daisy and Aunt Sadie wait for me on the porch. With each step, I am more convinced that we were right to confront Jerry. If our family and friends don't take a stand for us, what hope do any of us have?

"Everything okay?" Aunt Sadie asks.

"Not really," I say, climbing the steps to the porch.

The phone rings in the kitchen, and I go to answer it. I assume it is Lily, but it's actually Bee. After I tell her about the earful Mary Jane gave me, she sighs.

"People disappoint me sometimes," she says.

"Me, too," I say.

"The good news is, I found an attorney in Nashville who will take our case," Bee says. "The bad news is, she doesn't think we will get very far. It seems Jerry has friends in high places."

"Why doesn't that surprise me?" I twist the telephone

cord between my fingers until it starts to cut off my circulation and they begin to tingle.

"How's Daisy?" she asks.

"Surprisingly fine," I say.

"Maybe confronting Jerry was a good thing," Bee says. "At least she knows she doesn't have to go through this alone."

I tell her about seeing Matt Monroe on the trail, and how unnerved I was. A thought occurs to me, and I say to her that I plan to visit him. She asks why.

"To lay old ghosts to rest, I guess."

"Well, be careful," Bee says.

On most days, she is more cautious than I am. Although after what happened with Johnny, I've had a watchfulness that can be exhausting at times, as though predators lurk behind every rock. I find myself hoping that this isn't the case for Daisy, too.

Like Amy, Bee prefers to let sleeping dogs lie. Or at the very least, to avoid any conflict that might arise.

When I return to the front porch, Aunt Sadie is sewing quilt pieces while Daisy sits on the swing. It is strange to see Sadie sew by herself. Yet again, I am reminded that Mama is gone.

"That was Bee," I say to them. "She sends her love."

Daisy smiles, and Aunt Sadie excuses herself to go take a nap. With Sadie inside, I ask Daisy if she wants to drive over to see her mom. She answers with another smile. Although I have always known that Bee is Daisy's favorite, my status seems to be on the rise. Maybe teaching her to drive has something to do with that—or confronting her father. Either way, I am grateful for it.

Daisy is getting better at changing gears; her bucking bronco days are over. When we arrive at Sadie's, Lily is still in her summer nightgown and sitting on the porch swing having a cup of coffee. She hugs Daisy, who settles in next to her, and gives me a look telling me that we'll talk later about me teaching Daisy to drive. After we visit for a while, I kiss them both on the cheek and tell them I have somewhere to be. Not letting the moss grow on my idea, I get back in my pickup and head toward the Monroes' place and a date with history that a week ago I would have never anticipated. No time better than now, I think, to give myself courage. Waiting might only change my mind.

CHAPTER THIRTY-TWO

Daisy

Gran is barely out of sight when the telephone rings inside. I tell Mom that I will answer it, and she thanks me. On the fifth ring, I pick up.

When I hear my father's voice, my insides freeze.

"I can't believe you talked your grandmother into showing up at my office." He sounds angry.

My palms turn into a sweating mess, and I wish the phone cord would stretch to the front door, so I could tell Mom who it is.

"I didn't talk anybody into doing anything," I say to him.

"Oh, come on. You know what you did." Street noises fill the background. Is he calling from a phone booth?

"That queer grandmother of yours had better leave me the hell alone."

My wrist throbs from holding on to the phone so tightly. Paralyzed, I can't seem to stop listening or hang up.

"You need to tell everybody that you lied. Tell those

people that you were mad at me and made it all up. You hear me?"

Unable to speak, I try to swallow the fear choking me.

"You're going to regret crossing me, Daisy," he says. "I warned you."

All the hopeful feelings I've had since being in Katy's Ridge vanish. My cheeks burn.

When my arm finally moves, I slam the kitchen phone on its cradle with enough force to make the picture hanging on the wall swing on its nail. Seconds later, I run out of the house. I follow the road toward the lake. Mom calls after me, asking what's wrong. But I don't stop. Something about running feels necessary. I want to run away from my father's call. Run from everything that's happened.

At the sparkling lake, with nowhere else to go, I stop, and my tears begin. In the next moment my mom catches up with me, out of breath, and still in her nightgown and slippers. I never knew she could run so fast.

Her breathing labored, she asks what happened. Through tears, I tell her, and she pulls me into her arms again.

"I'm so sorry, Daisy." Her body is warm from running. Her embrace is everything I need. At a moment when everything feels wrong, she reassures me that everything will be all right. I want to believe her.

CHAPTER THIRTY-THREE

Wildflower

A newly paved driveway points the way to the Monroe place. Years ago, I slogged through mud up to my ankles to talk to Melody Monroe when she was living in that dilapidated old cabin. A large metal mailbox stands near where I park, the red flag up as though waving a danger sign. I promised never to return to this place. However, something is drawing me here.

Walking from here gives me time to prepare, though I'm not sure what I'm preparing for. I think of what Bee said about Jerry having friends in high places and that he will more than likely get away with his treatment of Daisy. Jerry won't be the first man to escape responsibility, nor will he be the last, and I have no idea what this has to do with Matt Monroe.

At the end of the road, a new cabin stands where the old one used to be and is triple the size. Trees cleared from around the cabin allow sunlight to break through where there used to be darkness. Landscaping surrounds the cabin. Robust native plants sit in rustic beds with large stones placed to get the most natural setting. To be honest, it looks like something I might have created.

The old outhouse is gone, as well as the oak tree where Ruby Monroe took her own life at the age of twelve. I remember coming here as a girl with Daniel after Johnny talked dirty to Mary Jane and me. Kudzu vines had swallowed the place. That first visit, a young, barefooted Melody opened the door, her eyes revealing a deep sadness. What would she say if she saw this place now? Does Matt Monroe feel all the ghosts around him?

For the longest time, I stand in front of the cabin and take in the transformation.

"Welcome," a voice says, coming out of the woods.

Startled, I give a short, flustered wave.

Matt Monroe places several pieces of fresh-cut wood to the left of the house on the evenly stacked woodpile.

"Cup of coffee?" He could be Johnny's twin, though an older, well-kept version. The resemblance resides most in the way he stands and holds his head.

"Sure," I say, suddenly questioning why I am here.

Matt takes off leather gloves and walks over to shake my hand. His hand is warm and soft, no calluses.

"It's hard to believe this is the same place," I say.

He smiles, and I think how lucky he was not to get Johnny's teeth in the rolling of the genetic dice.

"When I first got here, I thought I was crazy even to consider building something here, but I think it turned out okay."

"Better than okay," I say, which elicits another smile from him.

Katy's Ridge is changing. People who defected have come back. At least Victor has. And although Matt never lived here, he has come back, too, in a way, to claim the family homestead. He seems friendly enough, yet why do I feel like I am sweet-talking a snake into not biting me? And is my distrust in my imagination or based on fact? The resemblance helps to confuse me.

Matt leads the way up to the sturdy porch, where a small wooden table sits with one chair. I imagine this is where he eats his meals in the summertime, overlooking a view of the mountains provided by a chainsaw.

"I had no idea the Monroe property was sitting on such a beautiful piece of land," I say.

"It was a diamond in the rough, for sure," he says. "I've got instant coffee, is that okay?" Matt asks.

I nod. He invites me to sit, saying that he will be right back. He enters the house, easing the screen door closed so it doesn't slam. It is unusual to see a man living alone who isn't a widower. Although maybe he is. I know nothing about Matt Monroe and must admit I am curious.

Does he feel the pull of history here, too?

It occurs to me that maybe we are part of a reconciliation party, pulled together to heal the past.

You're beginning to sound like June, I tell myself, but there are worse things, of course.

Matt returns with two cups of steaming coffee on a wooden tray, along with two bowls of blackberry cobbler, complete with a scoop of vanilla on the top. He apologizes for not asking first, making it impossible for me to refuse. For a Monroe, he is polite, as well as cultured, perhaps fifteen years younger than me, maybe more. And his cobbler is fabulous.

"Did you know my mother very well?" he asks after we finish our desserts.

"Not well," I say. "Melody didn't come that often."

"The coroner's report in Rocky Bluff says that she died from an accident. A fall. And that her blood alcohol level was off the charts." He takes a sip of coffee as though noting a change in the weather.

"Twenty years ago, when she came back to Katy's Ridge, she was having a rough time and drinking a lot," I say. "That was right before she died."

"I mostly lived with my father," he says. "I saw her only a few times a year. I knew she drank a lot and had some rough stuff in her past. I never knew exactly what."

I think of Daisy, and how determined I am to help her work through anything rough.

In the silence that follows, it seems we are both questioning why I am here. I wish I had an answer for that. My imagination produces the ghosts of Johnny, Ruby, and Melody standing below the porch, watching us talk and wondering the same thing. How is it that we humans are supposed to finish up unfinished business? Does just talking about it solve it?

"I heard you live in Nashville. Do you like it there?" he asks.

"It's a great city," I say, already tiring of the small talk.

"But?"

"I guess I'm just a country girl."

He smiles, and I see who Melody might have been if life hadn't defeated her.

"Why did you leave Louisville?" I ask.

"Too many ghosts," he says.

I catch myself smiling. "It's not easy to get away from ghosts," I say.

"Do you ever think of moving back to Katy's Ridge?" he asks.

"Not really," I say, and wonder if this is true.

"Isn't your daughter that famous singer?"

"Yes, Lily McAllister is my daughter."

"Cool," he says, suddenly sounding younger.

I don't mention Lily is down the road at Sadie's place, or that she and Matt are actually cousins.

"So Lily and I are related?" he asks.

"You're cousins, I guess," I say, not revealing my surprise. As much as I have tried to bury the past, it keeps popping up. Unearthed. Exhumed by the latest Monroe.

"My mother mentioned when I was a boy that I still had family here."

Does Matt think his Uncle Johnny and I were sweethearts? Nothing could be further from the truth. I sit straighter, my feistiness warming up for the day.

I debate whether to be truthful. "For the record, I had no choice in the matter," I say, as the truth wins out.

Matt pauses, a pained expression on his face. He reaches for my hand, but I manage to pull it away. I suddenly don't want to be here.

"I should tell you something." He pauses as though putting order to his thoughts. "I've been researching my family tree, and you might find some of it interesting."

I wait. Matt's eyes find mine. "You mentioned not having a choice?"

I nod, already regretting my latest admission.

"Well, that kind of makes sense," he begins. "On the Monroe side of the family, I had a great-grandfather who evidently got his young teenage daughter pregnant and was run out of West Virginia by the sheriff. He ended up in Katy's Ridge with his son. That son was my mother's father."

I think of Arthur Monroe, his creepiness evident when Daniel confronted him about his son, Johnny. He was a drinker, too.

A heaviness sits on my chest. "So you're telling me that history was repeating itself when Johnny Monroe attacked me on a trail to the cemetery when I was thirteen, because Johnny came from a family of predators?"

Matt nods. "Sins of the father," he says. "Thankfully, I've never married or sired children."

For several seconds we sit in silence. It appears the gravity of the situation has not been lost on either of us.

"After I moved here, I went to a local fortune-teller," Matt says.

"June Sector?"

"Yes. You know her, of course. Everybody knows everybody around here."

I agree.

"She said something about generations repeating themselves until someone breaks the pattern."

"That's interesting," I say. "June said the same thing to me."

"How do you suppose we do that?" he asks.

"I have no idea," I say.

We exchange a smile.

"I've been giving the family graves a face-lift," Matt says, "and putting flowers on them, and telling different family members to rest in peace. But other than that, I'm not sure what else to do."

I tell him I'm not sure, either. But at the same time, it

seems that sitting here together and talking about these characters from the past is somehow part of the solution, too.

After another long silence, I tell him I need to get back to Lily and Daisy.

"Can we talk about this again?" he asks.

I tell him that I would like that. After our handshake, I leave the porch and start to walk back to my pickup. When I turn around at the edge of the clearing, he is still watching me. We exchange a short wave.

As I get back to the road, I wonder if I have misjudged him. Simply because he is a Monroe doesn't make him a bad person. My secret sense was right to guide me here.

CHAPTER THIRTY-FOUR

Daisy

While I pretend to read, my mom and Sadie spend the afternoon together. After their talk, Sadie suggests that the two of us take a walk to the lake. We leave Mom and saunter down the dirt road.

"Wildflower thought it would be good if we talked," she says.

I nod. Aunt Sadie is eighty-three years older than me, but she isn't wobbly or anything. She is my great-great-aunt. Until we came to Katy's Ridge this summer, I never gave family trees a thought, or whether a cousin was a first, second, or third. It all seemed too complicated—not that I knew I had any, anyway. But just like my body is getting stronger every day that I dig, now my awareness of family is getting stronger, too.

"A lot has happened lately," Sadie says. "How are you doing with that?"

Grown-ups tell kids what to do and don't ask questions. I try to say to her that even though my life is falling apart, I finally feel like I belong someplace.

Our walk is slow but has a rhythm to it, like one of Mom's slow songs that makes a hush fall over the crowd. Is this what Gran calls a "mosey"? She has been saying I need to learn how to do this. If so, Sadie has mastered the art. I match her rhythm, letting it settle into my bones. We get to the small dock at the lake and sit on a bench under the pines. Instead of wading into the conversation, she jumps right in.

"Wildflower says you have a different kind of secret sense, where you hear voices from the past?"

I thought I was all out of secrets except digging for treasure, but hearing voices is a secret, too. If anyone can understand, it would be Sadie.

"It's more like conversations," I say. "Like watching a scene on television between two actors, except I can't see them, I can only hear them."

The beginnings of a smile come to her wrinkled face.

"What do these people say?" she asks.

I think about how to answer her question. "Well, they talk about things that seem important in some way," I begin. "It's usually a conversation that somehow changes things, and it's not always for the good."

"Is it the same people that talk to you?" she asks.

"Different people, depending on who I'm with, and it doesn't happen all the time, just every now and again."

"Do the people in these conversations ever talk just to you?"

I pause again to think. "Sometimes, I have the feeling the voices want me to tell someone something. Or they want me to tell whoever I'm with what I've heard and maybe give them a message."

"A message?" Sadie looks at me as if peering through an opening into another time and place. "Can you give me an example?" she asks.

Sadie's face reveals no judgment, and she is taking me seriously. I tilt my head slightly to the left and my chin downward. "Sometimes I can tune the voices in," I tell her. "It doesn't always work, but I might as well try." I close my eyes to listen as we sit in comfortable silence. Tiny waves lap the shore as I open to the past.

A few seconds later, old-timey music begins to play, featuring a fiddle and a pennywhistle like Mom used once on a song. Several people talk at a gathering. The volume turns up on two of the people, and the other voices fade into the background. From the sound of their voices, I decide it is an older man and a young woman. By some means, I know that Sadie is the young woman.

"An old man is speaking in English, but it sounds funny," I say. "He's trying to talk you out of going somewhere. He calls you headstrong, and says you don't know what you're getting into."

"That's my Da," she says, her voice sounding like the young woman from the past. "He used those exact words when I told him I was coming to America."

"Well, he wants you to know that he was wrong, and that he is very proud of you, and that he loves you."

The music fades, and the airwaves close. Aunt Sadie's eyes turn red and tears pool.

"I'm sorry," I say, thinking I've done the wrong thing.

"No, no, no," Aunt Sadie says. "These are good tears."

Sadie sniffs and pulls a red bandana out of her pants pocket and blows her nose. She takes in a deep breath. "For all these years I've been sad that Da and I didn't end things well. Now I can finally lay it to rest."

I study the tight places that have formed on my hands from shoveling. It never occurred to me that the voices could be a good thing.

"My grandmother had the same gift," Sadie says, putting her bandana away. "She was known throughout the village as someone who could give and receive messages."

"Give and receive?"

Sadie nods.

"I didn't know it worked the other way, that I could give messages to the dead, too."

"Most things work both ways," she says. "With that in mind, please tell Da that I love him and that I think about him every day."

I do as she asks.

Sadie says things that I never hear anyone else say, except for Gran sometimes. But with Aunt Sadie, it's like her mountain medicine isn't just about plants, but words, too. Words that heal the broken places inside.

For a long time we sit in silence, as if we've found a treasure of a different sort and thanks must be given.

"Tell me what to do with it," I say finally.

"Listen to it," Sadie says. "And if it makes sense, pass on the message."

"If it makes sense?"

"Yes, well, you have to be careful, of course. For the most part, you will keep this gift to yourself unless you trust the person to receive the information."

"So, it's nothing bad?" I ask.

"No, child. It's nothing bad," she begins. "In fact, it's a perfect thing. You gave me a message from my Da that will comfort me for the rest of my days."

She squeezes my hand, and I let the medicine of her words sink into me.

"The thing about gifts, though, is that you need to protect them and use them wisely," she says.

"I'm not sure how to do that," I say.

"I'll help," she says. "We can talk about it more while you're here. I can tell you stories of my grandmother, so you don't feel strange and different."

"Do you hear voices, too?" I ask.

"No, not voices, but I have a sense when someone from the other world is near. For instance, I know you met my brother, Joseph, at the house the night you arrived. I didn't see him, but my secret sense told me that you did."

"It's true," I say. "It was one of the rare times when I got more than voices. I could see him, too. He was right there with her."

Sadie smiles. "You have no idea how glad I am to hear that."

"Does Gran have the secret sense, too?"

"She would have it more if she trusted it and actually used it."

"What about Mom?"

"She had it a little when she was a girl, but now I think she uses it to write songs."

I nod, believing this to be true.

"You, however, have received an extra helping." Sadie smiles. "I guess we were due."

In the meantime, the sun sparkles and dances along the

top of the lake. For the first time in hours I haven't thought about my father and how angry he is. Spending time with Sadie feels more important than worrying. I don't begin to understand how the invisible world works, but I feel as though I've glimpsed the real McAllister family treasure.

CHAPTER THIRTY-FIVE

Wildflower

On my way home, I go by Aunt Sadie's house to pick up Daisy. Lily is taking a nap, and when she wakes up, I will tell her that a new Monroe relative lives nearby who is different from the others, and that she may want to meet him. Aunt Sadie and Daisy are gone, but I can guess where they are on such a beautiful summer day. I walk down the dirt road toward the lake and think about Matt Monroe. I can't help but feel that our meeting was an excellent beginning to reconciling the past.

When I see Sadie and Daisy sitting on the bench at the edge of the lake, my secret sense confirms the importance of their friendship. Long ago, Aunt Sadie helped me heal, too. To have Sadie help Daisy is not only fortunate but feels like an act of grace.

Sadie turns as though she senses me coming. Looking back over my life, I cannot remember a time when Sadie didn't appear happy to see me. I breathe in the pine-scented air and think how unusual it is to see young and old sitting together. I join them.

For several seconds we don't speak, but settle in with one another as we watch the lake. Like the river that flows through Katy's Ridge, the lake also ebbs and flows, little waves lapping gently against the shore, their rhythms seemingly linked.

"We've been having a good talk," Aunt Sadie says to me.

"I figured you would," I say. "What have you been talking about?"

"Family inheritance," Aunt Sadie says, giving Daisy a wink.

Daisy offers a rare smile and seems more at peace with herself.

Aunt Sadie takes my hand, and I take Daisy's, the McAllisters united. My shoulders relax, and I let myself believe that everything is going to be all right.

Moments later, we decide that we are all hungry, and we rise from the bench and walk back up the dirt road to Sadie's house. A note sits on the kitchen table from Lily saying that she is running to the A&P in Rocky Bluff for groceries and will be back shortly.

From the kitchen, we hear a car drive up and a door slam. Is Lily already back from the store? Daisy runs to greet her. We wait for them to return to the kitchen. Instead we hear a man's voice.

Sadie and I walk toward the front door, where we find Daisy wide-eyed and still. On the other side of the screen door is Jerry.

"I've been looking all over for you," Jerry says to Daisy. "Get in the car."

"No!" I tell him. "Daisy is certainly not getting in your car."

Daisy steps back as though inching away from a copperhead.

Jerry steps inside. He is several inches taller than me, and my attempt to block him from Daisy only makes him smile.

"Get your things," he says to her.

"I'll telephone the sheriff," Sadie says to me, turning toward the kitchen.

"I wouldn't advise that, old lady," Jerry says.

"I can do whatever I like," Sadie says, her tone as serious as I've ever heard her.

"The sheriff already knows I'm here to pick up my daughter. I stopped by his office on my way here."

Sadie looks at him as if confronted with the same copperhead.

"Go get your things," Jerry repeats to Daisy.

Daisy suddenly looks younger. At thirteen, she is still a girl in many ways.

"Her things aren't here," I say to Jerry.

"Where are they?"

"Mama's house."

He looks at Daisy and points toward the car. "We'll go by there before we leave."

Daisy's eyes are filled with desperation and tears.

"Jerry, what are you doing here?" I ask, trying to sound reasonable.

"My daughter has fallen under a bad influence and is making up stories. My lawyer says I can get a court order to keep her away from you if I have to. He's already talked to a judge in Nashville."

My head throbs. Jerry looks like a lawyer himself, with

his suit, tie, and shiny shoes, and he seems to enjoy intimidating three females of various ages in their casual summertime clothes.

I realize Jerry's car is still running out in front of Sadie's house. He has no intention of talking or doing anything except making a quick escape.

"Daisy is staying here with Lily," I say.

"Lily's here?" He looks down the hallway as though waiting for her to appear.

"Well, she will be here soon. She had to run to the store."

"Right," he says, as though I've just given his leg a good pull.

"She has a lawyer, too, Jerry."

"I'm sure she does," he says, his teeth almost gritted. "Have her lawyer talk to my lawyer." He motions for Daisy to come with him.

Stepping next to Daisy, I put an arm around her shoulder to anchor her in place. At this moment, I wish I had Mama's shotgun. Physically, Jerry has at least sixty pounds on me and is six feet tall, to my five feet, two inches.

"Let's just wait until Lily gets back," I say, remembering how he softened earlier when her name was mentioned.

He narrows his eyes as if seeing a trap. "Daisy will be at my house. Lily knows where to find me."

I still can't believe Lily married this jerk, after a sweetheart like Crow. Meanwhile, Sadie and I exchange a look that reveals how helpless we feel.

"Sadie, call Daniel," I say.

Sadie disappears into the kitchen.

"I don't want anyone to get hurt," Daisy says. "Mom can come to get me later."

"But Daisy—"

"Mom will know what to do," she says.

Will she? I wonder. It seems the world is not set up for justice.

"Get in the car," Jerry says again. Daisy walks past me and out of the house.

"You leave Daisy alone, Jerry. You hear me?" The full force of my hatred comes out in a single look. It has no impact. He returns to his car, Daisy already inside.

As soon as he drives away, I scream my frustration. Never in my life have I wanted to kill somebody more. Not even Johnny, who left me for dead on the trail. In the kitchen, Sadie is hanging up the phone.

"What do we do?" I ask, sounding frantic.

"Daniel will be at the house when they pick up Daisy's things. He'll try to talk some sense into him."

I suddenly fear for Daniel. "I've got to do something," I say to her. My walk has fury in it, my fists clenched. "Daisy will not spend one more night in that man's house," I say aloud.

I get into my pickup. It starts with a gasp and a sputter, not up for a high-speed chase.

CHAPTER THIRTY-SIX

Daisy

"That grandmother of yours is a piece of work." My father wears leather driving gloves to hold his leather steering wheel. "I'm going to make sure you never stay with her again."

"But I like to stay with Gran." I hate how wimpy my voice sounds.

"It doesn't matter what you like." He drives faster on the narrow curves than is safe.

My father has never been overly nice, but he's never been too mean, either, not like now.

Compared to Gran's old pickup, my father's new Mercedes purrs. It is automatic, so the only challenge is staying on the road. We pull up into the driveway, and I wonder if he even knows that Gran's mom died. Standing in the shade of the Redbud Sisters is my Great-Uncle Daniel. His arms are crossed in front of his chest, his chin firm. But compared to my father, he seems old.

"Go gather your things," my father tells me. "And don't waste any time." I want to ask him what he will do if I do, but not enough to actually voice it.

I head up the hill while my father walks over to Daniel.

As I pass, Daniel asks if I'm okay.

I shrug. *Okay* is not the word I would use. I am determined. Determined to keep everyone safe and not make my father angrier than he already is.

By the time I get to the porch, I hear angry words exchanged between Daniel and my father, and I want to cover my ears. I hope Nellie doesn't hear them fighting or she might get frightened.

Inside the house, I put my things in my backpack. I hear the faint strains of a banjo and think of Grandaddy McAllister, who is of little help as a ghost except to serenade my exit. When I return to my father's car, Gran has pulled up and is standing next to Daniel, who tries to reason with my father. My father appears to get angrier with every second. Gran challenges him, and his voice gets louder. I realize I am trembling, but also frozen in place.

A man walks up the driveway at a quick pace. I recognize him. He was picking blackberries on the secret path to the cemetery. I try to recall his name. Matt something.

"Are you all right?" he says to Gran while looking at my father. "I was passing by and heard yelling."

He nods to Daniel and then looks at Gran again.

"This is Daisy's father, Matt," Gran says. "We're having a disagreement."

"You and your goddamn disagreements," my father says to Gran. "Daisy's mine. She goes wherever I say."

My stomach lurches, and I get a sudden taste of the oatmeal I had for breakfast.

"But she doesn't want to go with you." Gran stands firm. If she is as terrified as I am, she isn't showing it. But she is also at least six inches shorter than him, and I don't want her to get hurt.

Daniel asks my father to calm down so that they can talk, but this makes him even more aggravated.

"This is none of your business, old man. Or yours," he says to Gran.

My father pulls me toward the car. I forget to breathe. Gran tells him to stop, her voice frantic.

"You're the one who needs to stop!" my father yells. He then calls her a degenerate and looks at Gran with pure hatred.

I don't even know what that word means, but it must be bad. My father releases me and then lunges toward Gran. Daniel and Matt step in to prevent my father from reaching her. It is Matt who grabs my father and pins his right arm behind his back in some kind of karate hold. I gasp, and my heart races even faster.

"It's you who needs to be stopped," Matt says to him. "This ends here!"

After several seconds of nonstop cussing, my father squirms free. His face is red, his eyes full of anger. He mumbles something about calling his lawyer, but he has lost his bluster. He tells me to get into the car. Still frozen, I stay where I am. He tells me again, this time louder. The others try reasoning with him again. He reminds them that he is my father and has the right to take me wherever he wants.

Finally I unfreeze and get into his car. He gets inside, too, and locks all the doors with the push of a button. He grins at Daniel, Gran, and Matt as though he has outsmarted them.

With a look, Gran tells me to trust her, that she will

figure something out. I nod and tell her not to worry. But this is the most worried I have ever been. Driving away, the redness leaves my father's face, but I imagine he is still seething. My heartbeat stops racing.

As we leave Katy's Ridge, we pass places that are now familiar. The river where my cousin Nellie and I talked. The house that Bee used to live in. The road that leads to the school. Another road leading to the Sectors' place.

When June Sector told my fortune, she saw something in the cards that scared her. I wonder if the incident that just played out was it.

On the drive back to Nashville, my father and I do not speak. The silence feels almost as dangerous as his anger. I stare at my hands, thinking that I won't get to finish digging for the McAllister buried treasure. If I see Gran again, I will tell her about it so she can finish the job.

By two o'clock, we enter the ritzy neighborhood where my father lives. He pulls in front of his house and pushes the button that unlocks all the car doors.

"Go inside. I have to go back to the office." He doesn't look at me.

I hesitate.

"We'll talk later." The angry look on his face pushes me out the door.

I think of the fox Nellie and I watched when we were at the river. The rabbit sat unmoving to be invisible to the fox. In this scenario, I am the rabbit.

My father appears oblivious to the dynamics of foxes and rabbits. I doubt he has ever been a rabbit in his life.

"Louise is there, just knock on the door," he says before I close the car door.

Louise is their housekeeper. A black woman who lives on

the other side of Nashville. She makes their meals, does their laundry, and reads *People* magazine when she eats her lunch apart from the rest of the family. I suddenly realize how hungry I am. If I ask, Louise will make me a peanut butter and banana sandwich. I like Louise.

My father drives away. I shiver despite the oppressive summer heat.

Once inside, I will call Gran so she won't be worried. Days ago, she made me write the phone number at Granny McAllister's house in my diary. It comforts me to know that when I call, the phone will ring in the kitchen, and I will be able to picture Gran standing there weaving the long red cord between her fingers as she talks.

When I knock, Louise opens the door, looking surprised to see me. "Well, hello, Miss Daisy. I thought you were staying at your grandma's house."

"Change of plans," I tell her, stepping inside the massive foyer.

"Is she home?" I ask, motioning upstairs.

"Getting her hair done," Louise says.

We exchange a look of mutual relief.

"You want a sandwich?" she asks, as though she has picked up on my hunger.

"Yes, thank you," I say. "But first I need to call my Gran and let her know that I made it okay."

She nods. "Just put your things in your room and come back down. I'll fix you something."

Grateful for Louise's easiness, I climb the stairs and remember how just hours ago I was terrified that Gran or Daniel might get hurt. Before that, I was sitting at the lake with Gran and Sadie. Even with all that McAllister secret sense in one place, none of us saw this coming.

When I call Gran, she answers on the first ring. "Are you okay?" she asks.

"He dropped me off at his house and went to his office."

"Are you there alone?" she asks.

"The housekeeper is here. The wife isn't. Tell Mom not to worry," I say.

"I will. But we're all worried, Daisy."

"I know," I say. "I'm worried, too."

Gran asks for my number there, and I give it to her. She tells me not to hesitate to call the police "if anything happens." I hate that she even has to say those words. But I already know that calling the police won't do any good. The police chief has had dinner over here more than once, and my father is generous with their charities. He also knows lawyers and judges in Nashville. Some of them live in this neighborhood. Even at thirteen, I have figured out that a wealthy fox can get away with things.

"Once Lily and I talk, we'll call you back," Gran says.

"Mom's not back yet? She's been gone for hours."

"I know," Gran says. "She must have gotten waylaid."

I nod, forgetting she can't see me.

"Daisy, are you all right?" Gran asks.

"Yes," I say, not feeling the least bit all right.

"We're going to get you out of there," Gran says.

"Okay," I answer, but I don't believe it. My father has won. He is someone who always wins.

After I hang up the upstairs phone, I go to my bedroom and put my backpack on my bed. When I go downstairs again, my father's wife comes through the front door.

"What are you doing here?" She doesn't look glad to see me.

"My father dropped me off." I wonder if he told her about

us showing up at his office. I doubt it. They barely talk at dinner. I can't imagine them having a heart-to-heart about something important. According to my father, wives are to be clueless and attractive. A Mercedes for the home. Something that purrs and doesn't talk back. It makes no sense that he and my mom were together. Except I heard her tell one of her friends once that he was a father figure, since she'd never had a dad.

"He never tells me anything," the new wife says, more to herself than to me. "Louise?" she calls toward the kitchen. She smells of expensive perfume and cheap hair spray.

Louise arrives in the front hallway. She stands at attention like a soldier in a war except with her eyes lowered.

"One more for dinner, it seems." She brushes past me like she is a faster car passing me on the interstate. I have never known what to call her. Her name is Kathleen, and my father calls her Kathy when he is in a good mood. Kathleen is not someone I would ever call *Mom,* and I can't imagine that she would want that anyway.

"Just keep quiet, okay?" Our eyes meet.

I nod, knowing that, to her, this means to stay out of sight —except for dinner, where we pose as a real family. If he has anything to say at all, I imagine my father will come up with some excuse for why he had to retrieve me from Gran's house. But for now, I will keep quiet and go into the kitchen to hang out with Louise.

While I eat a sandwich, I invite Louise to join me in the breakfast nook. At first she says she can't, but then she sits to drink a cup of coffee while keeping an eye on the kitchen door for Kathleen. She pulls a *People* magazine from under a cushion. Lady Diana is on the cover.

While she clucks at an article, my mind wanders to Katy's

Ridge. How could I possibly miss a place I have only been for three weeks? But it seems something monumental happened while I was there. At the Fourth of July celebration at Daniel's house, I realized for the first time that I was part of something bigger. I belonged to a family tree with deep roots. The proof of my family ties filled several picnic tables.

Meanwhile, I regret telling Gran my secret. If I had kept my mouth shut, my father wouldn't be threatening to get a restraining order against her. And Mom wouldn't be all worried and guilt-ridden. Now, the only way to get through this is to forget. Forget about digging for buried treasure. Forget about finally feeling like I belong somewhere. Forget about Katy's Ridge.

CHAPTER THIRTY-SEVEN

Wildflower

Sadie and I sit on the front porch waiting anxiously for Lily to return from the A&P. She must have had other errands, because she is long overdue. We anticipate her coming here since she planned to make dinner for us. I think of Mama, who would be having a conniption right about now. The grief is still new. Raw.

Then I remember how Matt Monroe stepped in to help me, putting Jerry in an armlock. If he hadn't stepped in, Jerry might have shoved me down the hill or even worse. My gratitude feels as strong as the grief. A Monroe stepped in to save me from harm. I think of patterns breaking. Sticks in the spokes of bicycle tires. Good apples not falling far from the tree instead of bad ones. At this moment, I wonder if Matt and I could become friends. But first I must save Daisy.

I haven't told Sadie how heated the exchange became or how Jerry tried to come after me. I don't want her to worry more than she already is.

"I wish I'd told Daisy to lock her bedroom door tonight," I say to Sadie. "But surely she knows to do that, right?"

Sadie puts a hand to her chest as though to keep her heart from breaking open. "Surely," she says.

We hear the car, and then eventually the sound of someone walking up the hill. Lily steps into the porch light's reach. Carrying a bag of groceries in each hand, she smiles. She has no idea what has happened while she has been gone. I stand to greet her, telling myself to stay calm.

"I forget how steep this hill is," she says. "But it's good exercise."

"For sure," I say, wondering how to tell her.

Lily puts the bags on the bottom step. "I ended up driving to Harriman to get a decent bottle of wine," she says. "Where's Daisy?"

"I tried to call you at the A&P," I say. "I couldn't find you anywhere."

Lily drops her purse off her shoulder onto the bottom step, too, as though realizing something heavy is coming. "Mama, what's happened?" The concern is written across her face.

"Jerry came and got her, honey. We were over at Aunt Sadie's, and he just drove up and told her to get in the car."

"And you didn't stop him?" Her voice crescendos.

My attempt at staying calm crumbles. "That man is twice my size, Lily. He pushed me aside like I was nothing. Not to mention he told the sheriff in Rocky Bluff that he was coming to get his child," she continues, "and that we were a bad influence. I didn't have much choice."

Tears rush to greet her anger. "Mama, what are we going to do?"

"Did you call your lawyer today?" I ask. "You mentioned you might."

She pauses. "He thought that any kind of restraining order would antagonize Jerry into trying to get sole custody again."

"Jerry tried to get sole custody? You didn't tell me anything about that."

Lily looks at Sadie, and I wonder if Sadie knows something I don't.

"I didn't want to worry you," Lily says.

"Why did he want sole custody?" I ask again.

"He said I was an unfit mother because I was on the road all the time."

My fists clench to keep my teeth company. "But as your record producer, he wants you on the road all the time."

"I know," Lily says.

"Besides, being on the road doesn't make you an unfit mother. Daisy stays with me. It's not like she stays alone and sleeps on a park bench."

Lily hesitates again. Even when she was a girl, I could tell when she was keeping something from me, and this is one of those times.

"Lily McAllister, what aren't you telling me?" I look at Lily and then Sadie, who lowers her eyes as if the two of them are in cahoots. I've never known Sadie to keep anything from me.

"Mama, leave it alone," Lily says. Now she is the one reaching for calmness.

I put my hands on my hips as we stand eye to eye. "Tell me," I say. Rufus looks up at me as if I might start growling any second.

Lily and Sadie exchange a look, and suddenly I realize

what's going on. Instead of conniving something, they are protecting me. I see now that this secret has love wrapped around it. Until now, I didn't realize secrets could work that way.

My defenses drop. "I appreciate what you're trying to do," I say to them. "But it's best that you tell me the truth."

"Jerry told his lawyer about Bee," Lily says.

It takes me a few moments to realize what she's saying.

"So Bee and I are unsavory characters? Is that what you're telling me?"

"Mama, I'm so sorry. People are so stupid sometimes."

I let out a scream that sounds more like a groan. I want to pace out in the yard like an angry rooster, stir up some dirt, and peck Jerry's eyes out.

"I know, Mama. It's awful."

"Has he always felt that way about me?" I ask.

"He's always been jealous of how much power you have over me."

"Me? Power over you?" I let out a gritty laugh. "Since when do I have power?"

"Oh, Mama. You do. You just don't see it."

We sit together on the bottom step, putting our best thinking caps on, as Bee used to say.

Aunt Sadie has been a silent witness to all that's going on. She sits above us now in Mama's rocker. I turn to look at her and notice a weariness I haven't seen before. Drama is harder to bear as you age. I know this for a fact.

"What do you think we should do?" I ask Sadie.

She looks thoughtful. "I think you and Lily should go get her."

"Go get her?" I say.

Lily and I exchange a look as though in disbelief that we didn't think of this ourselves.

"If we do that, we need a strategy," Lily says.

"Do you need to call your lawyer again?" I ask.

"He's useless," she says, appearing deep in thought.

A lone lightning bug sparkles in the white oak nearby as though carrying a message of hope. Later this evening, hundreds will glitter in the trees like Christmas lights. Every night we've been here Daisy and I have watched their magical display from the porch.

"No one gets to tell me whether or not I can spend time with my granddaughter," I say.

Sadie and Lily look at me, their surprise turning to smiles.

"Do you want to drive, or shall I?" I say to Lily. "We'll come up with a plan on the way."

"Let's go get her," Lily says.

We stand and take the groceries into the kitchen, where Lily prepares roast beef sandwiches to take with us, and Aunt Sadie makes us a thermos of coffee. It is nine o'clock on a Saturday night, and we are about to drive to Nashville. I could call Daisy and tell her the plan, but if Jerry answers, he may figure out that something is up.

We're coming, Daisy, I tell her. *We'll be there in a couple of hours.*

Earlier, I told Bee about Jerry coming to get Daisy. I call her again, since I promised to keep her informed. She gets quiet when I say that Lily and I are driving to Nashville to rescue Daisy.

"What is it?" I ask her.

"This feels dangerous, Lou."

Now it is my turn to get quiet. "We've got to do something, Bee. Listen, I need to go."

"Wait," she says. "What can I do to help? I feel powerless over here."

I pause. I don't tell her that Jerry has used us as a reason for Lily to lose custody. That would break Bee's heart.

"Why don't you go and sit in front of Jerry's house in case we need you," I say. Lily tells me the address, and I give it to Bee.

"I wish I could get Daisy a message that I'll be right outside," Bee says.

I give her the phone number, too, but tell her not to use it unless there is an emergency. We don't want Jerry to catch on.

She agrees that this makes sense. "Even if I just go over there, it's better than sitting here doing nothing," Bee says.

"Exactly," I say, "and if we need reinforcements, you'll be there."

She agrees.

Two hours later, we enter Jerry's upscale neighborhood. Lily pulls in front of a sizeable red-brick mansion surrounded by a brick wall. A gate stretches across the front, but luckily, it is open. On the street, Bee waits in her car. Lily stops behind her and flashes her lights as though we are in a scene of a Hollywood thriller. Are the good guys here in time? Will the bad guy escape?

Bee gets out of her car and appears to be traveling incognito. She wears a sweatshirt, jeans, and a ball cap pulled low, her hair pulled back in a rubber band. We exchange hugs, sealing a conspirators' bond, despite the dismal reality that we are rescuing Daisy from a predator, her father.

"Let's do this," Lily says.

"Do what?" Bee asks.

We both look at Lily.

"I'm just going to reason with him," she says, "and if that doesn't work, I'll threaten him."

Bee and I exchange a look, maybe both thinking that this is the worst plan in history.

"Don't worry," she says. "I've got tricks up my sleeve."

"Tricks up your sleeve?" Bee asks.

"Tricks up my sleeve," she repeats.

The three of us get in Lily's car and drive through the large black iron gate. The drive is circular, allowing for people to be dropped off in front. Lily parks the car just beyond the door and turns off the engine.

"No lugging groceries up a hill here," I say, imagining that the kitchen is all of fifty feet away.

"I doubt they even go shopping for themselves," Bee says. "The housekeeper probably does it."

"He's done quite well, it seems," I say.

"Because of me," Lily says. "I'm his biggest client."

I suddenly fear for her, but we've got to get Daisy out of there. "You ready?" I ask her.

"Almost," she says.

She pulls down the visor and looks into the mirror. After applying fresh lipstick, she fixes her hair. It is eleven thirty. However, the lights are still on downstairs. My insides flutter, as though my secret sense is waking up from a long sleep and sensing danger. I remind myself that this isn't a drug den in a poor neighborhood but the home of a wealthy music producer. An executive who unfortunately has a lot of powerful friends who look out for one another.

My second thoughts give birth to third ones. Every few seconds, I look into the rearview mirror expecting Jerry to walk up and ask us why we're loitering in his driveway.

"Maybe this is a bad idea," I say.

"Too late now," Lily says. "I'm going in." She steps outside. Before closing the door, she leans down and asks: "How do I look?"

"Like a million bucks," I say.

"Good. Jerry likes money." She winks at me, but her smile is laced with jitters.

The doorbell echoes through the large house. I look to the upstairs windows, wondering which bedroom is Daisy's.

Help is on the way, I tell her.

The door opens, and Jerry's surprise is evident. Thankfully, he invites Lily in.

CHAPTER THIRTY-EIGHT

Daisy

At my father's house, I can stay up until midnight if I want to. It is his wife who goes to bed early, nine thirty, as though it is always a school night. It is almost eleven thirty. For the last hour I have written in my diary everything that happened today. I never miss Nashville when I leave, so it is odd how much I miss Katy's Ridge.

The house is quiet. The door opens, and my father steps inside. The suddenness of his appearance sends a shudder through me. I didn't lock my door, and I chastise myself for not thinking. In the daytime, it is easy to forget nighttime happenings.

It is my father who locks the door behind him. A clear, distinct click. He steps into the room and stops at the end of my bed. I sit against the bed frame, a pillow behind me. My breathing grows shallow, jagged, and I don't look up from my diary. Maybe if I don't look up, he will go away.

For a solid minute, he doesn't speak. He isn't angry like he was in Katy's Ridge, but I know he is here for a reason. He sits on the bed next to me, the mattress lowering with his weight. My body stiffens. I hold my breath. I feel upside down. Unclear which way is the sky and which is earth. I keep writing. If I keep writing, maybe I will be able to right myself.

Seconds later, the doorbell rings. I exhale. The spell suddenly broken, my father leaves my room. As soon as I hear his footsteps on the stairs, I jump out of bed and lock the door. My heart beats as though it is running all the way to Katy's Ridge, where life is more simple and safe.

Voices drift up the stairs. I try to make out who it is, grateful that they broke the spell. I go to my front window and open it, gasping my surprise. Gran and Bee are below my window. They look up. Bee waves, and Gran smiles despite the worry etched onto her forehead.

My fear vanishes. I smile. "What are you two doing here?" I ask in a loud whisper.

"We've come to rescue you," Gran says.

She isn't your typical knight on a white horse, but I'll take it. Unfortunately, my bedroom doesn't have any trees to shimmy down.

I ask who is talking to my father, and they say it is my mom.

"Mom's here?"

Gran nods.

I narrow my eyes to hear the voices better. But I can't make out what my mom is saying. My father raises his voice to get my mom to back down. I can't make out his words, either, but he is the type to threaten if he doesn't get his way. All of a sudden, there is another female voice, and I realize that Kathleen has joined them in the living room.

This should be interesting, I say to myself.

"What's happening?" Gran says from below.

I shrug, thinking that this is maybe one time when the gesture is appropriate.

"Pack your bags," Gran says.

"Why?" I say.

"If our plan works, you'll be going back with us."

I wonder if this is possible. I can't imagine how my mom will talk my father into letting me go back to Katy's Ridge. The one thing he told me on the drive here was that he wasn't going to let my mom win. Ever.

With a sudden shudder, I flash on him coming into my room. I've got to get out of here tonight. No matter what.

Following Gran's suggestion, I grab my things, putting them in my backpack for the second time today. A feeling of hope comes over me. I smile at the girl in the bathroom mirror, her fate still unknown.

The voices downstairs get loud again. Three voices.

When I go back to the window, Gran suggests I sneak downstairs.

I tell her I will try. Bee holds up crossed fingers, wishing me luck.

Earlier today Sadie, Gran, and I sat on the bench by the lake. Three generations of McAllisters together. A tribe of strong women. Sturdy stock. I remind myself that I am a McAllister, too. A thought that suddenly means something to me. I stand straighter and sling my backpack over my left shoulder.

When I open the door, the voices get louder. I freeze like a rabbit seeing the fox. Unable to move, I tell the rabbit part of myself that everything will be okay and that I will be safe soon. I think of Gran and Bee outside waiting for me. With renewed courage, I inch my way downstairs.

"Who do you think you are?" my father says to my mom.

"I'm Daisy's mother, that's who I am, and don't you forget it." Mom sounds strong.

Halfway down the stairs, no one has noticed me.

"Get out of my house," Kathleen says to my mom. Kathleen stands closest to the door, her arms folded across her chest. She is wearing a fancy bathrobe covering her equally elegant nightgown and matching gold slippers. I hug the rail so she won't see me. She looks younger than my mom, even though my mom isn't that old.

"I'm not leaving until I have my daughter," my mom says from the living room.

"We'll see what the police have to say about that." My father walks over to the telephone.

I stop mid-step, wondering if my father would try to stop me if I started running. I need to get closer to the door.

"Jerry, if you call the police I swear to God you will live to regret it," my mom says.

He chuckles and picks up the phone anyway.

"I can ruin you in this town, Jerry, simply by telling the truth. If it's me against you, I have more people who will believe me than you do."

He laughs. "You exaggerate your importance."

Mom pauses, and I can almost feel her desperation. "Does Kathleen know about your latest girlfriend?" she asks.

Putting down the phone, my father looks at his wife, whose expression appears to sour like a glass of milk out in the full-day sun.

"She's lying," my father says to Kathleen. But Kathleen's expression sours even more.

Whether truth or lie, Mom's warning has the effect she intended. My father has weakened. At least momentarily.

"We also have proof of what you did to Daisy," my mom says.

"Daisy?" Kathleen's eyes narrow.

"This is none of your business," my father says to her.

Kathleen turns to go to her bedroom upstairs. She sees me. I expect her to tattle that I've been listening. Instead we exchange a look that holds more kinship than hatred. When she passes me on the stairs, she lowers her head, as though she knows more than she is saying. Was she aware of my father coming into my room at night? Moments later, she slams her bedroom door, clearly for my father's benefit, given the forcefulness of the slam.

Aware that I have forgotten something, I make my way back upstairs to get the four cassette tapes hidden in the top of my closet. Proof. They will do me no good if my father is the one who finds them. I quickly put the tapes in the top of my backpack, as well as the small notepad with the list of dates that document the cassettes.

It would have never occurred to me to make tapes if I had not been recording myself reading sections from *Island of the Blue Dolphins* for an oral book report. The recorder was right there in the top drawer of my nightstand, the microphone easy to hide.

I sneak downstairs again, out of sight of my parents still arguing in the living room. My father accuses my mom of blackmail.

"I'll be finding another record producer, too," my mom says.

He laughs at her again, but something is underneath his

laughter that wasn't there before. Does he know that she has won?

Focused on the front door, I walk briskly downstairs.

"I'll be out in the car," I say to Mom, catching a glimpse of my father's surprise as I close the door behind me.

Once outside, I run to Gran and Bee. All smiles, they give me hugs. We wait on Mom, practically holding our breath. She finally steps outside with a thumbs-up, and we hurriedly get into the car. We drive through the gate and stop long enough for Bee to get into her car and leave. Mom drives, with Gran in the passenger seat and me in the back seat. My fast breathing finally slows.

Above the Nashville skyline, a full moon watches. I imagine the moonlight sparkling on top of the lake next to Aunt Sadie's house. When I ask where we are going, Gran says, "Home," and within minutes, we are on the interstate heading toward Katy's Ridge.

CHAPTER THIRTY-NINE

Forty Years Later

Wildflower

At ninety-four, my two great childhood fears have long been outgrown: dying young and Johnny Monroe. Johnny has been dead now for almost three-quarters of a century, and I did not die young. Far from it. My only regret is that I wasted so much precious time worrying that I might.

After Mama's death, I moved back to Katy's Ridge and lived in the old house. Aunt Sadie lived with me in the last years of her life. A more natural death, I cannot imagine. One evening she was laughing and celebrating her ninety-ninth birthday with family, and the next morning she simply didn't wake up. A smile graced her face as though all her questions were answered in that moment of passage.

"Mama, you need anything?" Lily stands by the bedroom door, a cup of steaming tea in her hand.

It is hard to believe Lily is eighty-one now, and Daisy is fifty-three. I still remember them so clearly as girls.

I chuckle.

"What's so funny?" she asks, handing me the tea.

"I was thinking about how we pretend to be all grown up, but at the same time, we are still the girls we used to be."

She smiles. "Well, that's a good thing, isn't it?"

"I hope so."

To my continued surprise, once Lily had her fill with traveling, she came back to Katy's Ridge to settle, opting for a simpler life, if there is such a thing these days. Lily now lives at Sadie's place by the lake and has a few horses and a small recording studio.

Lily admires the hummingbird quilt that I recently returned to my bed. After Mama died, I took it off and preserved it until now. Every night the past tucks me in and warms me. In my imagination, I can still see Mama and Aunt Sadie sitting together at the kitchen table, collecting piece after piece and sewing the squares. Somehow, it seems they stitched me together in the process.

I am not a person who stays in bed, but more and more I feel like lingering. Some mornings I find myself wanting to stay with my dreams instead of getting on with regular life. Not because I dream of flying or exploring the fantastical, but because, more often than not, they deliver scenes from when I was younger. Things I had forgotten. Things like the smile on Daddy's face when he opened one of my homemade presents as if I had given him jewels from Buckingham Palace. Other times, I remember the rhythm of Mama's broom sweeping the front porch. Or the smell of an apple pie baking in the oven, the juices bubbling with cinnamon. Last night I dreamed I was looking down at Lily as an infant in her crib as she slept, my love for her practically busting me wide open.

"Daisy will be here later this afternoon," Lily tells me. "She's bringing the girls."

Saturdays are for family time. Lily always comes over and makes my breakfast. Most Saturdays, she makes biscuits just like Mama used to make. Sometimes we'll have them with eggs and bacon and strawberry preserves from the pantry. Preserves that Sadie made herself the last year of her life. Other times we'll eat biscuits hot out of the oven with real butter and honey from the Sectors' beehives.

While I was lingering this morning, I remembered Aunt Sadie's call to me that long-ago morning when I was still living in Nashville. Daisy was staying with me for the summer. Life changed after that. Life does that sometimes. Changes in an instant, or over a single summer. That summer, I remembered what was truly important: family and a sense of place.

"You need some help getting up, Mama?" Lily asks.

"I'm not *that* old," I say to her, even though sometimes I feel like I am.

When one arm refuses to find its sleeve, she helps me put on my robe. Then she follows me to the bathroom, the old wooden floors singing their song to us along the way. I stand in front of the mirror over the sink and look at the wrinkled face looking back at me. I smile at the old girl that is now me, standing alongside my gracefully aging daughter.

"You're beautiful, Mama," Lily says.

"So are you, sweetheart." I take a mental snapshot, not wanting to forget us standing here together side by side. Mother and daughter. I wonder if she is doing the same.

"You ready for breakfast?" Lily asks.

My eyes widen for her benefit, though my appetite isn't what it used to be. We walk arm in arm to the kitchen, and I sit at the oak table, which is nicked with memories, some of which are older than I am.

Lily puts a plate of breakfast in front of me and then sits at the table. She always eats earlier than me.

"I'm feeling nostalgic this morning," I say to her.

"Are you?"

My white hair, captured in a loose braid, crosses over my shoulder, reminding me that while I wasn't looking, I became an elder.

"Eat, Mama." Lily pushes my plate closer.

"You were a good cook even as a girl," I say. "Not to mention, you could run like the wind, and had a singing voice that brought tears to the eyes of anyone who listened."

"Thanks, Mama." She kisses me on the cheek.

Lily's singing career was still going strong when she walked away from it a decade ago. But she continues to write songs. Every now and again, she attends an awards show, and I'll watch it on the television in the living room.

"You longed to travel back then," I begin again, "and you were in love with Crow Sector. Secretly, of course."

Lily looks past me as though remembering. "I never thought for an instant that we would end up back here in tiny Katy's Ridge," she says.

"Neither did I," I say. "But *never say never,* as the saying goes."

"Do you ever wish we hadn't left in the first place?" she asks.

"Not at all," I say. "We needed to get you to Nashville so important people could hear you sing. You might still be unknown if we had stayed in Katy's Ridge."

I think of Bee, who died four years ago. We talked on the telephone every day, and I was with her when she died, our friendship as strong as ever. After Mama's funeral, Bee never returned to Katy's Ridge. But all those people who rejected us are dead and gone now. Dead people are easier to forgive. If I've learned anything after living so long, it is that we're all, in our own way, doing the best we can. Of course, that's sad in some cases. The other thing I've learned is that frightened, closed-minded people are everywhere—north, south, east, and west—not just in the Appalachian Mountains.

"If we hadn't moved to Nashville, I probably would have married Crow and had six kids and a bunch of grandkids by now," Lily says.

"Hard to imagine," I say.

One child was enough for Lily, as it was for me. Of everyone in our family, Daisy is the most maternal, loving every age and stage. Her two daughters are teenagers now.

"Mama, can I ask you a serious question?"

"Of course," I say, taking a bite of biscuit for her benefit.

"Do you have any regrets?"

"Oh my, plenty of them," I say, without even thinking.

"Really?" Lily's surprise surprises me.

"Of course," I say. "I'm not sure how you avoid regrets in this day and time."

"Like what?" she says, looking genuinely curious.

I ponder my answer. "Well, I wish I hadn't stayed in Nashville as long as I did after your career got underway. I could have had more time with Mama before she died."

"But that's hindsight, right?"

"I guess."

"Anything else?" she asks.

"There's about a thousand times I wish I'd listened to my

secret sense when it gave me a nudge," I begin. "But the truth is, we have very little control over what happens. It has taken me a lifetime to realize that. Although I do believe that we can choose to love life instead of fear it."

I think of Daisy and that dramatic summer when the truth came out about her father. She spent every summer with me afterward and came back for numerous holidays. When it came time, she went to Vanderbilt and got a master's degree and finally a PhD in counseling. She married Adam Sector, and they built a house at the edge of June and Horatio's property. Adam and Daisy have the best marriage I have ever witnessed. Daisy has a private practice in downtown Rocky Bluff, and she also has clients who drive all the way from Nashville to see her. Thankfully, Rocky Bluff has come alive again and has the cutest little downtown area that even tourists want to visit.

Everything rises, and everything falls, I think. *And then it rises again.*

"Lovely breakfast," I tell Lily, though I've left half of it on my plate.

Turning my attention to my morning chores, I rise to put cat food in the bowl by the back door for the latest orange tabby to grace our kitchen. Her name is Pumpkin Spice, and I am convinced that she is a distant descendant of the original Pumpkin from when I was a girl.

With the breakfast dishes washed and put away, Lily helps me gather eggs from the chicken coop. Then we fill the two bird feeders in the back before sweeping the front porch like Mama always did. Finally Lily and I walk to the mailbox and back to get my exercise for the day.

Saturday rituals with Lily are something I look forward to.

"The day I can no longer walk this hill to my house is the day I'll be ready to die," I tell her.

"You say that every Saturday, Mama."

"Well, it's true."

"I know," she says with a smile.

When we return to the house, it is time for a nap. I take two short naps a day now, one after breakfast and my chores, and one after lunch.

"My naps are rehearsals for the final curtain," I tell Lily.

She laughs. "You're getting lots of practice then."

The hardest part of being this old is all the people who get off the stage before you. I think of all those original characters in the play that is my family drama. For those of us lucky enough to go three acts, it seems an unusually long touring engagement at times. I still miss Mama, and of course Daddy, and Aunt Sadie. Jo is my only sister left. After Daniel died, she moved in with Nellie, who lives in downtown Memphis. Nellie is a marine biologist who studies rivers and is currently unmarried.

"Wake me up if I'm asleep when the girls get here," I say to Lily.

She says she will and pulls the hummingbird quilt over me, tucking in the corners. Daisy had her girls late. She was almost forty and had trouble getting pregnant, so it's hard not to think of them as miracles.

As soon as I close my eyes, sleep comes, as well as the dreams. Daddy plays a song on the banjo that makes Mama smile, and she leans back on the sofa, her face relaxing into a happy life. Daddy's rich voice fills the room, his fingers softly picking a tune on his banjo.

"I'm very proud of you, Wildflower," he says to me in the dream. I let his words and music fill me.

When I wake up, Daisy is sitting in Mama's old rocker by my bed.

"Hello, sweetheart," I say.

"Hi, Gran." She smiles.

"You know, I still remember when you were thirteen and sitting up with Mama in that old rocking chair."

"Being thirteen is something I try to forget." Daisy laughs a short laugh, sounding just like her mom.

"Where are the girls?" I ask.

"They took a walk up the old cemetery trail, but they'll be back soon," Daisy says. "How are you feeling, Gran?"

A person can tell when they are cherished. The feeling is mutual. After that summer, when she told me her secret, we became close and remained close.

"Any day aboveground is a good day," I say, thinking of Victor. This was his saying before it was mine, and it always made us laugh.

Victor is the latest of my friends to go. He died six months ago. I put a roll of peppermint lifesavers in his coffin. We spent many evenings together playing Scrabble and talking about old times—one of the things old-timers do best. I saw his sister, Mary Jane, at his funeral. We barely spoke, our friendship needing more than forgiveness to revive it.

Often, Matt Monroe joined Victor and me in the evenings. The three of us became close friends over the years. I would like to think that Matt and I did our part to heal the past. Matt and Lily have become friends as well. Sadie taught them how to make her blackberry spirits before she died, and they have continued the tradition out behind Lily's recording studio.

Lily enters my bedroom. "Are you ready to move outside, Mama?"

I climb out from under the covers, my body voicing its complaints. "I wonder if when we die we toss off these old bodies like hummingbird quilts."

Daisy and Lily look at me.

"I may use that in a song someday," Lily says. She starts to hum as if already creating the song. Daisy and I exchange a look that says, *There she goes again.*

"I remember this quilt," Daisy says, straightening it on my bed.

"It made sense to bring it out again," I say.

"It's beautiful." She studies the stitching, admiring the skill put into it. One of Sadie's quilts ended up at the Smithsonian, donated by a wealthy woman in Nashville who had bought it from Sadie in the 1950s.

Meanwhile, Lily tries to tame my hair and then gives up, pronouncing me beautiful despite my imperfections.

The three of us make our way to the porch. It is a glorious summer day in the Tennessee mountains. One of those days when you realize why you live here. The honeysuckle is in bloom, along with the wild roses, their scents competing as though in a contest to see which is the sweetest. The morning fog is a distant memory, and the day is crisp and clear.

Heather and Holly walk up the hill carrying two bunches of wildflowers, freshly picked. Youth is an elixir to me these days. It's hard to believe I used to be as young and vibrant as the twins are at thirteen, the age their mother was when everything changed.

When they give me the flowers, I am overcome by the beauty. Orange tiger lilies mix with purple irises, sprigs of lavender, and white wild roses. Like their mom, they call me Gran, though I am actually their great-gran. To keep things straight, Lily is called Nana.

The girls exchange a look, pleased with themselves. Heather has hair to her waist, and Holly's is short. Heather is much more outgoing than Holly, whose shyness is infamous in the family.

"Can I re-braid your hair?" Holly asks.

I nod. It is another Saturday ritual that sustains me.

With a gentle touch, Holly releases the old braid, shakes my hair out and brushes it, and then begins anew. She weaves together the strands.

"Did you bring your instruments?" I ask.

"Of course," Heather says. "We know how you love it when we play."

From the time they could walk, Heather and Holly have played musical instruments. We found Daddy's banjo in the attic, and Lily had it restrung and restored so Heather could play it. Holly plays the fiddle or violin, depending on where you're from. Their father is very devoted and has taken them all over these mountains to learn folk tunes from the elders in the tradition, and they have become quite good.

Heather finishes my hair and takes a photograph with her phone to post on the World Wide Web. My ancient brain refuses to take in these newfangled electronics. We didn't have a telephone until I was grown, nor did we have indoor plumbing. A distant banjo plays in my memory. It would be just like Daddy to show up for our Saturday concert.

The eighty-second anniversary of Daddy's death is in three months. Even this many years later, I never forget the anniversary. We all have signposts in our lives of painful and celebratory things. It is the price we pay for living.

No one can escape it, I hear Aunt Sadie say.

I smile.

"I heard that, too," Daisy says, rocking in the chair that Mama always sat in when she stopped long enough to rest.

"You heard that?" I say.

She nods.

I sometimes forget that Daisy hears voices from the past.

Heather and Holly tune their banjo and fiddle. They sit on the top step of the porch, instruments in hand. Like their grandmother Lily, they don't have a moment's hesitation about sharing their gifts.

Heather starts first, picking out a tune, and Holly joins in. Pumpkin Spice jumps in my lap, and I pet her, closing my eyes and letting myself drift away on the music. Lily sings along, a melody without words, and at this moment, an emotion fills me that must be joy. I picture the fullness of the river and the expansiveness of the forest around me. Every note is alive, just like every inch of this mountain is alive.

When I open my eyes, Daisy is watching me. I wonder what she's listening to besides the music. But then I instantly know. My secret sense has been generous lately, having forgiven me for all those years I didn't pay attention. Together, we remember the day she found the treasure.

I SIT at the kitchen table, listening to the faint sounds of Daisy's shovel breaking ground. It has been a week since we returned from picking her up at her father's house. Then the shoveling stops. Seconds later, the kitchen door opens, and Daisy rushes in, her eyes alive with excitement.

"I found it!" she says.

She drops a metal box onto the table, leaving a nick on the table to remind us for years to come. It never occurred to me that she might actually find something as a result of all that digging.

"What is it?" I say. The box is rusty and covered with dirt, the size of two large cigar boxes. It has a latch, but no lock.

"It's your daddy's," she says. "Before Granny McAllister died he came to her bedside and reminded her of the metal box he buried out in the backyard. I think he wanted me to hear him so that I could unbury it."

"Daddy told you?"

Daisy nods, not taking her eyes from the box. "Should I open it?" She looks up to get my response.

"Well, I sure wouldn't do all that digging and then not *open it," I say with a smile.*

Daisy pauses, biting her lip.

"I don't think I ever told you how Daddy loved to send us girls on scavenger hunts," I begin. "Sometimes he would spend an entire Saturday afternoon hiding things all over this mountain for my sisters and me to find. As the youngest, I rarely won, but I had a great time scavenging for things."

We look at the box.

"In a way, it makes sense that Daddy would bury something for us to find years later," I say. "It also makes sense that he would save something for a rainy day even when it was already pouring outside."

Daisy nods.

"Well, open it," I say.

She wipes her hands on her jeans. At first the lid refuses to budge, but Daisy gets a butter knife from the kitchen drawer and runs it along the edges of the dirty latch.

"Got it," she says, slowly lifting the lid.

The contents are carefully wrapped in a piece of waxed cotton. Her eyes widen again, taking it all in. I step closer to see. She care-

fully lifts each item from the box, looks at each one, and then hands it to me.

Inside is a stack of letters between Mama and Daddy, from when they were courting and newly married. A red ribbon is tied around the collection that is in incredibly good shape given it has been buried underground for decades. Only the very edges of the pages have tattered.

Next Daisy hands me a small bag of gold coins. The coins are from Scotland, marked with a symbol of some kind. We giggle and note the heaviness of the leather pouch, marveling at its contents. Underneath the coins is an old deed for a piece of property in Glasgow. We open it and study the signature and date. It is signed by Daddy's father and is dated August 2, 1856.

"What do you think these things are worth?" Daisy asks.

I tell her I have no idea, but that we can find out.

From the bottom of the box, she pulls out more letters, written to me and my sisters on our twelfth birthdays. Handwritten notes from Daddy. Daisy hands me mine. As I read the letter, tears blur the words before me.

To my dear Wildflower, on the occasion of your twelfth birthday.

I am watching you bloom into a young woman, and I am so pleased by what I see. You are a kind and thoughtful person, full of curiosity and wit. Sometimes, I can't believe you are my daughter, because you are so much more than I deserve. Watching you grow up has meant the world to me. I remember your first steps as you held your mama's hand, and I remember watching you recite "I Wandered Lonely as a Cloud" from memory and with such feeling in front of your entire school.

I have always been so proud of you. My beautiful, courageous

Wildflower, I have no doubt that you will do great things with your life, and you will do them with great enthusiasm and love. The world is so lucky to have you, as I have been.

Love,

Daddy

Daisy and I exchange another look as we return from our journey to the past. The treasure amounted to enough to build a small library in Katy's Ridge, where Sweeney's Country Store used to be. The treasure to me that summer was Daddy's letter. But I am convinced the real fortune Daisy found in the summer of 1982 was herself, and her family.

In many ways, Daisy's fortune has been my fortune, too. If we hadn't come back to Katy's Ridge that summer, and if she hadn't found the courage to tell me her secret, I might never have left Nashville and come home.

Nodding to the melody, deep contentment settles over me. The old tune mingles with birdsong, as sunlight and shadows dance in the trees. Someday, I will toss off this old body like a hummingbird quilt. My spirit will walk outside and be greeted by all those who have gone before me. I imagine Daddy as a young man, and Mama, too, and my sisters and Daniel and Nathan and Aunt Sadie along with all her beloved dogs, as well as Pumpkin the cat, and his orange tabby descendants that we came to love. Reunited, it will be as if everything that happened on this old porch has been heaven, after all.

ACKNOWLEDGMENTS

Daisy's Fortune has been a joy and an honor to write. I discovered the fictional McAllister family in 2002 when I first heard Wildflower's voice in the middle of the night and she began telling me her story. I had no idea at the time that *The Secret Sense of Wildflower*, as those early writings came to be known, would even be published. Ultimately, it was my breakthrough novel. Kirkus Reviews deemed it one of their prestigious *Best Books of 2012*, and my writing career took off. The sequel, *Lily's Song*, came four years later after so many readers requested more of the story. When I realized there was one more generation that needed to be heard from, the Wildflower Trilogy was born, and I wrote the third and final book, *Daisy's Fortune*.

I have only recently realized that this trilogy is three generations of coming-of-age stories: Wildflower at thirteen, her daughter Lily at thirteen, and Lily's daughter, Daisy, at thirteen. Finishing this series has felt very satisfying to me as a writer. It feels as though Wildflower chose me personally to tell her story, and I am forever grateful for the opportunity.

I am also grateful to the following people who helped me bring this book to publication. First and foremost, my sweet, endearing readers. You have emailed me and told me what my books have meant to you. You have commented on my Facebook author page. You have posted glowing reviews. You have invited me to your local book clubs, where I had the great pleasure of meeting you in person. However, most of you I have never met. I love writing stories for all of you just the same.

Of great help to me on *Daisy's Fortune* was my daughter, Krista Lunsford, who types in my changes after all the drafts I edit by hand, as well as gives me feedback as she goes along. "Are you sure you want to say that, Mom?" She is invaluable.

Also, of momentous importance to my writing life is my business manager, Anne Alexander, who creatively and skillfully completes all the marketing and technical things that are so absolutely foreign to me as an author.

The first readers of this book were also incredibly helpful in offering their feedback: Cheryl Groeneveld, Susan Burnside, Maureen McGough, and Betty Bessette. Your comments and suggestions have made *Daisy's Fortune* a better book. Thanks also to my awesome audiobook narrator, Holly Adams, who brings my characters to life in such a magical way. Thanks to Laura Dragonette for her excellent copy editing and Lizzie Gardiner, who created the fantastic cover.

All of these members of my writing team have been an enormous help in getting *Daisy's Fortune* out into the world and into the hands of readers, and I am so thankful.

To my beautiful family and friends, I send you heaps of

love and gratitude for your encouragement and understanding over the last twenty-five years. You buck me up when I get discouraged, and you celebrate my successes. This journey would be so lonely without you.

Finally, to my current writing assistants, Charlie and Jack, my precious mutts who snuggle with me and bark at squirrels every day that I write. A dog biscuit awaits each of them as soon as I finish writing this sentence.

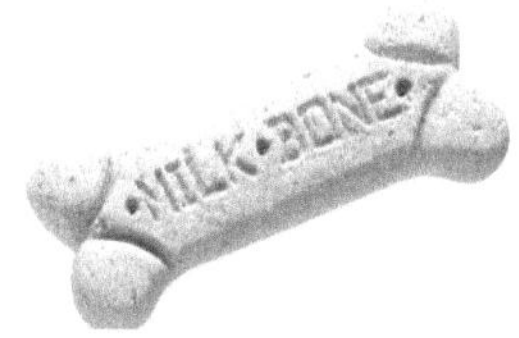

ABOUT THE AUTHOR

Susan Gabriel is an Amazon and Nook #1 bestselling author who lives in the mountains of North Carolina. Her novel, *The Secret Sense of Wildflower,* earned a starred review ("for books of remarkable merit") from Kirkus Reviews and was selected as one of their Best Books of 2012.

She is also the author of *Temple Secrets, Gullah Secrets, Trueluck Summer, Lily's Song* and other novels. Discover more at SusanGabriel.com.

TEMPLE SECRETS & GULLAH SECRETS

TEMPLE SECRETS

A town held together with secrets. A wealthy widow looking for an heir. One choice could shame high society into submission.

Eighty-year-old Southern aristocrat Iris Temple's health may be failing, but her wit is as sharp as ever. Before she joins her ancestral ghosts, she must pick an heir to take over her sprawling estate—and the book of secrets that's kept her family in power for generations. But between her scheming son, her estranged daughter who abandoned Savannah years ago, and her illegitimate half-sister, she's working with slim pickings.

While only her half-sister and cook have put up with her outlandish diet and constant bickering, she can't ignore the powerful hold her late father's 100-year-old mistress has over the two women. When someone leaks embarrassing snippets from the Temple family book, she half suspects the voodoo-practicing centenarian as the elites of Savannah teeter on the edge of revolt. With Iris fading fast, her ragtag bunch of potential heirs must reveal the leaker before the book's secrets tear the sleepy town apart.

Temple Secrets is a hilarious women's fiction novel with a Southern gothic flair. If you like wisecracking humor, headstrong women, and twisty mysteries, then you'll love Susan Gabriel's compelling tale of an unconventional inheritance.

Buy *Temple Secrets* and start unlocking the mysteries today!

Available in paperback, ebook and audiobook.

GULLAH SECRETS: Sequel to Temple Secrets

A family legacy in danger. A stranger in their midst. Do they have the strength to survive the gathering storm of secrets?

For the Temple women, the winds of change are blowing. And if they're not careful, it could sweep them all away…

Gullah Secrets is the sequel to the bestselling novel Temple Secrets. If you like Southern gothic literature, characters you won't want to close the cover on, and locations steeped in history, then you'll love this hilarious and warmhearted saga.

Available in paperback, ebook and audiobook.

TEMPLE SECRETS & GULLAH SECRETS

TWO-BOOK BOX SET ALSO AVAILABLE

ALSO BY SUSAN GABRIEL

FICTION

The Wildflower Trilogy:

The Secret Sense of Wildflower

(a Best Book of 2012 – Kirkus Reviews)

Lily's Song

Daisy's Fortune

Trueluck Summer

Temple Secrets Series:

Temple Secrets

Gullah Secrets

Grace, Grits and Ghosts: Southern Short Stories

Seeking Sara Summers

Circle of the Ancestors

Quentin & the Cave Boy

NONFICTION

Fearless Writing for Women:

Extreme Encouragement & Writing Inspiration

Available at all booksellers

in print, ebook and audio formats.